IN THE EYES OF GOD

THE BLENDING OF TWO SOULS

Neal Ritter, PhD

Introduction

I wrote this book to provide the reader with a deeper understanding and appreciation of concepts introduced in my previous book, *Truth Beyond Words*. For those who may have landed here inadvertently, I felt it necessary to add a bare-bones summary since I'm using "Truth" as a foundation for elucidating the ideas. Naturally, I recommend reading the former book before proceeding. Those who have done so may either skip the next section or use it to rekindle memories and, hopefully, inspirations derived from my earlier work.

To appreciate the following, the reader must begin with an understanding of a key premise. The ego is defined as the mechanism through which each individual interfaces with the outside world. It serves as a point of integration for our many thoughts and desires. An ego that encapsulates consistent and healthy beliefs allows for optimal functioning and a reasonable chance for happiness on a day-to-day basis.

However, there is more to the story. The ego enjoys being front and center when dealing with our more primitive impulses. Unhappily, it must share the stage. Since the beginning of time, we humans have felt a need to embrace something greater than what we experience in our mundane lives. We long for a sense of essence, of divinity, that transcends our individuality. My books describe the ongoing struggle between the ego with its selfish wants and needs and our higher Selves as we strive to break the shackles of our mortality. In the following pages, the reader will find a road map leading to discovery and enlightenment as they accompany a couple in their search for the Holy Grail.

Recap

With some trepidation and ambivalence, Linda schedules an appointment with a psychologist, Bill. She discovers that she has allowed herself to become boxed in by the opinions and criticisms of her father and husband. She breaks free of the trap of other people's opinions rather dramatically by ensnaring the psychologist in an elaborate fantasy of exhibitionism. When Bill is understandably shocked, she tells him quite bluntly that she doesn't care what he thinks. In so doing, she is declaring her freedom from social constraints.

In a rather desperate attempt to maintain control of her internal *status quo*, Linda becomes sexually aggressive with Bill. During a touch-and-go interaction, Bill manages, just in time, to reassert his professionalism. In the following session, she redirects her previously suppressed energy by expressing antipathy toward her husband, Rick. She then slyly maneuvers Rick into a near-physical confrontation with the hapless psychologist.

Even as her mood improves, Linda continues to be troubled by a vague sense of dissatisfaction. During therapy sessions, she realizes that something is missing in her life. Bill helps her discover that she feels disconnected from her "Self." He demonstrates how the words she uses habitually play a critical role in creating a sense of alienation from her true nature. He defines her vacillation as a struggle between her ego with all its material wants and her higher Self.

She eventually agrees to forego psychotherapy and replace it with some strange new phenomenon that Bill calls the transformation of consciousness. As part of this novel process, Bill introduces the concept of a witness to teach her to identify with her higher Self. Through this phase, Linda learns that she can no longer afford to think and speak haphazardly. Though Linda resists the semantic changes Bill recommends, she gradually realizes the importance of using words consciously. She discovers that her words have real power in affecting her world, especially when in a heightened state of awareness.

While she is focusing on her inner development, a former friend/archenemy, Barb, makes an unexpected appearance in her life. Linda's marriage has been drifting for some time, and Barb elects to take advantage by making a move on her husband. Meanwhile, Linda is learning the danger of using words to maintain her self-identity. Of critical importance, one of the words most central to her self-concept is jealousy.

Barb's efforts to subvert the marriage begin to work subliminally on both partners. A combination of Barb's sabotage, which throws Linda off-kilter, and the surge of energy that Linda is experiencing through her work with Bill culminates in a psychotic episode. Though Linda manages to regain her bearings, she continues to ping-pong in the battle between ego and Self.

Bill shares an ethereal experience with Linda, teaching her how to maintain her bearings while in a higher state of awareness. As she begins to experience life from a different perspective, she becomes fascinated with everything she is learning. Then complications arise as she is confronted by a welcome and an unwelcome change. Her life-long dream of becoming a psychologist unexpectedly becomes a real possibility when she is accepted into graduate school. At the same time, her husband begins drifting closer and closer to the arms of Barb, the infamous other woman. Rick's attempts to intellectualize and rationalize his passive role in the developing affair lead to a growing sense of self-condemnation and, ultimately, a decision to make his own appointment with Bill.

The drama unfolds on both fronts as Linda deals with the overwhelming demands of grad school and the resulting emotional and cognitive distress. As if that weren't enough, she discovers that her adversary has moved in on Rick with more than a bit of success. She is torn between her gratitude toward Bill for what he has shown her and her resentment because, in her confused mind, Bill is at fault for seemingly telling her not to be jealous.

Not surprisingly, Linda's emotional state becomes precarious. Bill assists her by showing her a sense of transcendence to encourage her to regain perspective. In stark contrast to the heavenly world he shared with her, she is confronted by the realities of unreasonable academic demands and a genuine threat to her marriage. Even as Linda shows signs of resilience, Barb goes to unimaginable extremes to undermine Linda's emotional stability along with her marriage.

Fortunately, Linda and Rick find a way to come together as they combat the challenges they are forced to confront. In a surprising twist, they find their relationship starting to come alive again. As things are finally going well, Bill introduces the possibility that they might share a relationship beyond anything they might have dreamed of, hence this book.

Preface

It began as a love affair lasting decades as I was fascinated by basic questions, such as why we are here and what makes us tick. While still in high school, I read the Bible cover to cover. I followed that up by reading the complete works of Sigmund Freud. Alas, the affair was never culminated.

I grew weary of secular interpretations of religion. In the face of my passionate efforts, I also found the field of psychology to be wanting. Between the abstract theorizing and the nitpicking experiments, I discovered that my studies provided little insight into the minds of others, much less my own. In its current state of evolution, the field swings wildly between overly theoretical ideas and minutely detailed experiments, neither providing great insight into what makes us uniquely human.

Thank you, my readers, for providing me with the fulfillment previously lacking as you are now absorbing the knowledge I worked so hard to obtain. My search culminated when, through some karmic event, I met a Western Master who was able to guide me in a direction that allowed insight into my troublesome questions. In this book, I'm grateful for being able to share life lessons that I've learned, cherished, and enjoyed along the way.

The previous book, *Truth Beyond Words*, began on a whim. I wanted to recapture some of what I had learned many years ago from the previously referenced Western Master, hoping to share it with a broader audience. I enjoyed the process and, before I knew it, had written a considerable number of pages. There was no planning for the book other than occasional brainstorming while in the shower. Instead, I was capturing the flow of regular therapy sessions. I simply went where the book took me.

Now for the moment of total honesty. Much of the content of my previous book has been known for centuries. Those who have been fortunate to have obtained "knowledge" have existed throughout time. Don't believe me? Read the Bible or other religious texts. Alternatively, read a few fables. In some, if not the majority of cases, the writers have known without knowing that they knew. They somehow were able to tap into the vast wisdom—collective consciousness—that flows through the universe.

Unfortunately, I won't be able to provide direct attributions for some of what is included since I recently rediscovered it while browsing through my notes from forty years ago. However, I will attempt to give credit where it is due. My modest contribution involves bringing ancient knowledge to light in a format utilizing my experience as a psychologist while adding a touch of spice to make things more entertaining.

I aim to present the core concepts clearly to compel and inspire self-reflection. I want to encourage readers to explore their inner potential and gain new insights into the vast possibilities within themselves. My goal is not fanciful storytelling. Instead, I hope to deepen the reader's understanding of powerful ideas that can motivate personal growth and breakthroughs. If this book can spark that process of inner discovery, I will have succeeded.

Since I am a psychologist, I also want to provide information for those who accept the great responsibility of guiding others along their path. The inherent limitation, just as in the previous book, involves the inadequacy of words in portraying nonverbal communication. There are myriad ways in which we attempt to express the products of our minds to one another that have nothing to do with words. Such forms of communication are impossible to capture by simply adding black ink to a white page. Even more critically, conveying a sense of the energy that drives the transformation process is impossible. With those drawbacks in mind, I can only hope that my writing achieves the lofty status of being not only provocative but evocative. I feel gratified to the extent that I can not only teach but inspire.

Out of necessity, some of what follows is "in the weeds." I hope those seeking to explore further into the more complex concepts will benefit, but not at the expense of readers seeking a more fundamental understanding. It will become evident that numerous core concepts require packaging and repeating in various ways to make them stick. However, knowledge, at its core, is not about intellect. In that vein, I want to convey my deep desire to include heart in the following words. Without love, what does it matter?

Midway through writing this book, a question occurred to me. Will readers think that transformation of consciousness is nothing more than literary fiction? The answer is a resounding no. It's as real as the book you are now reading. It's not a spooky idea I dreamed up to enliven the book. Instead, it has been integral to my life for the last four decades. Many of my clients and friends have been grateful for what that gift allows me to offer. So now, here's the actual book.

Table of Contents

Linda's Journal

May 12

Bill told me of the risks of anticipation. So why am I jumping up and down? Well, *duh*! I obviously know better. It's like indulging in that piece of chocolate even when you know you're shredding your well-intentioned diet. Sometimes it's just worth it.

Okay, let me stop myself. I've got to ask, why am I writing to myself like I'm talking to another person? I guess what it comes down to is simple. I want to. Life is about learning and having fun. I don't have to follow anyone else's rules as long as I'm doing this for myself. My first lesson from a year ago was genuinely emancipating. I learned, and then I realized over and over again ad infinitum not to allow myself to be controlled by anyone else and their opinions.

I've gone through all this falderal because I'm almost scared to write down what's about to happen. I don't want to do anything that might sabotage it. So, here's the deal. Rick and I are scheduled to meet with Bill for our first appointment as a couple in 2 weeks. *Hallelujah*! It might not sound like a big deal to anyone, but for me, it is mind-boggling for two reasons.

First, Bill is bigger than life to me. I won't say he's like a god because he might find out and then smite me down. And he isn't really, except that he kind of is. He not only taught me; he liberated me. He freed me from the shackles of the beliefs that had encumbered me and allowed me a peek at what is, can be, and ever more shalt be. Woah! That sounds weird even to me. Maybe I shouldn't get ahead of myself.

The second reason is just as exciting in its own way. Bill told me about the possibility of marrying Rick, my beloved husband, *in the eyes of God*. Of course, I thought I had already achieved that milestone. But then again, I thought many things about my world that had barely scratched the surface.

I've had a glimpse of the possibilities. Sharing it with Rick with the prospect of our becoming genuine soul partners is beyond anything I could have ever dreamed. I love him and always have.

What's more, I've come to trust him. Now, I see the possibility of joining him on a journey to heaven itself.

Is that ample reason to be excited? It must be because I feel like I'm about to explode. Okay, I need to remember the lessons. I've had fun indulging in my thoughts. It's time to bring it back to the present. My goal involves awareness. It's about the eternal now. I'm taking a deep breath and getting myself back to the present. I am confident that our work will allow me to find myself in an infinite and timeless reality.

Rick's Journal

May 16

Linda has been bouncing off the walls. But I'm not complaining. I've been jumping up and down metaphorically right along with her. If someone offered you ten million dollars, would you be happy? What I'm anticipating, or at least hoping for, makes that measly prospect seem like a joke.

Just for fun, I've thought of the comparison. Not long ago, the thought of financial security would have been my dream. Now, I look at it in contrast to the possibility of a blissful, eternal life bonded to the woman who means everything to me. Just for the heck of it, I want to play with that idea. Let's see, my past idea of fulfillment compared to what now lies before me. Boy, what a hard decision. After considerable thought, I think I'll opt for Door Number 2.

Not only is my relationship with Linda totally different, I've become a new person. Don't get me wrong. I'm still the same bumbling guy who stumbles roughshod through social interactions. However, it doesn't matter. It's not that I am indifferent to what others think. I just feel good about who I am. Even more so, I feel tremendously happy and proud about my relationship with Linda.

My life is incredible and full of possibilities. As I think of it, I'm getting a bit antsy. Things are going so well. I'm almost reluctant to risk having Bill overturn the apple cart all over again. And let's face it, that's exactly what he does.

Then I remind myself. I tend to get caught up in what's comfortable. It comes down to the fundamental decisions we all face throughout our lives. Do I want to keep things the same and risk dying slowly? Or am I willing to take a chance on what life might bring if I put myself out there?

Most people make that decision by not deciding. I do have to give myself some credit. It was challenging for me to initiate the phone call to schedule an appointment with Bill. If I hadn't, what would have become of my life? I would have probably had an extremely short-lived affair with Barb, trailed by a painful divorce. Likely, I would soon be sitting in a one-bedroom apartment, sipping beer and hoping my life would soon end.

Let's move past the gloom. While I'm basking in the bright sunshine, I know that storm clouds and their accompanying thunder are inevitable. Still, life is meant to be embraced. I've learned how silly it is to hide from the storm, sheltered by the false reality of my thoughts. Words are not real. I must remember that because I'm about to head right into the spiderweb of the illusions I have spun throughout my life.

Now that the time is approaching, I have reservations. I remember Bill's comment all too well as we ended our previous sessions about spending time in survival mode. Hey, I might as well face it. I've gotten used to being fat and sassy, and I like it. Then, I remember a common fallacy. Things never stay the same. I can wait for them to change or choose to be proactive.

The Agreement

I was thrilled to see Rick and Linda enter my office after a prescribed hiatus of several months. "Hey, guys! I was expecting your call. I'm glad you first took time to integrate what you have learned, both within yourselves and together as a couple."

As her usual adorable self, Linda responded, "It hasn't been easy to wait, but I realized that I needed to follow your guidance. I've experienced about twelve entire lifetimes since our last session. I've also gotten to know Rick in ways I didn't think were possible. Thank you."

Rick was not quite as humble, but his sincerity was evident as he said, "I haven't forgotten for a second the last thing you told us. I hope you know that you scared the hell out of us with that survival idea. Your idea of requiring us to risk our lives makes no sense. I hope you're not going to insist that we go through with it. Linda really listens to you, and I'm going to beg you to give us a pass on that jungle deal."

I chuckled before responding, "Got your attention, did I?"

Rick looked more than a bit miffed as he said, "Don't tell me you were just yanking our chain."

In that maddening way I have, I replied, "Well, yes and no. Admittedly, I wanted to give you some reason for hesitancy so you wouldn't insist on returning too quickly. I also wanted to clarify that we're in a high-stakes game. For the moment, I would like to start with the basics. Let's first establish why you're here and what you want to accomplish. The foundation is critical in any agreement, and all parties must understand and agree to it."

With little thought, Linda volunteered, "My goal is transformation for Rick and me as a couple. I want to have the kind of marriage you described. I want our happy ever after. Isn't that what we signed up for?"

I pondered a minute before answering. "As you have learned, transformation is a very different phenomenon. It happens all at once over the course of time."

Rick once again seemed somewhat irritated. "Can we just cut to the chase without playing word games?"

"Sure," I replied. "I will tell you what I have planned, and you can tell me how it works for you."

Linda took a moment to collect her thoughts. She ended up saying, "Bill, I trust you completely. I will follow whatever path you think is best."

Rick smiled in agreement, so I proceeded. "For you to get the maximum benefit from this experience, especially considering the investment it requires, I will give you my recommendation. We could do it down and dirty, and you would benefit to some extent. Or I can do my best to give you a thorough grounding, including background information to make the experiences more meaningful and useful."

It was immediately evident that Linda was all in. Rick seemed a bit more hesitant as he said, "I want to make it clear that I trust you as well. However, I want to be able to make an informed decision. What are you proposing?"

"The way I see it playing out is multi-layered. The most direct aspect is likely to be the most challenging as it requires complete honesty and openness between you. With your mutual agreement, we will review the session recordings of our earlier private sessions. Listening to your unguarded thoughts would give each of you additional insight into how the other is put together."

Linda was first to object as she exclaimed, "But those sessions were supposed to be completely confidential! I said things to you without giving any thought that anyone else would ever hear."

I nodded in agreement. "Ordinarily, I would never make such a recommendation. But then, what I'm proposing is not something ordinary. I'm assuming that you're still interested in psychology and psychotherapy."

She nodded her head enthusiastically. "You're saying that you will teach me some of the tricks of the trade along the way?"

"That will be a bonus. What you might learn should also benefit Rick in his legal practice."

"Okay, I won't say I'm jumping up and down excited about it. But I'm willing to go along with that step." Rick then asked, "What are you proposing beyond that?"

First, let me remind you that you both have experienced self-metaprogrammer transformation. In our earlier work, you both found the place within yourselves where you were behind your words. You could then label that place so that it would be accessible from that time forward. It has since allowed you to choose words from a place of awareness rather than being captive to random thoughts and habitual reactions. While it is relatively a baby step, it is critical in your development.

"We will review what you've learned in preparation for what I have previously described as becoming married "in the eyes of God," or as my teacher labeled it, supra-self transformation. It will allow you to expand your ego and consciousness to truly encompass one another. It's a big step, and it requires a major commitment. It's much easier to say that you want to become one than to go about it."

Linda tore, and Rick beamed before asking, "So that's the end point?"

"It might be better to think of it as a new beginning. Always remember that life is a process, and we're just making a few quantum leaps along the way. But to answer your question, I would like to begin by explaining the reasoning behind what you have been experiencing and what will likely be coming. I will use different examples and draw from numerous sources of knowledge so that you will be thoroughly grounded in the process and better able to apply it in your daily lives. There is the potential for one more gigantic step, but we must take things as they come."

With obvious enthusiasm, Linda said, "That's exactly what I'm looking for. I don't want to get hung up on understanding, but that doesn't mean I wouldn't find it of great value in my life and my future practice."

Not surprisingly, Rick was a little more reserved. "I see tremendous potential in what you're proposing, but I'm unclear about the timelines and exactly what you would expect from us."

"First of all, remember that we would be moving even further toward the final stage, which my teacher called supra-species transformation. You will learn more about that possibility on the way. It involves developing awareness beyond your individual mortality. While I won't insist on your venturing out on a tropical island or a barren desert, I do need to tell you that there is a genuine risk if we get to that stage. It requires total, if temporary, annihilation/transcendence of the ego."

Linda shuddered before nodding in agreement. "I want to go for the whole shebang. It sounds just like what I had hoped for, maybe even better."

Always the professional negotiator, Rick asked, "Would it be possible to blend all the teaching into a single phase?"

"Nothing in what I'm suggesting is set in stone. I've never gone in-depth with anyone like this before. What I'm proposing is not sequential or simple to delineate. It would be best not to look for a logical progression. I could offer you the security of lesson plans, but then we would be wasting our time.

"But I want you to be aware that there is another level out there in the far distance. We are now moving toward supra-self, which is mind-blowing in itself. At the same time, it is mild compared to the next potential level. How about we take it one step at a time and continue with the natural progression?" I couldn't help smirking as I added, "As if there were such a thing."

Rick looked lovingly at his wife. He finally said, "I want to become as close to Linda as possible. If what you're recommending is the way to do it, I'm all in."

Linda's Journal

May 20

We finally had our first session. Now I'm more excited than ever! Bill is offering more than I'd ever dreamed. He will teach me what he does and promise the possibility of a genuinely transcendental transformation. In the meantime, he will lead Rick and me to a marriage beyond my wildest dreams.

My biggest challenge is going to involve reining in my enthusiasm and excitement. I'm fully cognizant of the importance of staying centered and not allowing my thoughts to carry me away. I've got to say, though, it's tempting. I think the most critical word tool for me now is equanimity. I'm going to practice diaphragmatic breathing while keeping it in mind. Deep down, I know that everything will come in time. I need to have confidence in the perfection of the universe.

The great thing is that I can share it all with Rick. Over the last few months, I've come to know him. He doesn't tell me about all the minute-to-minute details of his life, which is good because I don't have time to hear them. However, we make time for each other and prioritize discussing what matters the most. Just by lying together in each other's arms, I feel a warm glow begin to light the room.

But there is a catch, and it's a big one. I will have to sit there while Bill plays the recordings of our sessions! Talk about taking a risk. Even with the trust I've developed with Rick, I will feel incredibly vulnerable. Fortunately, the lessons concerning embarrassment and shame are coming back to me. But it's one thing to hear them intellectually and quite another to put them to the test.

I wonder if I have sufficient trust in Rick to pull it off. Even more so, do I have enough faith in myself? Will our marriage survive? Then, I realize that I'm allowing my thoughts to play out their scenario. I am not my thoughts. So long as I'm being myself, I can handle whatever comes.

Rick's Journal

May 22

I probably came off as a wimp, but I'm still hung up on the idea of fighting off snakes and tarantulas in an untamed jungle. At least Bill didn't push on that prospect. I think I, once more, lapsed into letting my thoughts gain control. Fortunately, I've learned not to get down on myself every time I slip. Otherwise, I would be so depressed that I couldn't function.

Now, there is an even more immediate threat. I'm tempted to let my thoughts go wild on the scary prospect of having Linda listen to the recordings of my sessions. Bill seems to be stepping just a little over the line with that idea. But we did buy into his insistence on honesty and openness. It is, after all, what I said I wanted. When I start to have doubts, all I need to do is imagine the kind of relationship with Linda that he described.

But what if she learns things I would just as soon not reveal about my rendezvous with Barb? There go my thoughts again. Maybe I deserve to feel guilty. After all, I screwed up big time. How could I have risked my marriage, the most crucial thing in my life, just for a fantasy?

Instead of looking backward, I must look forward to the possibilities that Bill described. But wait. I'm supposed to be living in the present. It's all getting pretty confusing. Bill taught me how to find a place beyond words. I need to, no, I'm going to go back there.

I did, and now I almost have to laugh. It's so simple and obvious. I've been ruminating over thoughts as if they are what's real. What matters is right here in front of me. And it's wonderful beyond description. The possibilities of what the future holds are beyond comprehension, but they will unfold as they are meant to. I'm one lucky man.

Second Meeting

"Hey, guys!" I said in greeting. "I'm not going to begin with lawyer jokes, but we do need to settle the legal niceties. I'm going to ask you to sign a formal waiver of confidentiality. Any questions or further reservations?"

"I'm down with it," Rick expressed.

Linda frowned. Her concern about what was to be revealed was apparent and easy to understand. With some reluctance, she nodded her assent.

"I will tell you that there is an obvious risk in transparency. As will soon be evident, I'm going to be sharing that vulnerability right along with you. Let me begin with one of the most pithy quotes I've ever heard:

"Live so as not to be ashamed if whatever you do or say is published around the world –

Even if what is published is not true."

"The first line is powerful. But it's the second line that really brings it home. That quote comes from Richard Bach's book *Illusions: Adventures of a Reluctant Messiah (1977, p. 48)*. If you haven't read it, I highly recommend it. The author speaks from knowledge. To the extent that you maintain the standard embodied in the second line, you will truly lead a life uncluttered by ego. You will be completely impeccable."

"Just FYI, he also wrote *Jonathon Livingston Seagull (1970)* which was the more popular book and also worthwhile but not as powerful. In the latter book, he uses a seagull flying over land and sea to provide a metaphor for gaining perspective. As you might imagine, the former book most closely mirrors my life, so it's been more influential for me."

"Let's begin with Linda's initial session. As will be evident in listening, she was a bit hesitant as we started. That's not unusual and is a sign of good ego strength. Clients that come in ready to burst into tears are easy to engage. It requires considerably more skill to gain the trust of an ambivalent or distrusting client.

"As you will hear, Linda provided me with several subtle challenges…not the least of which was her attractiveness. And I certainly don't say that lightly. I had to deal with my issues as well as hers. I'm not excusing that fact. I realized early on that she was my teacher, and the lessons she offered were not going to be without risk."

Rick shuffled around in his seat but managed to stay quiet.

I continued, "In the early phase of treatment, support is usually a critical focus. The therapist must maintain their position without becoming unnecessarily confrontational or defensive when challenged. The goal is to establish credibility without sounding pompous or insensitive to the client's feelings.

"One of the true skills involves knowing when to respond to process rather than content. Instead of providing a substantive response, reflecting on the underlying communication can provide the key to opening a more genuine interaction. Ironically, therapy requires words, but much of the real communication is expressed through facial expressions, gestures, intonation, etc. I don't want to get too involved in lecturing, so let me back off and see if you have things you want to say."

Linda was eager to respond. "Listening to the session and hearing your explanation of what happened is fascinating. It allows me to step back from the immediacy of our meeting and see what you were doing and thinking. There is much more skill involved than meets the eye."

After giving it a quick thought, she remarked, "I want to make sure I understand what you mean by process communications. It sounds like it's an important aspect of psychotherapy."

I replied, "You're not clear on what I meant and would feel better if you had a better understanding. You have a concern that you might be missing something important."

Linda smiled and responded, "Pretty slick. You answered my question by providing an example. You reflected on my underlying concerns instead of responding directly to my question. I can see how it's an important aspect of genuine communication. Otherwise, conversations would involve nothing more than an exchange of words. They would be completely safe, but you would never really get to know the other person."

I looked at Rick and asked, "And what kind of relationships do you think are most likely to devolve into nothing more than an exchange of information?"

With some reluctance, Rick responded, "I know you're going to make me say it."

Rather than pressing him for the obvious answer, I requested, "How about give me an example of something you could say to Linda process-wise?"

After a noticeable grimace, he came through. "Linda, you seem especially effervescent this evening. I love it when you smile at me and say pleasant things. It makes my day."

"Whew. You're much better at it than I am. Do you think I can sign up for lessons? But just to be sure, let's see how you do with a negative."

This request proved to be a little more challenging. After a few seconds, he continued, "You sound cross with me. Are we on the same page with everything?"

"Linda, you've got quite a husband."

Her obvious irritation suggested she wasn't quite as impressed, so I persisted. "Since you're proving adept at the relationship game, let me ask a simple question. Why do women like it when men give them flowers?"

He almost seemed to be gloating since he knew the obvious answer. "Everyone knows that women love flowers. If you ask me, they're kind of a waste of money. I would say it comes under the heading of marital duties."

"Okay, Linda," I acknowledged. "I can see that there is still work to be done. Would you care to give your clueless husband a clue?"

"Rick, of course, I like flowers. They brighten up my day. But you're missing the point entirely. If you ever brought me flowers, I would be ecstatic. But it wouldn't be because of the flowers. It would be because you took the time to think of me and wanted to do something special that I might enjoy."

"There's an important concept here," I commented. "The key is that, in doing so, you would be putting aside your ego and thinking of what she might like."

Rick seemed uncomfortable with the direction our discussion had taken and was more than ready to change the subject. "I'm more interested in this whole attractiveness thing. I can virtually touch the sexual tension while listening to these first recordings. What the hell were you doing with my wife? And I was paying for it! I thought you were supposed to be a professional. And from what I can gather, Linda was doing more than her part in playing along."

"Regarding Linda's involvement, it's crucial to recognize that our purpose here is not to assign fault but to understand and grow from these experiences. Life, as we know, is not a performance staged for the scrutiny of others; it's a journey often marked by missteps and learning. But there are a couple of factors that led to her uncharacteristic behavior. As you now know, her ego sensed the danger ahead and was willing to use its heavy artillery to ward it off."

"The other reason, which I've never before revealed, is that my gift of awareness allows me to gain the interest of women who wouldn't ordinarily give me the time of day. I work to suppress it, but sometimes it seeps through. If I suspect I'm using it, I stop and look seriously within myself. If I allowed myself to seduce a woman using awareness, I would be acting out of ego. And we know all too well where that leads."

On a less serious note, I added, "Regarding my part in interacting with Linda, I'm a professional, but I'm not a machine. Maybe next time, you should choose a less attractive wife."

They both got a good laugh out of that one before I proceeded. "I was far from clean as I allowed my personal feelings to influence my interactions with her. It's not an excuse. It's just an uncomfortable acknowledgment of the obvious."

I reluctantly added, "A wonderful thing about therapy is that every client and every interaction is unique. For a person like me, with my diagnosis of ADHD, predominantly inattentive type, it is particularly a blessing."

Linda squirmed before protesting, "You've never told me anything like that. I thought you were supposed to be the one who had it all together."

"Remember, Linda. I'm still here. I have obstacles to overcome and challenges to meet. You've reminded me of that fact more than once, even if you didn't intend to. Now that we are in a different kind of relationship, I feel free to reveal things I would have never discussed. In any case, it's now Rick's turn under the microscope."

We began listening to his recording. "In retrospect, tell me how you felt as we began our first session."

While shifting around in his chair uncomfortably, he managed to proceed. "It was one of the hardest things I've ever done. I don't like showing weakness to another man. In my experience, personally and professionally, people will most likely turn it against you. In addition, I was still embarrassed by the time I burst into your office and basically threatened you."

"And yet you showed up for the session and jumped in the water, not knowing the temperature or the depth. Something must have motivated you to take that giant leap of faith. Let's explore the underlying factors that led to your decision. "

With a half-smile, he acknowledged, "You probably know more about that than I do. You had this whole thing figured out in advance and knew my insecurities about Linda. I thought I had to get involved or face losing her."

Somewhat begrudgingly, I admitted, "I put you in a nearly impossible place. For what it's worth, that wasn't my intent. As the reality developed, you had to make a choice. I don't have any reason to think that Linda would have left you if you hadn't decided to schedule an appointment. However, we both know that you and Linda were moving in different directions and at a different pace."

"You know, Bill," he said after some reflection, "I'll have to admit that I've held some resentment toward you. At the same time, I feel tremendous gratitude for all you have done."

"Don't get too schmaltzy yet," I cautioned. "There are still some major hurdles in front of us."

Linda's Journal

May 29

I knew that Bill was attracted to me, but I'm now getting the idea that there was more to it than he let on. It's exciting to think he really had the hots for me. But two things come to mind. The first is my ego. I know the dangers of going there. Fortunately, I've become more adept at recognizing and harnessing it. The worst thing I could do is immerse myself once again in fantasies.

The second is a little more complicated to acknowledge, but in a way, it makes his attraction to me even more gratifying. As I think about it, my physical presence wasn't the driving factor in his reaction. I didn't want to downplay how wonderful it was to feel wanted, but now I realize that he knew me even before I stepped into his waiting room. His Self recognized it way before he did. And I was too caught up in how I was coming across to see him on any level.

I loved the quote he shared with us and vowed to make it my goal in living my life. After all the years I spent caught up in concerns about how other people saw me, I feel genuinely liberated. I've always felt burdened by a sense that I needed to be perfect. Nothing I did was ever quite good enough. Now that I'm in grad school and learning about eating disorders, I realize how lucky I am that my driven, perfectionistic style didn't lead me to becoming anorexic.

Seeing the bigger picture as I listen to my initial session with Bill is terrific. What seemed at the time to be a somewhat awkward conversation I now see as a beautiful tapestry. He knew exactly what he was doing as he weaved our discussion in addressing my resistance and gaining my trust. Looking back, I can only laugh at my early doubts about him. However, I will say that it makes sense that I wouldn't easily allow a stranger to access my inner thoughts and insecurities.

Rick's Journal

June 1

It was harder than expected as I listened to another man dive into the mysterious waters of Linda's most profound thoughts. My impulse was to tell him to stay out of our business. I'm glad I didn't hear the recording sooner. There is no telling what I would have done. I knew she had gone to see a psychologist, but somehow, I told myself that it was pretty much like a regular doctor's visit. Now I realize it involved risk for her, me, and our relationship. I don't even want to think about what might have happened if she had ended up with the wrong person.

Surprisingly, I learned worthwhile things from listening to his interactions with her in the recorded session. I can see how I can use the ways he dealt with her resistance and initial distrust in working with my clients. It brought home to me the importance of keeping my ego on the sideline. I will listen to my clients and follow where they need to go rather than always attempting to control and even bully them during our interactions. I can even see how I've sometimes come across as unintentionally condescending in the past.

I was thrilled that I could come through when he asked me to develop process statements. I guess I flunked, though, with the question about giving her flowers. I'm still struggling a bit with that one. It just seems so impractical. But I can see how putting her priorities over mine can make a difference.

I was glad he realized how hard it was for me to make the initial appointment. I was stunned to see how quickly he tuned in to my hidden agenda. I was serious about wanting help. But deep down, I was more interested in discovering what had happened during his talks with Linda.

Third Meeting

I began by asking Linda, "I'm curious about what happened that led to your decision to make the initial appointment. I know you were troubled by a vague sense of dissatisfaction, but you never really explained your reason for pulling the trigger."

She reflected for a moment before saying, "I'm not sure. I guess it was my discussion with some of the ladies at the club. They were friendly and pleasant to talk with, but I felt we were playing some stupid game. Somehow, I knew their attitude toward me would be completely different if I left the room. I didn't want to keep living a two-faced life. Since Rick was rarely around, they were my main source of support, and they weren't genuinely supportive at all."

"You chose to risk moving beyond a safe, unfulfilling life. Looking back, was it really a choice?"

"Well, I would like to take some credit, but I guess you're not going to give me that."

"Linda, why would I give you credit for allowing the universe to play out its game?"

"You sound like it's all preordained," she objected. "Do you not believe in free will?"

"Now you're getting way above my pay grade. I choose to play the game with the idea, whether or not illusory, that I have some influence on where it goes. I can't say if that's right, but it's a heck of a lot more fun that way."

"You've got a point. It's more enjoyable to think of it as a game and that I can influence it. I wander back and forth, thinking everything that happens is real and then realizing it's all just in fun."

"Well, Linda, it's all about as real as it gets. We must maintain the illusion of reality, regardless. Otherwise, we lapse into psychosis or solipsism."

"Regardless of the philosophical issues, I'm glad that you were able to give me hope and bring me back to living my life."

I replied sympathetically, "It was incredibly simple to do while also being impossible considering where you were at the time. As Einstein posited, "You cannot solve a problem with the same mindset that created it." You had to find a way to step outside of the problem. As an independent force, all I did was suggest a simple imagery exercise allowing you to escape the box, even temporarily."

I added, "Just for the sake of information concerning psychotherapy, it's critical to ask the client to re-evoke their various sensory memories during an imagery exercise because it encourages them to relive the experience rather than simply recalling what happened in words. The memory becomes much more real and present if they can re-experience smells, sights, sounds, or touches. You may find it surprising, but a totally different part of the brain is involved. Words are great for categorizing memories and storing them in a safe place, but they also deny us access to the actuality of our memories.

"Attempts to do psychotherapy strictly at the level of words are largely a waste of time. Insights, in isolation, are satisfying to experience but ultimately of little value. In fact, they can become their own trap. Clients must feel the impact of any new realization if they are to receive benefit from it. To understand why you acted as you did with me, it would also be worthwhile to consider the phenomenon known as demand characteristics. The situation inherently called for you to lend me credibility, even though it wasn't yet earned."

Linda enthusiastically interjected, "I really want to know more about how you weave your magic spell. Before meeting you, I thought psychotherapy was mainly one person talking while another listened sympathetically."

I agreed, "Unfortunately, and all too often, that's what ends up happening. Mental health professionals get involved in the grind of listening to one client after another. It's easy to go with the flow rather than do the hard work required. They get paid the same either way."

Linda looked puzzled. "Why is it so hard to help people? Don't therapists care?"

"People don't get into the field unless they want to help. But factors are working against them. First, people say they want to change, but they mean only if it's convenient. Or, in other words, as long as their ego isn't threatened. Just as importantly, mental health professionals sometimes lack the skills necessary to engage people at a deeper level. There is also another, more subtle factor. Sometimes, people just don't click."

She was obviously intrigued as she asked the natural question. "What do you do differently that invites a person to become involved beyond just talking?"

"Linda, I'm by no means unique. In fact, there are others who are much more skilled in developing rapport and in providing traditional psychotherapy. Since you're interested in becoming a therapist, I'll tell you more about my approach as we proceed. And you're right. Considerable skill is involved in assessing the client, developing a treatment approach, and guiding their progress."

"You're being too modest, and it doesn't become you. At least tell me how you go about it."

"For one thing, I must admit you threw me off stride during our initial encounter. I generally go in with a clear mind. By that, I mean that I give my clients total attention. It's a Zen thing. In saying that, I need to add that I maintain a level of awareness that guides me even as I'm focused on my clients.

"Unlike what I did with you, I don't engage in self-reflection. By being totally in the now with them, I can flow wherever they need to go. But there is more to it than simply mindfulness. It's necessary to continually sense when to support and when to challenge. Again, it's not a thinking thing. It's something that's developed with experience and intuition."

Linda could barely contain herself, "I feel like a kid in a candy store. Listening to the recording, I could hear what was happening without worrying about how I came across. I was so involved, though mostly subconsciously, with how I appeared to you that I couldn't truly appreciate what was happening. I love that you could flow with me, knowing when to be empathetic and when to probe."

It was time for things to get interesting, so I shifted the conversation from intellectual matters and introduced the topic of Barb. I turned my attention to Rick and said, "As we listen to the first recording of your sessions, it's obvious that you had gotten yourself in over your head before you even knew you were in the water. Are you ready to start talking about it?"

"Come on, Bill. You don't waste any time, do you? It's obvious that I rationalized and justified my way into trouble. It all seemed innocent. When I realized what was happening, I felt trapped and miserable. I never stopped loving Linda, but I did allow myself to become infatuated with an illusion. You helped me with that pretty much the way you did with Linda, but I still managed to keep digging myself in deeper and deeper. The harder I tried to get out, the easier it was to get sucked in. I felt like I was stuck in a mental quicksand.

"I'm going to give you a break and begin by focusing initially on my interactions with Linda. It will be less confusing if we don't jump back and forth. To that end, one of the early and most important concepts I introduced was that of the witness. I became aware of that term through the writings of Carlos Castaneda, an anthropologist and New Age author who greatly influenced my thinking. He dispensed knowledge by relating lessons he learned from an Indian sorcerer. He described the process as 'stalking yourself.'

"My teacher labeled it as the observer-operator or ob-op. Whatever you call it, it is important to begin developing the ability to step outside yourself while maintaining awareness. In so doing, you unmask the ego. You also begin recognizing your capacity for making decisions consciously rather than responding reflexively or simply out of habit."

"As I recall, Linda, my request for you to begin stalking yourself was likely the first time you started wondering just how weird I was."

With a brief laugh, she admitted, "Well, it certainly wasn't the last. I was looking for a psychologist and found myself with a brujo."

I acknowledged, "I certainly didn't intend to mislead you. In my practice, I try to slip in concepts and techniques that will provide genuine benefits without causing my clients to run for the exits. The important thing is that you started implementing the idea to the point where it became natural. It was critical as you were preparing for the separation from ego, which is the crux of the initial stage of transformation. Fortuitously, it also helps with psychotherapy, though not in such a direct way.

"While we're laying our cards on the table," I added, "I've got to admit that you played me like a fiddle. I was assisting you in gaining insight into your dependence on the opinions of others, and you nailed me with that rather engaging story about inviting the delivery driver inside while you were naked."

Once again, I was rewarded with the melodious sound of her laughter as she said, "I couldn't believe your reaction when I told you that made-up story about exposing myself. I reveled in watching as your face turned from red to green and back again. In retrospect, I think I was trying to regain some control over our interactions. While our talks had benefited me, I still resented that you had uncovered a weakness in how I dealt with others. I didn't want to repeat my mistake by letting you feel you had too much influence over me. It was the most fun I've had in years."

She half-heartedly attempted to suppress a giggle before saying with utter and complete insincerity, "Sorry about that."

I regained my bearings and continued. "As you may remember, I've mentioned that counseling sessions sometimes consist of little more than entertainment for the counselor. Well, you can certainly put me down as having been entertained. It took some effort at self-control to get back to your issue concerning interactions with family members."

Rick interjected, adding his two cents, "I had no idea that Linda felt I was controlling her. If anything, I would have said it was the other way around. I've always done my best to make her happy, but it seemed like the more I tried, the worse things got."

I inquired innocently, "What did your efforts entail?"

Rick was eager to explain what he had contributed to the marriage. "I've worked ten and sometimes 12 hours a day so that she can have the things she wants. I've ignored flirtatious secretaries and dealt with obnoxious clients. I've eaten, you know what, to keep the money coming in. Most people would say I've been the perfect husband."

Linda could barely contain herself. "Have you been listening to the recordings? I enjoy material things, of course. But that's not what life is all about. I would much rather live in a shack as long as I could be in an involved and loving relationship. I made that offhand comment, intimating that Bill was questioning our marriage because I wanted your attention. I didn't see the possibility of your charging into his office. However, I'll have to admit that it did excite me. It was the first sign I'd seen in years that you really cared."

"Bringing things back on track," I commented quickly; "I've got to hand it to you, Linda. You were easily the most stimulating client I've ever had. This brings us to our next big challenge."

As we listened to the recording, it was fascinating to watch the reactions of each of them. Linda was squirming uncomfortably as she listened to herself. She had been trying to blame everything on her husband. Rick was starting to fume. His face was turning red. As far as how I looked, I can't begin to imagine what an outside observer would have described.

I continued, "When a therapist hits the point of 'yes, but' with a client, it's an indicator that there is a need to change tactics. That defensive maneuver occurs when the client's ego is unwilling to release its stance. Nothing can be gained in butting up against an ego determined to maintain its position. The therapist can try to go at it from a different angle, wait for a more propitious time, or surprise the client by shifting and siding with the ego.

"In the latter case. which is known as 'going with the resistance,' the therapist surprises the ego by negating its defenses since there is nothing left to guard against. Additionally, the client suddenly realizes their rigid position no longer benefits them. It was a risky move, and it played out accordingly. Due to the unpredictability of results that might follow, I doubt that such an unpredictable maneuver is even taught in graduate school."

I explained to Linda, "It makes sense that your sudden insight about how you allowed others to control you led you to shift the blame, and Rick was a more than obvious target. When I surprised you by suddenly agreeing with your position that he was at fault, it was necessary for you to defend him.

"Although I got the desired result, I knew I was taking a risk. Let me emphasize that there is no blame here. You were operating with an agenda. We all do. In our current endeavor, the goal is to make those agendas more conscious and purposeful."

Linda looked sheepish as she replied, "You're certainly being generous. Deep down, I knew I was being bad. I should have known how Rick would react when I was egging him on. Not to justify it, but at the time, I felt ignored and depressed. And I had no idea he would burst into your office. He's never done anything impulsive like that before."

Rick snorted, "You pretty much made a fool of me. But what followed was even worse."

We began listening to the recording that revealed my awkward and intimate sexual encounter with Linda. After an uncomfortable pause, I reminded myself of the previously referenced quote about not feeling ashamed before proceeding. "You've likely heard of the Ten Commandments. Well, I slipped on the one about coveting. I will follow Linda's lead in saying that I can't excuse or justify it. But I would like a chance to explain."

I continued, "Psychologists, like physicians, must maintain objectivity and professionalism. It's especially critical because our jobs allow, and even require us, to intrude on the lives of relative strangers in ways that would otherwise be unimaginable. Additionally, psychologists, just like physicians, are human. And psychologists don't have the luxury of having a nurse stand watch. Moreover, it's much less revealing to undress physically than to lay bare your most intimate thoughts.

"As much as we try, and I didn't do a very good job at all, we strive to treat people with the same respect regardless of their looks or status. We don't always succeed. Some professionals even abandon the effort. You can read about them in the newspapers."

My erudite explanation had not turned down the heat as Rick and Linda were both noticeably crimson-faced. Rick did his best to remain in control, but the struggle was evident. He finally erupted by saying, "My God, I trusted you! I let you in on every part of my life. Now I've learned that you were playing footsie with my wife! And to make things worse, she was playing along."

"I would like to help by saying it wasn't as bad as it sounds. But it was as bad as it sounds."

My words of comfort somehow missed the mark as he growled, "I'm glad I didn't know what was going on. Otherwise, I would be spending the rest of my life behind bars. I'm not sure if it would have been you or Linda … maybe both. But something bad would have happened."

As unpleasant as the scene was, it had a definite upside. Until you meet a person in anger, you don't really know them. As with romantic relationships, business relationships are easy until egos get in the way. It's impossible to achieve total honesty and trust until you have gone eye-to-eye with another person through the spectrum of emotions. To the extent that you're satisfied with a superficial relationship, there's no need to take chances. Just realize that you'll never get to know the other person."

Linda wasn't going to evade responsibility either, as she said, "I allowed myself to get swept away in a fantasy. Again, no excuse. I was aware of what I was doing. I did it because it was fun and got my juices flowing. I wasn't thinking about the consequences, and I'm so glad it didn't go any further. But it opened me to the possibility of growing with Bill in a different, nonsexual direction. That's what led us here, and I'm incredibly grateful."

After the dust had settled, I summarized by philosophizing, "Remember that life is a process. Events along the way are stepping stones. It's up to us to choose the direction in which they lead. In this case, they allowed us to discover the awesome possibilities that now lie before us. While none of us would ever repeat the things we did, they opened the door for what is to come."

Linda's Journal

June 5

I don't know what I expected from our joint sessions, but it wasn't exactly this. As horrible as it was to reveal my sexual interest in Bill in front of my husband, it was also liberating. It was like having my worst secret out in the open. I despised it, but I loved the release it provided even more. I'm so glad for that quote about the shame he provided previously. It's surprising how many opportunities I'm finding to utilize it. And every time I do, I feel just that much cleaner.

How great is it that he is teaching me about psychotherapy? It's a nearly lifelong dream that comes true during every minute of our sessions. I enjoy the philosophical talk but cling to every word he says about psychotherapy. It's almost unimaginable to be able to first experience it, then listen to the recording, and afterward learn from him what was really happening. I wish every budding therapist could have this experience.

I don't mean to gloss over how awkward it was having Rick listening to my overt sexual fantasy about exposing myself to a stranger. I meant for it to be something fun, but I found myself involved in my creation. It had a much greater impact on both me and Bill than I ever imagined. Looking back, I can see that it was so effective because we both bought into it. We genuinely shared a moment of off-kilter sexuality that threw us both for a loop.

It was a thrill listening as I applied the coup de grace. I somehow sensed that Bill was caught up in it with me but didn't realize the extent until I told him I had made it all up. In all the time I've known Bill, that moment stood out as the one instance where I caught him off guard, leaving him utterly surprised and overwhelmed. He was still a bit red-faced when I left his office. I now realize that I had unintentionally set up what was to come.

Rick's Journal

June 5

Bill surprised me by bringing up my involvement with Barb early in our meetings. I saw in a flash the multitude of missteps I had made. I felt like I had hit the jackpot when Bill offered to postpone listening to my recordings. Now, I almost wish he hadn't. Believe me, it's going to be on my mind.

I knew this business of listening to Linda's sessions would be interesting. But until now, I had no idea just how interesting it was going to be. I couldn't believe that Linda had it in her. Her story about exposing herself to the delivery man was unlike the Linda I've known, yet she made it sound so real. I must admit that I got turned on as she told it.

And Bill. When I think of psychologists, I imagine someone sitting beside a desk, half-listening and taking notes with feigned interest. What I heard on the recording was a long way from that. I heard him struggling to maintain his professionalism while she was toying with him. I was blown away by learning that Linda could be so naughty. It helps that I now realize that the whole scene was the product of her ego struggling to stay in control.

I'm amazed at how much I'm learning. Now, I can hear Linda's lessons with a fresh mind. It's like he's teaching me the same things he taught her but in new ways. In the process, I'm able to grasp them more profoundly. Even the most straightforward ideas prove to be much more than they appear. And the things I'm discovering about our relationship are incredible. There is a lot to learn.

Fourth Meeting

"As I explained to Linda, transference is a genuine phenomenon. While it may seem redundant, I will begin by reminding you about the ego. As I've mentioned, it's necessary to explain important ideas many times over for people to hear and truly grasp them on different levels. Linda wanted to shake up her life. At the same time, she wanted to do it in a way that allowed her ego to maintain control. Her unexpected sexual interest in me allowed the perfect playground. She could act out her fantasies while ceding me responsibility for whatever happened."

Rick exclaimed, "Woah there, Bill! I'm still trying to maintain my cool about the whole thing. I'm far from being ready to accept some intellectual excuse."

As before, Linda was ready to come to my defense. "It really wasn't him. It was me. I felt ignored by you and safe with him."

Despite my self-protective instinct, I felt obliged to acknowledge an obvious fact. "Linda, if I had maintained a professional stance with you, things would have played out differently. As you know, I've been given a powerful ability to influence people. In my defense, I've seldom misused it. But I did with you. While it's painful for me to acknowledge, you were largely a victim in our interactions."

I ventured, "Let's not get stuck on that incident. Sex is a part of life. In what some might say would be an ideal world, our feelings of attraction to others would end once we get married. It doesn't work that way. So, let's consider that a lesson. What came next was the deflection. Linda was unhappy. Rather than consider her own, i.e., her ego's responsibility for her dissatisfaction, she turned to the most obvious target."

Since we all seemed eager to accept responsibility, Rick did his part by volunteering, "I can see it now but had no idea at the time. I was proud of my role in providing for my family and was blind-sided when she blamed me for how she felt. I both do and don't feel bad about how I came after you."

"Okay, you guys. This episode is one we're having trouble moving past. Let's move to the next lesson. There are Freudian terms to explain it, but let's stick with my terminology. Linda, how would you explain what happened?"

"It won't earn me any points in class, but it's obvious that my ego refused to accept my role. It was much easier to blame you and Rick, but as they say, I reaped what I sowed. I hate that I set Rick up to burst into your office to defend our marriage as I did. But, looking at it now with perspective, I can see that it was a perfect and necessary step in my progression."

"Regardless of your professors' thoughts, I'll give you an A+. Let's discuss what happened next as we discussed the roles you play in everyday life."

Linda paused before saying, "As I think about it, the contradictions between our various roles contribute to internal confusion. Rather than consciously recognizing the dissonance, we suppress it and become dishonest within ourselves. I love that you showed me how to rise above roles to begin getting to know who I am."

"It's been said that we are born knowing who we are and then spend the rest of our lives forgetting. As another way of saying it, we lose our purity as we learn to assume more and more layers of roles. As we listen to the recordings, it's clear that you had begun to question your relationship with Rick, which brings us to an important point."

Rick went first. "If I had previously heard you are having doubts about our marriage as you were describing on the recording, I would have been mad and confused. I thought that things were fine, just the way they were. However, it makes sense now that I understand the possibilities of an aware relationship.

"Linda, I can see how, when you thought about diving into our relationship at a deeper level, you had reservations. Bill suddenly changed the rules on you. Things got real. It was no longer you wanting more. It became about whether you wanted more than you had thought you wanted. I've got to hand it to him. He's pretty slick."

Linda looked relieved. "So, you're not upset that I had reservations?"

Rick continued, "Linda, my love. Now that I have some sense of the possibilities and the associated risks he was offering, I realize that you would have been a fool not to think long and hard about it."

The love between them was noticeable as he spoke. Linda reached over and held his hand with a gleam in her eyes.

I gave them time to enjoy their shared bliss before continuing. "When I first introduced the idea of constructs, I'm guessing you were somewhat baffled. What do you think of it now?"

Linda was eager to respond. "Do you know how many times I wanted to curse you? It seemed like you were going out of your way to make my life difficult. I was thoroughly pissed that I couldn't just think and talk like a regular human being around you. Even when I started to get it, I didn't like what I was getting. Gradually and somewhat reluctantly, I've come to accept that the things we take for granted are not as simple and obvious as we would like to believe. We do construct our view of reality without even realizing it."

"For informational sake," I added, "You might read *The Crack in the Cosmic Egg* by Joseph Chilton Pearce (1971). The book provides an excellent and insightful description of how the socialization process shapes and limits our view of the world. We then find ourselves unable to see beyond the fragile eggshell we have unwittingly created. He also describes what it takes to break the cosmic egg that eventually defines the boundaries of our reality.

"For those who manage to do so, an immense new universe with unlimited possibilities unfolds. It may sound simple, but it's anything but. It requires transcending what you have been taught for a lifetime. Throughout history, our greatest discoveries have resulted from people shattering the egg that blinded them to what has since become commonplace. Think about electricity and exotic things like flying machines."

Linda sighed, "I would love to read everything you suggest, but do you know how much work I have to do?"

"Actually, I have a pretty good idea. I've been there and done that, remember? It's like a right-of-passage ritual in which the professors think that since they had to go through it, they want to see you plow the same ground to prove your worthiness."

"But" Linda interjected, "What they expect of us is almost inhuman. In my Psychodiagnostics class, the professor detailed his expectations. It amounted to 60 hours per week. And that's just for one class."

To let her know I appreciated her dilemma, I commented," The educational system was not constructed with the idea of developing and encouraging healthy, motivated students. The educational bureaucracy was designed for the comfort and convenience of the teachers. As it happens, teachers are not particularly interested in disruptive influences. As a society, we tend to sacrifice creativity and ingenuity for predictability."

While understandably disgruntled, Linda asked the obvious question. "Don't we want professionals to be selected from the best possible candidates? I hate to think that the system rewards conformists who do nothing more than work to maintain the status quo."

"Linda," it's worse than that. I guess we could call this growing-up day for you. Conformity is only part of the puzzle. The students who get ahead are often the ones we affectionately refer to as 'brown nosers.' They're the students who stroke the egos of their professors."

She looked somewhat strained as she objected, "I guess I need to play devil's advocate. If they are willing to toe the party line and are effective in schmoozing with the profs in the process, maybe they will turn out to be the best therapists. They are smart enough to play the game and must have reasonably good social skills. With those attributes, they should be able to make their clients feel comfortable."

I reminded her, "Effective psychotherapy has nothing to do with comfort. It's not two old friends sitting around sipping a cup of tea. If a client signs up for that, I have no problem with it. On the other hand, such relationships tend to become long-term friendships and have little to do with dealing with real issues. It's, unfortunately, an all-too-common practice to bill insurance companies as if there were actual treatment involved."

I continued, "I'm glad I can help you take a fresh look at things I've already learned the hard way. It's so easy to revert to old patterns of thinking. Comfort is seductive. Find an easy chair to sit in and grab a bottle of beer if you're satisfied. Good for you. Just let me know when you're done so we can begin the funeral arrangements.

"On the other hand, you can choose to live. We continually face the decision to seek comfort or to take a chance on living. Either direction entails pitfalls. You must discover for yourself if the risks involved outweigh the rewards. And here's the kicker. It's a decision we all make on almost a minute-to-minute basis. Do I stay where I am, or do I move forward? That easy chair can be tempting. It's safe, and it isn't going anywhere. And if you get too comfy in it, neither will you."

Linda sighed, concluding, "In listening to the recording, I can't believe how close I came to backing out of this whole thing. My ego kept trying to convince me I didn't need to see you. But something about you kept me from drifting into the comfort of my prior existence."

I nodded in agreement. "You experienced a flight into health. It's not unexpected. Deep inside, your ego was panicked. It wanted to convince you to stay safe. It started with the idea that you didn't need to see me. As our interactions became more intriguing, that plan didn't work. Naturally, you then tried to change strategies by thinking you could make our work intellectual by assuming a student role so that you wouldn't have to take risks."

"As usual," she said with a degree of resignation, "You wouldn't permit me any relief. You know, you can be relentless."

"Truth is," I admitted, "I would have let you go if you had stood in the place of being okay. When there was hesitation after I challenged you, I knew that we had more to do. As you know, I'm fascinated by fairy tales. Do you remember Wizard of Oz? In the end, Dorothy was asked if she was the queen. She hesitated in her response. When asked again, she stood in the place of being the queen. Only then did everyone acknowledge her.

"If you go through life being half-assed, you will have a half-assed life. It's essential to be selective in choosing what to commit to. But when you make that choice, you must put all your being behind it. If either of you has even the slightest hesitation about what we are doing at any point, we need to address your concerns or say our farewells.

Linda's Journal

June 12

What a great session! I think I'm finally beginning to appreciate and understand the dynamics of psychotherapy. When Bill described my flight into health, he brought the point home. I can now see the intense internal battle I was experiencing. The kinetics were amazing as I moved simultaneously toward and against him. The struggle I was experiencing involved him externally but also me internally.

Psychotherapy is so much more than just a discussion. It involves every human emotion in an ongoing push and pull. I love psychology and psychotherapy. I can't wait to see where this journey leads me. Adding Rick to the equation should make it twice as fun.

Listening to Bill's stumbling hesitancy during the recorded session as the temperature rose, it became clear that I wasn't the only one struggling. The intensity of the battle overwhelmed him as both our egos and our Selves became engaged. I'm so lucky that some small part of him could step back from what was going on to call time. I can't even imagine how many marriages are ruined because neither party does so.

Even though we were in a professional relationship, heat is heat. Once it gets going, it's hard to stop. If you allow it to carry over into your fantasies, as I did, it's nearly impossible. Calling it transference is a way of intellectualizing it. To me, it's better understood as an externalization of the battle that raged between myself and my ego. My attempted flight to health was another example of the dynamics involved.

Rick's Journal

June 13

There was a definite highlight to our last session. It was gratifying and enlightening to see Linda experiencing confusion, horror, and guilt in her way. There were things that each of us had done which were unacceptable. In Linda's case, the main issue was her inappropriate interest in Bill. Her attempt to blame me for her problems was also upsetting. I did my part by getting mad and bursting into Bill's office.

The beautiful thing is that we could step back and forgive ourselves and each other. We found a way to look at major stumbles without feeling that our marriage was being threatened. Strange to say, but I almost think that the things that happened served to bring us closer together. We had become too safe in our relationship. There were ongoing squabbles, but we never risked talking about anything real. It's funny. As Bill is taking us further and further away from what I've known to be a reality, I'm paradoxically finding that my way of looking at life is becoming more solid.

I liked the description of the cosmic egg of beliefs that encapsulates and defines us. I can see how it's necessary to recognize it if we are ever to have any chance of cracking it open. I hadn't thought about the roles involved in my life. But he has a point. There is an inherent dissonance in the ways I act in various situations. I typically don't even consider it. At the same time, it contributes to inner discomfort. I've always had this nagging feeling that things just aren't quite right.

Fifth Meeting

I began by saying, "It's probably not your favorite topic, but obviously, nothing is off-limits in our discussions. Do you happen to remember the time when you went bonkers?"

Linda appeared to be deep in contemplation as she stroked her temples and furrowed her brow. "No… no… wait, there was something. You don't happen to mean the time that I tried to dissolve into you?"

"Good one, Linda. Nothing to see here. Nothing to remember. I'm sure it had no impact on you. Just another day at the beach," I scoffed.

"It wasn't one of my prouder moments, but I would certainly like to learn more about what happened."

"Now that you're well removed from the situation, I think examining the entire scene in some detail would be worthwhile."

"As much as I don't want to do so," she relented, "I really, *really* do want to. If there were ever anything I wanted to know more about, it would be that."

"Use ob-op," I encouraged, "And tell us what happened."

"Okay. While I had no idea at the time, Barb was already working her evil magic on me. It's not logical in the way we usually look at things, but she had cast a spell. In my work with you, I was already agitated, and my sense of reality had been shaken. It's hard to accept, but I had regressed to the point of being a silly little girl. I shudder to consider the impact on Rick."

Rick was happy to have a chance to join in at that point. "You think your idea of reality was thrown off kilter? You can't imagine what it did to me. You're the foundation of my life. When you went crazy, so did I."

I didn't want to miss my chance to jump in the ring, so I volunteered, "The situation was a first for me as well. I've never called a client over a missed appointment, and I've certainly never gone to their homes. It was a further indication that we have a connection beyond what any of us could have understood."

With an exasperated look, Rick commented, "Bill, from the start, you've really messed with my head. I was rocking along slow and steady. Then you turned my world into a nightmare. I don't know what to say other than 'thank you.'"

There were smiles as we shared a sense of relief, having lived through that unsettling event together.

Linda's unquenchable thirst for understanding prompted her to ask, "What was behind my regression? I get it about being triggered by my unresolved business with Barb, but surely that alone wasn't enough to drive me over the edge."

"You're undeniably right," I acknowledged. "Do you remember Jesus wandering through the desert for 40 days? It might seem different on the surface, but the ego battle he was experiencing was much the same. Like you, he was ultimately able to resist the temptation to succumb to worldly temptations. In other words, he achieved a major victory in his struggle with ego."

Linda was obviously nonplussed at the comparison as she objected. "So, I go a little crazy, and then you say I'm like Jesus? Maybe I need to go all the way off the deep end and see what happens."

"Linda, you already know. You've flirted with craziness more than a few times. Let's bring Rick into the picture. I can barely imagine what it must have been like for him."

"Nothing out of the ordinary," he joked. "My wife goes nuts. A strange man enters our bedroom and spends time with her while I sit in the living room. She walks by totally naked. I don't see what the big deal is."

"Once again, it's a good reminder of the importance of perspective," I suggested. "Looking back, can you now see how that incident shaped the development of your relationship? It shook you out of your cocoons and enlivened your slumbering marriage."

Linda was the first to register her surprise. "Leave it to you to find a gigantic positive in one of the worst days of my life. Looking back,

I'm amazed at how my ego tried to regain its footing during the next session by telling you that I would become a prostitute. I had no idea I could be that creative or that audacious."

"From there, things really started picking up steam," I commented. "Your concerns were basically resolved. We built trust, which removed a huge roadblock. Here's a new and vital concept. You're very aware of the battle with the ego. Taking it a step further, a similar struggle accompanies every relationship of any depth."

Rick chimed in, "I can't wait to hear this one."

"People understandably have reservations in dealing with others. You can't just open your emotional wallet and say, 'Have at it.' With time and trust, however, a bond develops, which is greater than simply two people interacting. In a sense, a higher, joined entity takes on a character of its own and transcends the individual egos. You can judge the depth of a friendship or, for that matter, any type of relationship by examining the extent to which that occurs. It doesn't even require any special awareness. It's more of a letting go.

"If you trust another sufficiently to allow them to see the real 'you,' an extraordinary bond develops. That's why you've been personally wounded when something happens to someone you truly care about. They genuinely have become a part of you."

Rick nodded in agreement. "As I reflect on my relationships, I can see the game of risk I've played. I want to get to know people better, but do I really? What if I reveal myself, and then they back off, leaving me hanging? What if I genuinely care and something happens to them? Additionally, it's too easy to allow a thoughtless or misunderstood word to cause a rift. There is a pleasure-pain balance involved in interpersonal relationships."

"And here's an interesting point," I interjected. An aspect of that risk is emotional capital. How much and how many people should you care about? If you emotionally invest in one person, does that mean you have less capacity to have feelings about another? Alternatively, does caring, in general, enhance your ability to care for more people? Further complicating the issue, are you cheating the people you already care about by letting more in?"

Linda commented, "I just had an interesting thought. There's a sort of parallel to the zero-sum game concept. We tend to think of things finitely, like everything must balance. But in reality, emotions don't work that way. The more you allow yourself to experience, the more you can feel."

"Yes, I agree," I said. "Math doesn't apply in the usual way."

Rick mulled over the idea. "Can we extend the idea to pets? We lost a dog that I was crazy about. Afterward, I couldn't take the emotional risk involved with adopting another. Linda and I had quite a heated and prolonged discussion about it. To me, it just wasn't worth the eventual, inevitable heartache. Why cause yourself to feel unnecessary pain?"

Linda chortled. "Sure, you can be Dr. Spock if you like. Just leave me out. I want to be human. What is life if you don't have feelings? If you don't want to risk pain, you might as well go ahead and die."

Not having learned my lesson, I tiptoed back into discussing sexual stereotypes. "It's a shame that men are supposed to suppress their feelings. How can denying emotions be a sign of strength? I certainly agree that the ability to modulate how we express them is a necessary and important sign of maturity, but it's horrible to extend it to say that men who have feelings are sissies or girlies." I glanced at my watch and said, "But I'm not sure this discussion is the best use of our time. Let's re-calibrate and meet again next week."

Linda's Journal

June 20

These sessions are certainly not without emotional risk. First, I had to sit and listen to the embarrassing sex scene. I should have expected that Bill was not about to let up. This week, he wanted me to re-live my psychotic episode. I love this process, but it's not a bowl of cherries.

As hard as it was and as much as I wanted to resist it, I trusted Bill enough to use that horrible time as a learning opportunity. The result was truly awesome. This time, I felt incredible compassion for myself. I could see all the events that led up to my craziness and the helplessness and confusion I was experiencing. I felt no shame, guilt, or anger. Or maybe I should say that I felt all three and more. It's just that I was feeling them and, simultaneously, not feeling attached to or invested in them. To be more precise, it was a profound episode of 'seeing.'

It's really kind of funny the way my ego tried to bounce back. I've got to give it credit. I thought that telling Bill, during our individual sessions, that I was going to become a prostitute would put him back on his heels. As it turned out, he was ready for me. I'm so glad that he knows what he's doing. If not, I (my ego) would have won, and it's obvious what would have followed. What a loss that would have been!

I don't want to get too wrapped up in it, but there was a bonus. Bill proved that he cared about me by coming to my house. I'm sure it wasn't easy for him. He has a thing about boundaries. Thank God for that. Something else positive came from the ordeal. After he shared that experience with me in its entirety, how could I not trust him?

Rick's Journal

June 20

She told Bill that she was going to become a prostitute! Who is this woman? Incredibly, I've been married to her for years, and never in my wildest dreams did I imagine she could come up with a statement like that. I discovered that she was a real pistol. And it was loaded. It's no wonder that I had been afraid to pull the trigger.

Bill brought things together for me when he talked about relationships as having a life of their own. It's funny, but I've never thought of it so organically. It helps make sense of my disequilibrium. When Linda went off the deep end. I thought I was losing it as well.

I'm almost surprised that I dealt with it as well as I did. Even though Linda and I had been living separate lives, our relationship was the glue to my sanity. The world can get chaotic. Knowing that Linda was there, even when we didn't get along, was critical to my stability.

In retrospect, the whole scene was almost comical. After our phone call, Bill entered our house with obvious trepidation. But I could also tell he cared. While his focus was quite appropriately on Linda, he showed consideration for me throughout the incident. Even when Linda walked by without the benefit of clothing, he held it together. When he asked how I was doing, I felt the dam begin to break. I don't trust easily, but I began to think I had found a man I could have confidence in.

I've even started to re-examine this whole feeling idea. I've always been told that such nonsense is for the lady folk. Could it be that I was cheating myself and even Linda? The very idea of opening myself up to emotions scares me. It goes against all my conditioning. Now I have to wonder, is there a world I have purposefully shut out? Might it be worth considering? I'm feeling antsy just thinking about it. I think I'll put it on the shelf for the time being.

Sixth Meeting

I announced, "It's time we step back from what we've been doing."

Linda's reaction was shock, followed by concern. Rick was intrigued until a disturbing thought caught up with him. "Please, please, please tell me that you haven't bought us plane tickets to Costa Rica or Eastern Mongolia, wherever that is."

I grinned, "I'd almost forgotten about that. I had some pretty terrifying nights in the wilderness in preparation for my final transformation. Have you given any thought to which jungle you would like to visit? Or maybe you prefer more of a desert ambiance."

Linda broke the tension by commenting, "You really are a rascal, aren't you? You can hide it for so long, but it always comes out."

I laughed. "You got me dead to rights. I like to play. I like it even more when others play with me. I have to be careful not to do it at their expense. As you know, I'm playing with a different deck of cards."

Linda said, "I love the playful part of you, just not when I find myself squirming. How about explaining what you meant when you said stepping back?"

"It's obvious we've come a long way from when I first met you," I explained. As we've worked together, we've drifted so far from psychotherapy that I can't even see it from here. But there's good news in store. It no longer makes sense for me to charge you for our visits ... if that's okay with you."

Somewhat predictably, Rick whooped, "You mean we get all this for free! Are you Santa Claus?"

While I enjoyed the pleasant interplay, it was time to get serious. "Despite how it may have seemed at times, ethics and professionalism are extremely important to me. We are now sharing in a way that is far beyond psychotherapy. I still have things to teach, but our relationship is now much more equal and intimate."

Linda squealed, "I love it. Does that mean I can hug you now?"

"Help yourself. As long as Rick is here, I would love it."

She did, and I did. Happily, Rick seemed to enjoy our unexpected show of affection.

Getting back on track, I said, "Along those lines, I'll tell you a little more about my personal life. I met a wonderful woman a few months after my first meeting with Linda. God knows it wasn't always easy, but somehow, we worked through a tumultuous courtship and ended up married. Ever heard of 'Taming of the Shrew?' Of course, there is the remote possibility that she might characterize it a little differently."

Linda leaned forward, almost begging, "I've got to hear more."

I'm sure you remember that we worked on issues with jealousy through our sessions."

"Do I ever!"

"My wife, Julie, genuinely struggled with jealousy. She had a dream in which I was unfaithful. Afterward, she wouldn't speak to me for two weeks. As you might imagine, trying to bring reason to another person's dreams creates a helpless feeling. You can now see how the gift of transformation helped us deal with those tumultuous times. Through all the craziness, and I'm not putting it all on her because I was caught up in the emotional maelstrom as well, we were able to come together in awareness."

Linda somehow managed to look appreciative, even as she sneered, "Thanks for sharing the Cliff's Notes version. Do you *really* think I'm going to be satisfied with that? Give!"

"I don't think reliving my personal soap opera with you would be beneficial. On the other hand, I do think it would be worthwhile to reveal the outcome."

Linda didn't seem particularly happy, but she said, "I guess I'll have to take what I can get."

Rick groaned as he commented, "You're going to tell us that you learned to put her needs before your own."

"Sounds logical," I agreed. "But the place we attained is very different. It's not some noble position of self-sacrifice. I don't put her needs before mine."

Linda tried to put her hand over her mouth, but a brief "Oh!" escaped.

"Remember, in supra-self-transformation, you cease, on a higher level, to be separate individuals. You truly become one. By giving the needs of the other greater priority in the way that Rick mentioned, we would be indulging in separateness. At worst, doing so would reflect paternalism or even martyrdom. Putting your partner's wants and needs first is a great way to present your relationship, but only if your primary interest is patting yourself on the back.

"In contrast, Julie and I see our individual needs as equally important and work together to meet them. If we both want the big slice of pie, we decide who is the hungriest or who is the bigger fan of sweets. We don't strive for egolessness or sainthood. Instead, we have opted to become one ego, directed by our higher Selves that we are now in the process of joining."

Linda couldn't contain her curiosity. "Please tell me in great detail about your transformation with Julie. You don't have to tell me everything…just who, what, when, where, how, plus any other items that come to mind."

"Linda, I'm eager to share some fantastic news with you. The fact is that it hasn't happened yet. We're certainly moving in that direction, but we're taking our time. There is no doubt that we're married 'til death do us part.' We are not, however, jumping headlong into a bond that would last through eternity.

"Bringing it back to you and Rick for a moment, I wanted to mention some of the nuts and bolts of getting to the next goal we have in mind. You two are doing well in allowing your relationship to blossom in awareness. I want to make sure that you're maintaining a balance between spiritual development and the realities of coexistence in your everyday lives. To that end, I think the time is right for you to consider marital therapy. That work is out of my lane, but I can make a referral. I want to ensure that your relationship is as clean as possible on this level before introducing you to the next."

They both nodded in agreement. Rick volunteered, "As high as we've been flying, we still have silly issues, like who is going to pick up the dirty socks."

"No reason to feel bad about it," I counseled. "Reality is. You can't fly all the time. Mundane matters exist and must be dealt with. You won't reach some pinnacle that allows you sufficient altitude to escape the inevitable conflicts of everyday life. However, you can learn to deal with them from a different level so that the resulting skirmishes become almost comical."

Linda playfully observed, "I love how you tell us you can't describe the transformation and then turn around and tell us all about it. It's a good thing that I like and respect you. Otherwise, I would be tempted to kick you in the butt."

"I love that you said that," I responded. "You just provided an example of what I'm trying to say. You mentioned an understandable annoyance, but you said it from a place where it's rather funny."

It appeared that Linda was contemplating my remark before she concluded, "Once again, I see your point. There was a time I wanted to shoot you for seemingly contradicting yourself. I'm now in a place from which it all makes sense. Words aren't important. The intent behind them is. If the intent is off, so will be the word choice."

"Lesson learned," I concluded. "Of course, it's obvious by now that the learning never stops because there are so many levels to traverse in getting to know the Self. Before we get back to the recordings, there is an incidental matter I would like to address. I'm sure you've heard of L. Ron Hubbard's Scientology. I wanted to make a distinction between being 'clean' in my terms and 'clear' in his.

"I was a fan of his skill in writing science fiction novels. Maybe I should disclose a personal conclusion that might endanger me if it got out. His disciples would not be happy having me express this opinion, but I believe that he started Scientology as, more or less, a joke. He was brilliant, and I think he just wanted to see what he could get away with. I've visited that space, so I have some sense of it."

I continued, "The foundational goal of Scientology is to become clear. According to my understanding, that goal has nothing to do with releasing ego attachments. Instead, it involves an attempt to release all tension together with associated troublesome thoughts. It's a worthy goal, even if the methods for attaining it are rather amateurish.

"What I find most bothersome is the construction of a pseudoscience that purports to be a religion. Ultimately, its true purpose involves gaining control over its followers. It's another example of what happens when a person attains an enhanced level of awareness and subsequently allows their ego to take over. In contrast, when you are clean, you rise above the petty attractions of this world. You can enjoy them, but there is nothing that can hold you.

Linda gushed, "I love how you mix in information while guiding us toward transformation."

"I also enjoy our discussions but remember there is more to it than meets the eye. Even though we are now on an equal footing, I'm continuing to hold the place of being your teacher. My words are not intended to inform so much as to distract. The preparation goes on at a deeper level."

Linda looked both intrigued and disappointed. "And I suppose you're not going to explain any further?"

"I'm sure you've heard the expression, 'in the fullness of time.' That's my answer. What I could say would make no sense until you're in the place to hear it. There is no game involved. It simply is what it is."

Linda's Journal

June 27

I'm ecstatic that Bill is seeing us more as peers and even telling us about his personal life. How ironic is it that he has also experienced the agony of jealousy, just from the other side? I can't even imagine what it must be like to be married to him. I write that with a sense of awe and not a trace of envy.

I wonder how he does it. He somehow picked up on the re-developing friction between Rick and me. Little things had started to become big. My ambivalence concerning marital therapy has disappeared. Rick is willing, and I say full steam ahead.

My curiosity concerning Bill might sound strangely out of proportion. I mean, it's not like Rick isn't my main emphasis. It's just that Bill has had such an incredible influence on every aspect of my life. What I wouldn't give to somehow peek inside his skull. More and more, I'm discovering that there is an actual human being in there.

Strange to say, my breakthroughs are becoming almost routine. I'm not saying in any sense that they are insignificant. They're anything but. What did I ever do to deserve all this? In any case, I finally think his message about words sunk in. There is an attainable place in which I don't have to watch the words I use. I say it's attainable only because I sometimes catch a glimpse of it. It might sound trivial, but it's much more than that.

The key is intent. If I become pure, the words will come out right. I compare it to shooting a three-point shot in basketball. You practice and practice. But there is a point at which you don't even have to think as you let the ball fly.

Rick's Journal

June 28

I never would have imagined thinking this way, but I'm sort of happy with the marital therapy idea. I really and truly want to be a good husband. But the fact is, I'm not very good at it. I get so wrapped up in the things that are important to me that I forget to give Linda her due.

Bill surprised me with the way he described his marriage. I had always thought that the idea was to put your wife first. I and most other husbands remember to do that when it's convenient. But then there is a game on TV or work that needs to be done. Afterward, I feel bad, at least until the next time it comes up.

The way he explained it makes sense. Our goal is mutual happiness. I don't have to prove myself with grand gestures. It's okay for me to do things that I enjoy. It's also acceptable for her to do things that make no sense to me. By the way, who came up with this mani-pedi nonsense? In any case, I don't need to understand. I can simply enjoy her enjoyment as we move together toward becoming one.

Our relationship with Bill has reached another level. I'm relieved about the free sessions, though that doesn't seem like nearly such a big deal to me anymore. I couldn't possibly put a value on what he shares with us in any case.

Seventh Meeting

It was not typical for Rick to interrupt our recordings, but this time, he couldn't help himself. "My God, Linda. I still can't believe it. You told him that you were going to become a prostitute? You mentioned it before but hearing it on the recording brought it home. It's like you decided that you hadn't played with my head enough when you went off the deep end earlier. What the hell were you thinking?"

Initially, Linda was understandably defensive. But it didn't take her long to gain her footing. "Rick, you must remember I was dealing with that sadist sitting over there. He had me so that I didn't know up from down. I wasn't going to let him control me, so I decided to turn the tables on him. As it happened, he didn't let me. No matter what game I tried to play, he wouldn't allow himself to become hooked. My ego wanted to fight him, but I was intrigued."

I asked, "Can you now appreciate my strategy when I diverted you to a discussion about semantics?"

"In retrospect, of course. At the time, I was still confused. Now, I can see that you were taking advantage of my vulnerability to teach a lesson that I was reluctant to learn. I didn't want to give up my self-definition of being a jealous person. Jealousy was, after all, at the core of my identity. As it turns out, it was at the center of my ego."

"As much as it was important to put the construct of jealousy in its proper place, there was a follow-up lesson of much greater importance. Tell me about where you are with that now."

"I'm a little embarrassed. I hadn't thought much about it before listening to the recording. I had philosophy classes in college but had never heard of the 'is of identity.' Initially, I thought you were making a mountain out of a molehill. I'm now developing some appreciation for the way language can trap us. It's so easy to casually say that somebody is___ or something is___. But in doing so, we are saying that there's nothing more to them. When you say that someone or something is this or that, you define them and limit your capacity for seeing them as anything else."

"I truly hope you will both keep that thought in mind. Any time you say that John Doe is stupid, crazy, or even handsome, you will have put him in a box. Every future contact with him will be defined and directed accordingly. Because our brains work to keep things orderly and in line with our expectations, it's likely you will unwittingly create interactions that will confirm your initial thought or statement."

I shifted my attention to Rick for the moment, "You may remember when I mentioned personality disorders in the context of our discussion of Barb."

He nodded and grinned. "Sure, using that label allowed me to get beyond the fantasy I had created. She was no longer some perfect, magical creature who recognized my magnificence and worshipped me as all women should."

I somehow got the sense that I appreciated his attempt at humor more than Linda. I remarked, "If you'll remember, you later became incensed at my implication that there might be an underlying flaw in how Barb presented herself. I hope it's now obvious that I intended to teach rather than to denigrate someone you cared about. I don't know how much the lesson took hold at that moment, but with the benefit of listening to the recording, what is your take?"

"I shuddered when you first mentioned listening to these recordings, but I'm now glad that you suggested it. I remember intellectually the way you explained it at the time, but hearing it again really reinforces your message. Words are intended to be our tools rather than our masters. But they can be either. There are times when it's helpful to put people in a box by defining them. Much more frequently, we err in the other direction. We define people and then miss out on the enrichment they might offer. People whom we might write off as old, stupid, or ugly are still souls, just in a box that may initially seem unattractive. If we take the time to unwrap it, an incredible gift may be waiting inside."

"Excellent insight, Rick. Because it's such a key component in the portion of the lessons that involves semantics, I really want to bring home the point concerning the 'is of identity.' If you say that a equals b, you are stating that b is nothing more than a. By the rules of mathematics and logic, it cannot have other characteristics. When a person says that Joe is a bad kid, something I witnessed another psychologist saying during a deposition, they are saying that Joe has no redeeming qualities. He is doomed to badness. As a side note, the judge was not impressed by that characterization. The young man and his mother won the case."

Rick seemed intrigued. "Wow. That's something I will definitely keep in mind. When opposing counsel makes that sort of statement, and they will, I know just how to turn the tables."

"It's the reason that I never say that a client "is" a borderline personality disorder. They may fit all the diagnostic criteria and should be dealt with accordingly, but that doesn't mean there is nothing more to them. The same with people whom I've diagnosed with antisocial personality disorder. I wouldn't trust them and believe that often, the public needs to be protected from them. Due to some unknown combination of genetics and environment, they become people who don't fit in society. I'm saying that not so much as a judgment but as an unfortunate acknowledgment of reality."

Linda felt a need to object. "You seem like such an understanding person, yet how you put that sounds so harsh."

"Linda, I can appreciate the sentiment of turning the other cheek. But if you keep doing so until your body is nearly lifeless, what have you proved? Maybe the aggressor has other wonderful qualities, but there is a point at which it really doesn't matter. Based on my experience, sometimes the best you can hope for is the likelihood that people who have been given certain diagnoses will burn out physiologically as they age. Eventually, they will present less of a threat to themselves and others. I truly hope that advances in psychology and medicine will change that pessimistic prognosis. But for now, it is what it is."

"Now, let's get back to Linda. It is, after all, her turn."

She shook her head vigorously. "No, it's perfectly fine. I think Rick could use the heat. But come to think of it, I would like to ask about something that's been on my mind. When I first came to see you, would you say I was depressed?"

I wanted to answer her question without getting into the lecture her question deserved. Despite my better instincts, I took the bait. "Remember what we were just discussing. What would I have been doing if I had thought of you as being a depressed person? Do you see how easy it is to slip back into the 'is of identity?' If I had dealt with you in that way, I would have been dealing with depression rather than with you as an individual. That's one of the limitations of psychology utilizing the medical model. In that scenario, I would have simply applied the appropriate treatment protocol and hoped for the best.

"Fact is, I didn't diagnose you at all. If we had been going through your insurance company, which I simply don't do, I would have come up with something relatively innocuous, like Adjustment disorder, unspecified. But that would have been a stretch. That diagnosis would have gone on your record. Additionally, there was no specific stressor, and you didn't fit the criteria for clinical depression."

"But I was unhappy," she protested.

"You were experiencing ups and downs, and the downs had started to become more common than the ups. But you still had times when you felt okay, and importantly, you still had the capacity to experience enjoyment. A primary symptom of clinical depression is alexithymia, in other words, the inability to feel good about anything. People who are experiencing that horrible symptom quit participating in life because nothing makes them feel better. Unfortunately, many of them feel hopeless and don't have the energy to seek help."

Apparently, it was time for information gathering as Linda continued in questioning mode. "Can you help me understand the difference between people who are simply down in the dumps and people who are genuinely depressed?"

"As long as we are on this earth, we are bound by the limitations of our physical beings. We are subject to the whims of the extremely complex interactions of neurotransmitters with associated electrical activity involving our neural circuitry. It's my opinion that thoughts are largely a result of quantum activity, but more on that later. Suffice it to say that I think the field of neurobiology has largely been chasing its tail."

They both seemed interested, so I continued. "To a limited extent, we can influence this complex neural activity through our thoughts and, consequently, our moods. That's what psychotherapy is all about. Whether through genetics, environmental factors, or residuals of past experiences, there are times when our bodies turn against us. In mild cases, antidepressants can be beneficial, though an undetermined amount of their value is due to a placebo effect. People can also become psychotically depressed. In those unfortunate instances, they experience a cataclysmic disturbance of neural functions that overcomes their ego to the extent that they can no longer maintain any semblance of normality."

Linda nearly begged," I love it when you talk about psychology. Would you indulge me by sharing a little more?"

I like to clear up misconceptions about mental health, so I continued. "When we hear about mental illness, we naturally think of it as a disease. While it's tempting to think of it as analogous to an infection, it's not nearly that simple. While we still have a lot to learn about the brain, the great majority of people who seek treatment have behavioral-emotional problems resulting from past and present experiences associated with maladaptive ways of thinking. As a result, their ability to cope effectively is compromised.

"We try to fit mental illness into the medical model because it's easier to understand in that context. Additionally, it qualifies clients for insurance, which makes everyone except the insurance company happy. In actuality, most people seeking treatment have a dimensional rather than a categorical disorder. In other words, they have degrees of feeling sad or nervous. Those are natural states of being that we all experience at times. They are simply more troubled by those feelings, sometimes to a level that interferes with their ability to deal effectively with the challenges of everyday life.

"Complicating matters, there are disorders that are best understood as categorical. For example, either you do or you don't have schizophrenia. You can't be just a little bit schizophrenic, though there are high-functioning people who continue to work and sometimes maintain relationships even with the handicap of a thought disorder. Medication can definitely help with quashing auditory hallucinations and paranoid thoughts, and even, to some extent, the symptoms of disorganized thinking.

"Bipolar disorder is a little fuzzier because too many people get diagnosed with it simply because they have a history of moodiness. I can't tell you how many clients I've seen who have told me that they or someone in their family has had that diagnosis. Genuine Bipolar disorder is categorical, and people who are properly diagnosed should be medicated, though their cooperation with taking meds is likely to be less than ideal."

Linda's next question was quite obvious, and she was far from the first to ask it. "Why wouldn't they take the meds? I can't imagine anyone wanting to go through the hell of extreme emotions with all the real-life disasters that accompany them."

"Now we're getting into an area with complex legal-ethical complications. Many of the people with whom I've worked who have had a Bipolar diagnosis say that they only feel like themselves when they're in the up phase. That's when their creativity shines through. There is ample evidence throughout history of people with a retrospective diagnosis of Bipolar disorder who have achieved marvelous things. Many of those same people have also done terribly destructive things when their unchained and inadequately modulated thoughts escalated to psychosis."

I was accustomed to psychotherapy, which, in large part, involved allowing the client to provide the direction and content of discussions. I was again wandering outside my comfort zone, but Linda persisted, "Keep talking."

"Depression is typically one of the easiest presenting problems to treat, though I'll admit I've run across a couple of people with intractable symptoms. The easiest answer in those situations, at least the one that provides me some solace, is that they are psychotically depressed. For those unfortunate souls, their brains are a battlefield of dysregulated neurotransmitters and misfiring neurons. To the extent that they can or will reveal their inner thoughts, I've learned that their egos have become so beaten down that they can make little sense of reality."

Linda seemed distressed. "Please don't tell me that there are people you can't help. I thought you could do almost anything."

"Thank you for the confidence, even though it's misplaced or at least exaggerated. Mental health professionals can help the vast majority of people who genuinely want to improve their lives. Maybe I should emphasize that I'm talking about two clients out of hundreds. Allow me to switch to something more positive. Back when I was involved with a professional school, one of the degrees we offered was in Holistic Health Education."

Linda's interest peaked once again. "I'm so glad you're going to tell us more about that time."

I chuckled. "I could tell you stories about that crazy period in my life, but I would risk losing any of the minuscule credibility I've managed to build with the two of you. In fact, my wife has several times told me to write a book about those experiences. As it turns out, my writing skills could most generously be described as nonexistent."

Linda shook her head. "Fortunately, you don't have to write them down. Just tell us."

She was attentive and engaging. As a result, she steered me down a path I hadn't anticipated. In self-defense, I routed the conversation back to the previous topic. "Rather than getting into my personal experiences, let me explain a vital aspect of mental health that has gone almost unnoticed. I think that the problem can partially be traced to attempts to shoehorn psychotherapy into the medical model. As I mentioned before, the latter is dichotomous. You're either sick or you're well.

"Consequently, we talk about mental health professionals 'treating' their clients. I hope that someday we will get to the point of describing our work as promoting and encouraging our clients' well-being instead. I'm sure that you've gone through times when you felt especially healthy and happy for no identifiable reason. I've discovered that it's quite possible to live drug-free while feeling high throughout the day. The great thing is that, in doing so, you aren't weighed down by the cognitive mush or the unpredictable side effects that accompany drug use."

Linda shrugged and said, "At the risk of sounding repetitive, you know what I'm going to ask."

"Well, I will tell you a somewhat amusing story. During my internship, I met a man who described himself as a healer. He had no licensure and was elusive when asked how he had developed his skills. Regardless, he had marvelous abilities. Some aspects of his treatments were quite painful as they included deep tissue work, but the results were more than worth it. I was fortunate to learn from him and even incorporate some energy work in my early practice.

"One of the first instructions I received from him was to eat a watermelon. I thought it was no big deal until he told me he expected me to eat the whole watermelon. I complied and then spent a sleepless night going to the bathroom every few minutes. The next day, he belatedly clarified his recommendation. He laughingly told me that he had meant to eat the rind and the seeds rather than the entire melon.

"The salient aspect of the story involves the well-earned faith I had in him that caused me to be so naïve. Before meeting him, I had gone through life feeling okay. But it was totally different when I was able to wake up buzzing with energy and feeling truly happy to be alive. It's going to sound a bit psychotic, but I even thought that I could tolerate being tortured because I so cherished every moment."

"I like your story, but I want to hear about the good stuff," she politely demanded.

"Surely you don't want me to trounce any further on my credibility. Let's get back to the recordings."

Linda surprised us both by standing up and gently slapping me. "You're such a tease. I hope you know that I genuinely love-hate you."

Rick joined in. "I should probably feel jealous that she said that, except I feel the same way."

"I appreciate the cathexis, or at least I think I do. At the least, it shows that you're both more than a little involved in the process."

We had wandered a bit off course, so I attempted to right the ship. "Thinking back to our multi-purpose sessions, I'm working with you in preparation for supra-self-transformation while also providing you with information you can use in your daily lives. A secondary purpose involves assisting you both in your professional development. Regarding the latter goal, I hope you can recognize the ebb and flow of our current and past sessions as we move back and forth from tension-filled moments to straightforward information sharing. While it may seem natural, and I hope it does, it's akin to directing a symphony. We progress from the innocuous to topics that are fraught. Then we journey back again, all leading to the crescendo of transformation.

"The professional goals for each of you are quite different as Linda is interested in providing psychotherapy, and Rick wants to improve his skills in arguing cases in the courtroom. But you should both benefit as you begin to think of performing your work as a means of directing the melody. Whether you are dealing with a client or an opposing attorney, you will be making music while they are still trying to figure out which instruments you are playing."

I suddenly had Rick's attention. "I don't know how familiar you are with my work, but it's cutthroat. Each side is constantly maneuvering to seek advantage. I've already benefitted from learning how to use perspective. Is it possible that our further work will give me an additional edge?"

"Rick, I'm glad you asked that question. It illustrates the challenge we face. In answer, yes, it can provide a huge advantage. You're not going to be as thrilled with the follow-up. Remember, you must always ask yourself if you're acting from ego. To the extent that you look inside and find a positive answer, it is imperative that you back off and recalibrate. I guarantee you'll have to learn your lessons along the way. But I hope that you keep my caution in mind. Do you remember a Biblical reference about being able to move a mountain if you have sufficient faith?"

They both nodded. "Well, here's the catch. If you have developed that level of faith, i.e., awareness, you would have no interest in moving mountains. If you had reached that pinnacle of essence, you would have effectively become the mountain. On the other hand, if your ego tries to move a mountain, you may have some luck if you operate from a higher level of awareness. But the mountain will likely come down right on top of you."

Linda's Journal

July 5

I thought I was really getting somewhere with my revelation that having a clean intent allows you to make good word choices naturally. Bill told me that it's not quite that simple. I think he was reminding me that I'm not there yet. I still must pay attention to what I'm thinking and saying so I don't lapse into bad habits. It's still kind of a pain to do so, but it's becoming more natural.

As I look back, the last session provided some necessary reminders. I had let the idea of my witness start to fade away. My witness is critical in helping me remember that reality is not real, except that it really is. Once again, I start wondering what sort of craziness I've gotten both me and Rick into. Then I remember how helpful it is to utilize my witness in stepping back from life even as I become fully involved in everything I do. It's a powerful feeling to be invulnerable, especially when I'm most vulnerable.

Rick and I are just starting to share our reactions to the sessions. We've both been too overstimulated to just sit back and talk. As it turns out, his thoughts, both positive and negative, parallel my own. He also feels overwhelmed at times. In using that word, we've agreed that it fits in two ways. We are blown away by all we are learning, as well as how it transcends anything we had ever imagined. We're both in awe.

It was also helpful to remember how much the opinions of others had controlled me. That's not to say that it was all bad. The pressure I felt to excel led me to success in many ways. I probably wouldn't have met and married Rick without it. I'm saying that simply because Rick and I wouldn't have run in the same lanes. However, there's got to be a better way to motivate your children. I'll have to add that to my long list of questions.

Rick's Journal

July 5

I'm so glad that Linda and I made the time to sit down and talk. When I say made, I mean it quite literally. She is incredibly busy. But we must still keep our priorities in mind. With all the time pressure we're under, friction occasionally develops. I'm kind of glad we're starting marital therapy next week, even though it's going to add to our scheduling woes.

I continue to be amazed as I listen to how Bill led Linda through similar lessons. I loved hearing about his method of dealing with obsessions. Certain thoughts still have a way of grabbing me at times. An essential aspect of this awareness idea is catching them early before they pick up steam. I now realize that if I let them go too far, I become irrational and lose my emotional equilibrium.

There is no doubt that I'm a better lawyer as a result of my time with Bill. Previously, I would have laughed if anyone suggested I see a psychologist in order to improve my practice. I've noticed that people are more deferential and attentive when I speak. At the same time, I'm choosing my words rather than allowing my mouth to go off on its own. It wasn't something I really wanted to hear, but I will definitely have to take his caution about using power under advisement.

Eighth Meeting

"I've never had children. But putting you through the wringer as I did, I can empathize with what parents must go through. Knowing I was setting the stage for you to rise up and then plop right back down was not easy for me. But as you know, love requires letting go."

"Thank God you didn't completely let me go. You gave me the space to learn needed lessons, but you were there when I needed you. I hated what I put Rick through during that time."

Rick, being the really good guy he is, was understanding. "My love, everything happened for a reason. I'm just grateful that it worked out as it did. I've got to admit I went through a lot of confusion.

"My friends often joke about how moody their wives are. They say they usually end up just trying to stay out of their way. I adopted that strategy myself at times as well. But I had faith in you and in my love for you. Sometimes, I wasn't so sure about that man sitting right a few feet away, but I sure like how it's all developed."

Rick looked at her with puppy dog eyes, and I wanted to bring them back to earth. The best way to do so involved reintroducing a somewhat touchy subject. "Linda, I can't count the times I said something to annoy you. Quite possibly, my pestering you about the words you were rattling off was the most offensive. Would you agree?"

"I may have to put on boxing gloves before I take that one on," she laughed. "I was doing my best to learn from you. Still, at times, I felt like all you were giving me crap just for the fun of it. I'm naturally a social animal. I enjoy conversation; however, I am not with you. I felt like a child in a Catholic school. Just the slightest wrong word, and you would slap my hands."

"True," I admitted. "But if I didn't, you know what would have."

"I had to learn the hard way. I know… I know. You tried to tell me. It was like the situation parents go through that you mentioned at the start of our meeting. I had to find out for myself."

"It's like growing up," I acknowledged. "There are no shortcuts. You've got to go through the school of hard knocks and find out for yourself. The price of talking and thinking automatically is something you can no longer indulge in. You simply don't have that luxury when you enter the path to awareness."

Linda seemed introspective and reflective. "On the surface, awareness allows you to rise above words, so they are relatively unimportant. But then, when you use words through awareness, they become super important. Words are no longer trivial. They have a definite impact on reality."

Rick said, "What a pain, and yet what a gift. The more I use my words like lasers, the stronger I become. It's far from easy, but I'm learning how to avoid using my own words against me. I have, or it would be better to say, had many bad linguistic habits that I developed over the course of my life. Giving them up is a real challenge."

"I really like the way you're using your words. Just let me suggest one small refinement. Think of it not as giving them up but instead as replacing them. If you find yourself using depressogenic words, stop yourself for the split second necessary to think of a healthier way to think."

"How about an example? I'm not the sharpest tool in the shed."

"Rick, you're making this too easy," I joked. "Linda, maybe you can clarify for your self-proclaimed, slow-witted husband."

She giggled. "You know there's nothing I enjoy more than correcting him. It's kind of fun to watch someone else go through your torture regimen. It helps me see how easy it is to fall into the is-of-identity trap. Rick, please don't lead me to think of you as nothing more than a garden implement."

"Excellent, Linda. I applaud your insight. This leads me to another important concept. If you remember, I insisted on you using me as a mirror. In retrospect, tell me what you make of that."

"Once more, you were pretty slick. My ego wanted to find a way to get to you…to minimize the threat you imposed. I kept thinking I could outsmart you. At one point, and I hate saying this, knowing Rick is sitting next to me, I was even ready to seduce you. It's not that you're not wonderful and all that. But now I realize it was my ego not wanting to let go."

I was pleased at how well she was learning a seemingly simplistic but quite complex concept. "I'll have to admit, you almost tripped me at first. Then, I slipped into awareness and became liquid. There was nothing about me to hold onto or push against."

Rick inquired, "How in the world did you do that?"

"If you think back to your recent experiences, are you starting to find that happening?"

"Wow! I'm glad you mentioned it. As I think of it, there have been plenty of times. Other lawyers have used their old tricks to try to bait me. Even friends and acquaintances have said things that would have caused me to react before. Now, I'm more likely to go with the flow. And when I decide to take a stand, they had better watch out."

"Good point! The idea is not to become a nonperson. Instead, you want to think in terms of being an aware person. You can then let things blow past you. But you have also identified a place within yourself where you are invincible. It's necessary to use it with discretion, but it's a great place to know that you can access."

Linda inquired, "I agree with what you're saying, but how can I use it as a therapist?"

"Linda, I trust you enough to share a rather arcane bit of knowledge with you. There is a little-known and seldom-practiced technique known as emotional driving. To use it, the therapist must be as pure as the driven snow because it can go wrong in so many ways. Keep in mind that I'm just sharing information with you right now. Don't even think about using it at this point."

Linda complained, "And at what point do you quit being a tease? Just tell me what's involved, and I promise not to use it until I'm ready."

"Okay, I trust you. Emotional driving is an active expression of mirroring. In emotional driving, the therapist follows the client into whatever emotional space they enter in an attempt to hide. If they become sad, the therapist becomes sad. If they get angry, the therapist goes right with them into the space of anger, and so on. In doing so, the therapist must be absolutely clean. If any trace of ego accompanies the mood shift, the client will latch on to it. The battle will then be over, and both participants will have lost. And just to be totally clear, the therapist doesn't get angry at the client or sad in a sharing way with the client. Instead, they enter the pure state of the feeling with none of the usual baggage, such as blaming, defending, or even supporting.

"It's totally different from typical psychotherapy. A person observing would likely be confused and even incensed. They would probably think, 'What business does the therapist have getting mad at their client?' But that's the thing. Despite appearances, the therapist would not get mad at or cry with their client. Instead, they would simply be entering into the same space with them. If done without ego, the results can be astounding. The client's ego finally recognizes that there is nowhere to hide. The exposure of the ego is emotionally impactful. It's a powerful way of introducing a client to themselves."

Linda seemed a bit awestruck. "Boy, do you have a bag of tricks? I don't know whether to applaud you or run from you."

"You've certainly tried your hand at both if I remember correctly. Flattery has its charm. Being human, I can't help but relish a bit of admiration, perhaps even more than the average person. That's largely because I recognize the whole affair for what it is—a game. I'm conscious that getting caught in your judgment or anyone else's spells potential trouble. But, shifting gears, are you interested in hearing about the first time I navigated the terrain of emotional driving?"

Even though we had ventured off in a rather obscure direction, they seemed interested, so I proceeded. "It wasn't in a professional setting. Soon after my transformation, I went to a party and found myself talking to a gorgeous girl. She was in a bitchy mood. Rather than taking offense, I consciously went into contrariness right along with her. Because her unpleasant demeanor wasn't chasing me away as intended, she became downright angry.

"At that point, I saw myself starting to back down and become apologetic. Instead, I decided to enter her program and allowed the feeling to escalate until I stood nose-to-nose, yelling right with her but with no ego involved. Since she still hadn't escaped, she broke down and said she wanted to kill herself. Relentlessly, I went into a suicidal space with her. After a couple more weak attempts at evasion, she broke through and was right there with me."

Linda was obviously fascinated. She looked at me hungrily and demanded, "What happened next?"

She entered the space of ecstasy as she was able to move past her ego and into essence. But I had bitten off more than I was ready to chew. I then had to convince her that she didn't have to fall in love with me simply because I had helped her find a deeper level within herself. It was at that point that I realized what women are talking about when they say that men don't understand them.

"Bringing things back to our business, this is a good time to remind you that I'm nothing more than a copycat. People much smarter than I have discovered these ideas. I'm just lucky enough to have stumbled onto them."

Linda had to ask, "Since you're saying that these ideas are not new, is there a chance I will study them in my third year?"

I'll have to admit that I got a kick out of her question. "Graduate school is not where you go to learn about what matters. That's not to say that you won't find useful information. But don't expect great revelations. If your professors were talented psychotherapists, do you think they would be teaching?"

I was pleased that Linda then came to the defense of her professors. "But you've already said that they are really smart. And I think that they are invested in my success."

"You're making a good point. Rather than criticizing the professors, it would be more appropriate for me to comment on the limitations of the system. In truth, I had the benefit of some great teachers along the way. When people make genuine jumps in learning or have Eureka moments, it's not because they're following a linear path. To do so, it's necessary to step beyond the bounds of traditional knowledge.

"The wisdom of the past is not codified in a manner that allows it to be easily transmitted. Remember, you can't teach knowledge unless you already know. You can repeat established facts and ideas, as typically happens in the classroom, but that ends up being no more than parroting the words. I'm glad that this topic came up. It's a good reminder that we're facing the challenge of using words to deal with something that is truly beyond words."

Linda's Journal

July 12

The shift in my relationship with Bill is becoming evident. While I like being his student/client, I also want to be more in control of what we're doing. For better or worse, I made a successful move in that direction. I discovered a tiny chink in Bill's armor; he likes to teach.

In retrospect, he probably knew what I was up to. But he indulged me. I wonder how often his regular clients find a way to divert him. I know I had little luck in my previous attempts to wiggle off his hook. Maybe it wasn't so much that I redirected him as it was that he knew I was seriously interested in what he had to say. There was no aspect of protecting my ego involved in my questioning. I don't think he would have wandered off into content if there had been. His way of relating is quite different since we are no longer keeping up any pretense of psychotherapy.

Independent of whether I enjoyed some minor victories, I learned a lot. I agree with everything he said, but I'm having trouble accepting his pessimism concerning people with certain disorders. I want to believe that there is some way we can help them. He talked about not writing off people with the way we unintentionally use our words. I hope the same mistake doesn't doom clients based on their diagnosis. I guess I'll have to find out for myself.

I'm proud of myself for jumping another barrier in getting to know Bill. I know that my emphasis should be on Rick, but at the moment, it's clear that Bill is my primary protagonist. In any case, I was fed up with his reluctance to share personal information. I stood up and gave him a little slap. I've always been deferential to authority figures, and it's unbelievable that I crossed that line. At the same time, I'm glad that I did. I'm doing what I can to redefine our relationship.

Rick's Journal

July 14

Things are improving daily between Linda and me. I think that marital therapy is going to help even more, though it's going to seem super strange to talk to a stranger about our sex life. Of course, weirdness has become part of my daily routine.

As an attorney, I make my living out of words. I love that I'm learning how to use them as tools in a very focused and productive way. I'm especially going to nail opposing counsel with the misuse of "is of identity." They are going to, inevitably, make declarative statements about my clients that are going to come back to haunt them. I was impressed by Bill's example of an attorney saying that so and so "was" a bad kid. Talk about prejudicial! Now, I know how to explain to a jury just how bad it was.

I overreacted a few months ago when Bill was talking about personality disorders in the obvious context of Barb. I was terribly sensitive and confused at that time. The way he used the term was ingenious. It allowed me to see her in a totally different context. He was right. He didn't diagnose her or say that she had a personality disorder. He simply gifted me with an incredible word tool. There are times when it's wise to put people in a box and then set the lock. I'm not going to use that trick unconsciously as most people do. It will simply be another card to keep tucked carefully under my sleeve.

Ninth Meeting

Linda began, "I've got to tell you how thrilled I am that you're finally opening up about your life, at least a little. On top of that, you're teaching me things about psychotherapy that I never would have learned in school."

"Does that mean you can now appreciate why I've been somewhat opaque with you?"

"Well, it doesn't mean I liked it, but you are at least starting to dribble out a little information. Now, I totally get your mysterious and somewhat removed stance. You weren't trying to make it difficult for me, but you were making it hard on my ego. I just felt that if I could find one solid thing about you, I could put my finger on it, I could start understanding you. Of course, you would also have lost your power over me, which is exactly what my ego wanted."

"Let me share a little Psychotherapy 101. Unfortunately, most therapists either missed that course or, more likely, it simply isn't taught. I'm guessing the latter. Here's how it begins. It is of the utmost importance that therapists avoid discussing their personal lives or, even more critically, their own problems with their clients. I don't even have pictures of my family in my office, though I have no problem with others who do. Beyond that indulgence, a therapist has no business saying something like, 'I went through a difficult divorce myself a couple of years ago.'

"Your clients are not there to learn about you. While therapists may think that talking about things they have in common with their clients makes them more relatable, the fact is that they are changing the nature of the relationship. Psychotherapy should not be allowed to devolve into friendship. Let's just go ahead and label that as Rule Number One.

"But as is often the case, there is an exception. It's perfectly fine and even beneficial to tell stories beginning with, "I once had a friend who....' Such examples can often assist a client in finding a solution to a problem. By phrasing the lesson in such an impersonal manner, the therapist can suggest constructive options without becoming entwined in a personal relationship."

Rick volunteered, "While I don't know anything about psychotherapy, I can tell you about a recent trip to my physician. I was having some knee pain along with crepitus. The doctor told me that it was nothing to worry about and insisted that I feel his knee as he flexed his lower leg. He didn't even examine my knee. To tell you the truth, I felt cheated. I hate going to the doctor and certainly didn't make the appointment to learn about his issues. I'm guessing that both doctors and therapists get bored hearing other people's problems day after day and, subsequently, fall into the trap of talking about their own. It's a very human thing to do, but it's not in the best interests of their patients."

Linda was anxious to learn more. "I've got to know, what's Rule Number Two?"

"It's incredibly simple. It's also an easy trap to fall right into. People make this mistake regularly in their everyday lives, but it's inexcusable when a therapist does it."

Linda's patience was once more wearing thin. "Instead of doing a dance, why don't you just tell us what it is."

"In actuality, the things I say are more likely to be memorable if I dress them up. By prefacing a simple and rather obvious notion, I can say it in a way that is more likely to make an impression. I want to make sure that it will stick in your mind so that you will catch yourself if you start to fall into that trap."

Linda looked downcast and defeated. "I often feel like you're holding a piece of candy but keeping it just out of reach. I get mad at you, and then I learn that you were doing it for my own good. Then I get even more mad at myself."

"Very good, Linda," I surprised her by saying. "What an excellent opportunity you've provided for a lesson."

Instead of staying frustrated, Linda decided to make an emotional shift and half-smiled in response. "And what will it be this time, Herr professor?"

"Rather than keeping you in suspense, I'll tell you the rule. Then, I'm going to ask you to re-examine what you just said. Rule Number Two is don't ever tell a client you know just how they feel. If you do so, I will find you, and then I promise that I will smack you. And it will hurt."

Rick asked, "What's the problem with that? I hear people say that all the time when they're trying to sympathize."

"Sympathizing is not in the job description of a psychotherapist. In a sense, it's treating the other person as lesser or needy. That's, as Linda would have me say in my new identity as Herr Professor, verboten. Just as importantly, saying that you know just how someone feels minimizes their experience. You don't know just how they feel because you haven't been in their shoes. You don't know the millions of life experiences that have led them to their current state.

"I'm better at breaking rules than establishing them, but I can assure you that I've never broken Rule Number 3. If you ever say to a client or basically anyone still breathing, 'Don't be nervous,' I will summon a thunderbolt from the heavens."

Rick looked at me quizzically, "What's the big deal? Aren't people saying that because they want to be helpful?"

I scoffed. "If you want someone to relax, is it a good idea to have them self-reflect on their discomfort? In doing so, you're simply confirming that the world sees them as looking nervous. I can't imagine anything more anxiety-producing.

"I'll even throw in a corollary. If someone is about to engage in something risky, the worst thing you can say is, 'Be careful.' They are already aware that they are planning to do something dangerous. Telling them to think about it instead of trusting their unthinking brain is the worst thing you could possibly do. It would be like walking a tightrope and looking down rather than simply stepping forward. I even avoid telling people, 'Good luck,' because the underlying message is they will need it."

"Let's give Linda a shot at taking apart what she said a minute ago."

"Okay," she agreed reluctantly, "I'll give it a try. I said I get mad at you, discover your intentions were good, and then I'm stuck with the anger. It has to have someplace to go, so I end up turning it on myself."

"Good summarization. How could you have handled it differently?"

"Anger just is. It's natural to have negative feelings when things don't go according to our wishes or expectations. If we dwell on our reasons for feeling upset, we'll find reasons to keep our lousy mood chugging along. What's more, we will likely create situations that aggravate it.

"Come to think of it, that's how people become enemies. Instead of recognizing and releasing their anger, they maintain a provocative attitude. Their friend is then likely to react in a defensive or even aggressive manner that justifies the feeling. Subsequently, everyone loses."

"You've got it down cognitively," I advised. "Now the trick is putting that knowledge into action. I'll give you another term that I've found helpful. First, remember that we're no longer engaged in psychotherapy, so the rule against self-revelations doesn't apply. Though I will admit that disclosing deeply personal things while in my office setting still makes me want to shiver."

I gathered myself before continuing. "There have been times when I've had troublesome feelings that, as you just described, are self-perpetuating. For example, I went through a period during my internship during which everyone I knew seemed hostile. I was disturbed by it and didn't know what was happening."

"Sounds miserable," Rick empathized. "I've had times like that myself, but I know better than to tell you I know just how you felt."

"Good one, Rick. By putting the earlier lesson into words as you just did, you made a major step toward being able to remember it. Taking in information passively does not lend itself to learning. If you really want to grasp a concept, you must play with it by comparing it to other things you know and considering how it might fit in your life.

"Not to get sidetracked, but the lack of emphasis on active learning represents one of the major flaws in our educational system. The information I'm providing can seem dense. Anything you can do to bring it into practice will make it more real for you.

"But back to what I was saying, my teacher liked to use the term interlocked. When I was going through that irritable time, it was fortuitous that another driver pulled out in front of me. And while I was feeling that way, it didn't take much to get me going. I reacted by honking my horn and offering an unfriendly hand gesture, which I seldom do ordinarily. That simple, out-of-character act woke me up. I realized that I had been interlocked with anger and could then release it.

"How were you able to do that?"

"I shocked myself into coming to my senses. There will inevitably be times in which you find yourselves in a mood. The funny thing is that moods seem to have a life of their own. Once they're established, your ego won't want to let go since the moods justify and strengthen its hold. The first trick is to acknowledge that you're in one. Then, you can use awareness to rise above it. Strange as it may seem, moods have a way of putting a bag over your head.

"People are reluctant to admit, even to themselves, that they're caught in one. For example, have you ever heard someone say, 'How dare you say I'm in a bad mood?' It's like my example of being stuck in a box. You must find a peephole before you can start to find your way out.

"Let's transition away from psychotherapy into something very different as we're getting to a critically important segment on the recording. On the surface, it might seem trivial. But as Linda experienced the first level of transformation, she was able to truly step beyond the world of words."

Linda became excited. "Are you going to tell us how to do it?"

She was taken aback as I said, "You may be surprised to learn that the two of you are now in the role of apprentices. I'm going to share the tricks of the trade. Just know that the information I'm going to provide is not sufficient to allow you to do the work at this point.

Words will help you make sense of the process, but it's not done using words."

Rick appeared to be puzzled and yet interested. "So, you just go up to a person and do some kind of hocus pocus, open sesame sort of thing?"

I chuckled, "Well, it's not quite that simple. I'm sure you won't be surprised by having me begin by contradicting myself. Words are actually of great importance in the process. To do the first level of transformation effectively, it's necessary to begin by mapping the cognitive strongholds of the person's ego. The next step requires finding a way to breach its defenses. Then, speaking on a semantic level, it's necessary to encourage the person to break free and hold the space long enough to recognize, identify, and mark it. Most people are somewhat surprised because, while they may have been at that level of awareness at times in their lives, they previously had no map to find their way back to it."

Linda said, "What you're describing sounds challenging but doable. But you said there is something more involved, and I'm pretty sure I know what it is."

"Rather than attempting to explain it, I'm going to ask the two of you to take a shot at putting it into words."

Rick was the first to step in. "As I remember our first sessions, it seemed like we were just talking like two people do. Then, before I knew it, there were times when I started feeling a little weird. Not in a bad way, but I felt off balance. The feeling would come and go during the sessions. It didn't take me long to recognize that it was strongest when you wanted to drive home a point."

Linda was eager for her chance. "I agree with everything that Rick said. But the most salient thing to me was the light that I saw to varying degrees, depending on what we discussed. When we moved into essence, the light was the brightest I've ever seen. At those times, it was almost like I ceased to exist as an individual."

I concurred. "Both of your descriptions are right on, considering the limits of our inevitably futile attempts to use words to describe something that has nothing to do with words. I often use the term energy to describe what is involved, given that there is nothing better to call it. Given my circumscribed ability to comprehend such matters, I see the light as the purest form of energy. It is the source of creation. During transformation, that energy/light is the catalyst."

"Is it different at the successive levels of transformation you mentioned?"

"It is, and it isn't. You might think of lighting a match compared to setting off a hydrogen bomb. There is virtually no comparison. As we prepare for supra-self-transformation, an energy comparable to lighting a city block will be necessary. While it's not enough to be overly frightening or destructive, it will certainly be sufficient to get your attention. As a gentle reminder, keep in mind that we are talking about binding your souls through eternity. The heavens don't take such matters lightly."

Linda commented, "You have this way of exciting and scaring me at the same time. Do you enjoy being like that?"

The out-of-character act woke me up. I realized that I had been interlocked with anger and could then release it.

"How were you able to do that?"

"I shocked myself into coming to my senses. There will inevitably be times when you find yourselves in a mood. The funny thing is that attitudes seem to have a life of their own. Once they're established, your ego doesn't want to let go since the moods justify and strengthen their hold. The first trick is to acknowledge that you're in one. Then, you can use awareness to rise above it. Strange as it may seem, moods have a way of putting a bag over your head.

"People are reluctant to admit, even to themselves, that they're caught in one. For example, have you ever heard someone say, 'How dare you say I'm in a bad mood?' It's like my example of being stuck in a box. You have to find a peephole before you can start to find your way out.

"Let's transition away from psychotherapy into something very different as we're getting to a critically important segment on the recording. On the surface, it might seem fairly trivial. But as Linda experienced the first level of transformation, she could truly step beyond the world of words."

Linda became excited. "Are you going to tell us how to do it?"

She was taken aback as I said, "You may be surprised to learn that the two of you are now in the role of apprentices. I'm going to share the tricks of the trade. Just know that the information I'm going to provide is insufficient to allow you to do the work now. Words will help you make sense of the process, but it's not done using words."

Rick appeared to be puzzled and yet interested. "So, you just go up to a person and do some kind of hocus pocus, open sesame sort of thing?"

I chuckled, "Well, it's not quite that simple. I'm sure you won't be surprised by having me begin by contradicting myself. Words are actually of great importance in the process. It's necessary to map the cognitive strongholds of the person's ego to do the first level of transformation effectively. The next step requires finding a way to breach its defenses. Then, speaking on a semantic level, it's necessary to encourage the person to break free and hold the space long enough to recognize, identify, and mark it. Most people are somewhat surprised because, while they may have been at that level of awareness at times in their lives, they previously had no map to find their way back to it."

Linda said, "What you're describing sounds challenging but doable. But you said something is involved, and I'm pretty sure I know what it is."

"Rather than attempting to explain it, I'm going to ask the two of you to take a shot at putting it into words."

Rick was the first to step in. "As I remember our first sessions, it seemed like we were just talking like two people do. Then, before I knew it, there were times when I started feeling a little weird. Not in a bad way, but I felt off balance. The feeling would come and go during the sessions. It didn't take me long to recognize that it was strongest when you wanted to drive home a point."

Linda was eager for her chance. "I agree with everything that Rick said. But the most salient thing to me was the light I saw in varying degrees, depending on what we discussed. The light was the brightest I've ever seen when we moved into essence. At those times, it was almost like I ceased to exist."

I concurred. "Both of your descriptions are right on, considering the limits of our inevitably futile attempts to use words to describe something that has nothing to do with words. I often mention energy to describe what is involved, given that nothing is better to call it. Given my circumscribed ability to comprehend such matters, I see light as the purest form of energy. It is the source of creation. During transformation, energy/light is the catalyst."

"Is it different at the successive levels of transformation you mentioned?"

"It is, and it isn't. You might think of lighting a match compared to setting off a hydrogen bomb. There is virtually no comparison. As we prepare for supra-self-transformation, an energy comparable to lighting a city block will be necessary. While it's not enough to be overly frightening or destructive, it will certainly be sufficient to get your attention. As a gentle reminder, remember that we are discussing binding your souls through eternity. The heavens don't take such matters lightly."

Linda commented, "You have this way of exciting and scaring me simultaneously. Do you enjoy being like that?"

"Let's be clear: what we're encountering here transcends verbal descriptions. You need to understand that it's not just beyond language; it also surpasses our emotional grasp. Naturally, this journey will stir up profound emotions, yet the very essence of what we consider human feelings will eventually give way to an experience far more immense and awe-inspiring—even language buckles under the weight of the concept.

"Consider a well-known phrase from an ancient text: 'In the beginning was the Word, and the Word was with God ...' We're venturing into realms predating the very invention of words. That realization alone speaks volumes."

Rick wasn't quite prepared for this high-flying rhetoric and was seeking a sense of grounding. He was a bit shaken and desperately wanted to make sense of what I had been saying. "As I understand it, when you first started working with us, you were mapping out how we think. While addressing our presenting problems, you were also working at a level beyond the obvious in preparation for what was to come. Do I have that right?"

"You're absolutely spot on. But as I've mentioned, we're dealing with multiple levels. Linda, is there anything you would like to add?"

"You bet. The key to it all is energy. You weren't just talking to us as one person to another. You were talking to our physical beings to prepare us for what we were about to experience. It might have seemed like ordinary conversation, but something much greater was going on. In retrospect, it's kind of funny. I had no idea what you were up to. If I had, I would have been tempted to hide in the basement."

Rick was totally involved but was still trying to get his bearings. "When people see a therapist, shouldn't they be warned about this kind of voodoo?"

"Rick, you've hit on an important point. Let me assure you that, as far as I know, other therapists are much more conventional. And that's good because most people are seeking something more predictable. But with you guys, I had a sense, a sort of knowing, that it was time to do more than typical talk therapy. As you remember, I sought an explicit contract with each of you to go beyond traditional psychotherapy. And you agreed to take what Kierkegaard referred to as a leap of faith. You made that jump, not knowing where or even if you would land."

They both shook their heads as they contemplated what in the hell they had gotten themselves into. Linda said, "I can't believe it. All I did was make a simple phone call. I had no idea that you were going to turn me, my marriage, and everything else in my life upside down and inside out. Maybe there should be some sort of warning by your name in Google searches. It should say something like, 'Don't call unless you're willing to go through hell on the off chance that you might end up in heaven.'"

"That's a good one, Linda. I wonder how many takers I would get. But as I've been careful to explain, you've signed up for something much different and far greater than the service I typically provide. As a caution, I don't want you to think you're special. I wouldn't go so far as to attribute our meeting as chance, but don't think for a second that it's because we are some exalted beings."

Linda's Journal

July 20

Bill was very clear from the start. He said that he would be explaining things numerous times in various ways so that we could get what he was saying on multiple levels. Well, I just got to another level. Rather than being redundant, he is getting his points across in ways that will finally sink in. And now they are. My black-and-white way of looking at the world is becoming technicolored.

As I'm struggling with my Statistics course, I find myself thinking that I'm stupid and I'll never get it. The more I get angry and frustrated, the more I feel like giving up. I get up and get a drink of water. Then, I make a conscious decision to approach each formula one step at a time until it finally makes sense.

Here's what's funny: I change my thoughts to tell myself to enjoy what I'm learning rather than having my thoughts work against me. Believe it or not, I then relax and start figuring things out. I'm probably one of the few students in history who has ever gotten a kick out of a Stat class.

I try to catch myself when I'm having ill-advised, random thoughts. Unfortunately, I'm not always able to do so before they cause trouble. Sometimes it's little things. I get angry because I'm stuck in traffic. When I finally got to the store, I was irritable and unfriendly with the cashier. Of course, then I'm unhappy with myself.

On a much grander scale, my thoughts do become programmatic. I wanted to be chosen to run a study for my favorite professor. Not surprisingly, he chose me. That's a reason to celebrate, but where will I get the time? Along with all the other lessons, I have to watch what I wish for.

There's another genuine reason for concern. I've felt conflict with one of my classmates from the start. I must admit I sort of wanted her to fail so I wouldn't have to deal with her. She did. Now, I have to live with it. Did I play a role in her failure? It's impossible to say, but I know I experienced a wake-up call. I know I've said it before, but I will no longer be impatient with Bill when he talks about linguistics.

Rick's Journal

July 22

On the drive home, we discussed Bill's apparent fixation on language. We both feel like we would rather be spending our time with him learning the vital things. As I thought about it later, I began to accept that he knows the direction we need to take. If he thinks concentrating on words will help us, I'm all for spending time on words. It's funny. Just changing my way of thinking about the situation relieves my frustration. Once again, Bill knows what he's talking about.

Of course, the goal is to go beyond words. I feel like I'm doing that when I don't fall into the traps other lawyers set for me. I keep my ego free when they use accusation and innuendo to make their point. I think of myself as a mighty oak that can bend with the wind but stand tall and firm when the time is right.

"My paralegal noticed the difference in my demeanor and complimented me. It would have been so easy to think about how great I was doing. My ego is incredibly sly. If I give it an inch, it will convince me that I've got it all down and don't need anything or anybody.

I kind of like the idea of becoming his apprentice. It wasn't too long ago that I would have laughed at the thought. I'm glad that he took the time to explain some of the nuts and bolts of what he does. Of course, that doesn't mean that I understand it. What I truly appreciated was his description of the energy that underlies transformation. It was the most upfront he has been in talking about the underpinnings of his work. At the very least, it gives me some frame of reference in dealing with the weirdness I sometimes experience during our sessions.

I do have to admit that I experienced a slight hiccup when I heard Linda's recording. She came right out and admitted that she attempted to seduce Bill. I would have lost it if she had said that a year ago. I can't believe that I sat there in relative calm. I'm learning that the ego takes no prisoners in its struggle to maintain its place on the throne. Since I realize that it was simply Linda's ego doing its thing, I feel much less threatened. While I love her ego as a part of her, I recognize it as transitory. It's just a vehicle she is now using on her voyage to forever.

I can't believe it. Now I'm starting to talk like Bill.

Tenth Meeting

"As you have undoubtedly noticed, one topic keeps rearing its head.

Linda frowned as she spoke. "I think I know what you're going to say, and I can appreciate how important it is. But it's also a bit intimidating to realize how much our thoughts and verbalizations affect our everyday reality."

"I'm glad that you labeled it as intimidating. It's a powerful word. It demands the respect you are learning to give to your word choices. Even people not dealing with awareness would be well served to be more prudent in what they think and speak. As surprising as it may be to hear, people tend to think they are nothing more than the words rattling around in their heads and spewing out their mouths. From that viewpoint, people see no reason to try to direct or change them. They feel free to just live their lives unconsciously."

Linda admitted, "My introduction to the power of words was far from pleasant. The first time I went nuts, I really had no idea I had played a role in what had happened. As we review the recordings, it's becoming crystal clear. I let my thoughts of jealousy run on auto. I didn't see myself as having any choice in the matter as I effectively drove myself crazy."

I commented, "It's not the kind of issue you can simply recognize as a problem and then attempt to solve it. Our thoughts can forgive the expression and have a mind of their own. Becoming their master is a tremendous challenge, one that few people even attempt to face. It's much easier to simply eschew responsibility for them. How do you handle that tendency now?"

"You're certainly right. It doesn't just disappear. The imagery you shared with me, however, is compelling. I must watch myself, using the witness you mentioned. I need to catch my thoughts and worries early before they gather strength. If I do so early enough, I can just let go of them. If they have started to gather steam, I visualize a vibrant, glowing, golden spiral with the letters of the words stretching out and rising up and up until they go 'poof!'"

Rick piped in, "And don't forget about me. I went through something very similar."

Linda was in the mood for a playful argument. In a change of direction, she shook her finger at him and said, "You have to wait your turn. It's my time in the limelight."

"Okay, Linda," I cautioned jovially. "Just because we're done with the sex part, don't think that it's all downhill from here. Let's talk about the related lesson you learned."

Linda concurred. "Learning to deal with obsessions was a huge plus. But it's fascinating how it evolved into something much more significant. Before, we talked about being influenced and even controlled by other people's opinions. I had learned about that trap on numerous levels, but it came home when I could literally see in my mind's eye how I had been boxed in by the words others used to criticize and define me."

"There's a related and inevitable subject we may as well address."

They both looked at me with a mixture of dread and curiosity. After a brief and uncomfortable pause, Linda broke the ice. "I'm almost afraid to ask. As soon as I start feeling like I know what's happening, you say something that throws me for a loop."

"Not to worry. You've both already begun wrestling with this issue. The question is quite simple. What is reality?"

Rick seemed almost annoyed. "Why do you have to go and spoil a good party? We felt good about lessons learned, and then you throw us a curve ball."

I responded, "Don't pretend that the question hadn't already been on your mind."

Linda shuddered slightly before admitting, "I'm almost afraid of what you're going to say."

"You're going to be both relieved and disappointed in my answer. Reality is. We can't define it and have little control over it. What we can do is live with it consciously. Shit happens. We can get stuck in the muck, or we can experience and even embrace the unpleasantness that is, at times, inevitable. In the meantime, we can enjoy the freedom our Selves experience as they realize that our lives on this planet are, more or less, a fantasy. How's that for a statement?"

"Actually, I love it. I can't tell you how much I now cherish my witness. It allows me to fully experience things that are, on the surface, really crummy because my higher Self is looking down on it all and laughing."

I beamed, "You're getting the cosmic joke. That's a major step forward. Congratulations."

"Hold on," Rick objected. "I know this isn't a competition, but what is she getting that I'm not?"

I advised, "How about using perspective? Look at yourself dispassionately as you're asking the question. From a higher level, see how ridiculous it is to consider Linda's insight in a competitive light."

Rick sat back with a frown but soon leaned forward again with a smile. "Thank you. Thank you. Thank you. It's so wonderful to share Linda's breakthrough. I forgot for a moment that she was a part of me. My ego had to make one more attempt to grab hold. I just had to regain perspective. It's ridiculously easy to lose but so wonderful to rediscover."

"You both get points, not that it matters. Who is keeping the score? Moreover, who cares about the outcome? When you begin to face the nature of reality, such questions become humorous. Who is who? Or, for that matter, what is who? We find ourselves back at the starting point. Reality is. Our thoughts define it for us automatically; alternatively, we can use them to define it. There is a big difference. Which do you choose?"

Linda laughed as she said, "If you have to be such a damned guru, I wish you could at least make things a little simpler."

"Rather than speaking as a guru, let me address the issue logically and scientifically. As I mentioned a while back, our sensory organs, of necessity, filter out most of the enormous amount of information available at any given instant. Most of what comes in fails to get beyond an early stage of processing. We likely use more brain power in discarding sensory information than we do in interpreting what we absorb. From the small amount of stimulation that is processed, only a minuscule amount reaches the level of conscious awareness. And even that has been through the wringer of a multitude of electrical and chemical interactions."

"I see what you're doing," Rick commented. You're keeping us uncomfortable by having us consider every idea from multiple levels. We can't just settle on an answer we've found that allows us a sense of comfort and stability. You keep pushing us further. I'm starting to get why Linda doesn't like you."

This time, Linda failed to come to my defense. Instead, she said, "I know you're telling all of this for a reason, but I've got to say. Rick has a point."

Using crude humor as a defense, I said laughingly, "Well, then. I'll just take my cookies and go home."

As I started to stand, they both got up and playfully restrained me. "Don't think we're going to let you go that easy," Rick insisted. "You've gotten us into this. Now you've got to get us out."

I signed with a mock resignation. "Well, when you put it that way. Getting back to my point, we don't perceive what is really 'out there' by any stretch of the imagination. The spectrum of information we can absorb is far different, and in some cases much more limited, than that of other animals.

Then, our brain plays a trick on us, which is basically for our own good. It filters that information according to models we have developed through the process of socialization. The information that reaches the level of conscious awareness is nothing more than a distorted and manipulated version of what we assume to be the outside world. What we experience is, instead, information that conforms to our own conjured-up models. In large part, we are effectively autistic."

Linda grimaced. "I wish I'd stopped when I was ahead. Forget my earlier complaint. I like you better as a guru than as a scientist."

Linda's Journal

July 27

I started glowing when Bill said he liked my use of the word "intimidating." Then my witness woke up. I'm so pleased that I caught myself starting to fall into the same old trap. I really, really know better. At the same time, it's so easy for me to start doing pirouettes just because someone likes something about me. I now realize that it puts me under their control. There is no need for me to keep dancing.

Reviewing the lesson on obsessive thoughts was undoubtedly worthwhile. I'm challenging myself to detect any time a thought starts to become overly important. I can maintain my equilibrium if I can catch a worry or even something exciting before it grabs me. I especially like using visualization to imagine a train of words running off the tracks and crashing.

It would have been great if I'd known how to do that earlier in my life, but I doubt that I would have had the discipline to use it. When my date was 30 minutes late for senior prom, you wouldn't believe where my thoughts took me. The most valuable word picture by far involves nothing more than a box. That's where I visualize myself anytime I get caught up in what others say about me.

Rick's Journal

July 28

I can't believe I caught myself feeling jealous of Linda's insight. I guess I still have a ways to go. If she makes progress, we make progress. That darn ego of mine. Wouldn't it be great if we, as a society, could enjoy the achievements of each individual? What I just wrote epitomizes one of humankind's great, unresolved struggles. We know that competition provides the necessary fuel for progress. At the same time, it serves to pit us against one another. I guess that's why some people despise capitalism. I'm open to a better way. I just don't see one over the horizon.

I guess I shouldn't be surprised that Bill pulled another one on us. "What is reality?" Come on now. At least I'm not paying for the sessions anymore. Making things worse, he had a point. I like to feel the ground under my feet, but it's starting to give way. As he warned earlier, true progress is not achieved incrementally.

As much as I've benefitted from my time with him, I don't want to become a philosopher. But once again, there is a method to his madness. He is teaching us to avoid getting caught up in the petty events of our daily lives so we can continue to focus on the big picture. I'm okay with that plan, but I'll admit that there is more to it. He really is encouraging us to question our sense of reality. And there is even more. He is showing us. I wish we could skip that part. Frankly, it scares the hell out of me.

I sometimes wonder if he's trying to wring me dry of all my preconceptions concerning what is. I shouldn't bother wondering. That's exactly what he's up to. What's worse is that he can back up his arguments logically. It's annoying. I would pick up and move on if I didn't respect him. But who am I kidding? These sessions are the best thing that ever happened to me, not to mention our marriage.

Eleventh Meeting

"Well, now we find ourselves solidly grounded in mid-air," I commented wryly. "How are you doing at this point?"

Once again, there was a pregnant pause as they considered my question before Rick ventured, "I'm glad you asked. It's easy to get lost in these super-abstract ideas, especially since you move us into unfamiliar spaces with little or no warning. The truth is, I find the concepts you talk about to be seductive but try not to overthink them since I have things to deal with here on earth."

Linda agreed wholeheartedly. "I love the philosophy, especially since you have a way of making it real. But sometimes, it still scares me. I have to step back and ask myself, 'What in the hell am I doing?'"

"And what is your answer?"

Stifling a brief laugh, she said, "As you well know, having one foot in the heavens and one foot on the ground takes some getting used to. In many ways, it makes life easier. I also find that sometimes I have a tendency to drift away. I can easily become overly absorbed in other levels of awareness. I then must remind myself to come back to earth. I keep in mind your warning of the necessity of maintaining discipline. You, or maybe it would be better to say, I, have made quite clear the consequences of traveling further than I'm prepared to go."

Rick's answer was, not surprisingly, somewhat different. "I'm naturally a more down-to-earth guy. Even lawyering is a bit out of character for me. I like to work with my hands in the dirt. I think that's why this business is a little harder for me to accept. The things we're doing are unquestionably real. I guess you could call me confused and even a bit disoriented at this point."

"Good self-analysis from both of you. You're progressing right on schedule, if there is such a thing. Keep in mind that you're adjusting to an entirely new view of reality. It's kind of like suddenly finding yourself on Mars. You want to find a familiar convenience store, but the street it used to be on has disappeared. Then you look around and find that you're in a totally alien environment. The reality supports you're accustomed to seem tenuous, and you're unsure of the new rules."

They both nodded enthusiastically in agreement. Linda said, "I'm beginning to understand what you're doing. You help us figure things out so we can adjust to our current level of reality. Then you give us a little bump, and the process starts again. I can also see the delicate balance involved. If we take off on our own with the new energy, we'll likely feel lost and overwhelmed."

I commented, "As horrible as it was when you took that unplanned trip to the Twilight Zone soon after we met, it's obvious that the value of that lesson was not lost."

Rick complained half-heartedly, "How come I didn't get a chance to explore the world of looney tunes?"

"The answer is not simple, but I'll give it a shot. As you remember, you were exposed to Linda's shifts and her developing energy along the way. Without realizing what was happening, you, your body, and your psyche were allowed time to make corresponding adjustments.

"When she really lost it, the consequences of this work suddenly became very real to you. You had no desire to risk that sort of craziness. And, as you said, you naturally tend to be more rooted in the everyday reality. That's neither good nor bad. It simply means that you are following a somewhat different path. We just have to make sure that you both land in the same place."

Linda gushed, "Ooh. Does that mean we're getting closer to the next level of transformation that you mentioned? I can't wait."

"Anticipation is a natural aspect of the human experience. It fills us with excitement and allows us to escape the humdrum of our ordinary lives. But I also need to throw in a caution."

"I think I see where you're headed," Linda said. "As you taught me, excitement can lead to anxiety and potentially to disappointment as well if you allow it to get out of hand."

"Yes," I agreed. "There is even more to it than that. When you think about what is ahead, you easily lose appreciation for what is right in front of you. The temptation of forward-looking thinking has the same risks as backward-looking thinking. In either case, you lose the value of your current experience. Consider the aptly titled book *Be Here Now* (1970) by Ram Dass, aka Richard Alpert, Ph.D."

With a wrinkled brow, Linda asked, "Why did he have an alias?"

"Allow me to go back a couple of generations. I mentioned that I planned to discuss some of my early influences, and he was certainly one. He was a professor of Psychology at Harvard and an associate of Timothy Leary of LSD fame. Like you, he had achieved many of his goals but was dissatisfied with life as he was experiencing it."

"Wow, I'm super curious. I know what I did with my predicament. What did he do with his?"

"He made numerous forays into different levels of awareness propelled by powerful psychedelics. He also spent time with gurus who showed him how to turn the spaces he visited into places. In other words, rather than simply experiencing a 'high,' he developed a roadmap of states of awareness during his inner travels. Dr. Alpert was a brilliant man who set out to achieve knowledge. He didn't do drugs recreationally. Rather, he took them with purpose. Because he wasn't just looking for a high, he could remain sufficiently aware during his trips to analyze what he was going through."

"In the book you mentioned, did he learn things he could share with the world?"

"Absolutely. In fact, he began to have followers. As in my case, he quickly learned that it was a treacherous and unwise way to go. He eventually left the academic world and joined a spiritual community, minimizing his contact with ordinary society. I can tell you from experience that the post-guru adjustment can be tricky."

"Is there anything that you can share from his book?"

"Our discussion quite naturally led me to think of him, so I'll tell you one of his vignettes. I went to a seminar in which he described the perfect pizza. He first thought of all his favorite ingredients. He liked so many toppings that he had to stop and consider which ones would best blend. He didn't want to pick up the pizza, so he had to determine the ideal time to have it delivered. Once it came, it still wasn't everything he had hoped, so he put on some music. The pizza made him thirsty, and he opened a bottle of wine. Then, it occurred to him that it would taste better if he smoked some weed. Still seeking perfection, he decided to sit in a warm bath while eating. Do you get the point?"

Rick said, "As I think about it, it's a lesson that we hear repeatedly but never quite learn. We can only be happy in the present. As long as we are seeking something out there, we can't fully enjoy what we are experiencing."

"Yes," I agreed. "It's that old thing about being happy with what you have rather than being preoccupied with what you don't. Linda, how about bringing it back to our current discussion?"

"That story is a good reminder. Things are perfect as they are right here and right now. The key to happiness is in realizing it. I'm with two men I love, though the ways I express that love are quite different. And I'm learning things beyond what I imagined to be possible. I guess you could say I'm quite happy. The trick will be carrying it over to times when things don't seem so ideal. I think I can manage it. I just need to remember to use perspective."

"How about the aspect of looking ahead?"

"I remember your lesson about viewing time as nonlinear. In a sense, transformation has already happened. It's in me and a part of me. Surprisingly, I somehow believe that to be true. I can't tell you how good that makes me feel."

Linda's Journal

August 2

I honestly never know where Bill is going next. I think he intended to give us a breather in our last session. He provided numerous much-needed reminders but didn't set off a bomb underneath our feet as he sometimes does.

Strange to say, but I'm now grateful for the time I lost it. As horrible as it was, it freed me from my stuck sense of reality and opened me to new possibilities. Bill knew what he was doing, and I can't say he didn't warn me. Of course, I thought I knew better. I felt that, at least to a degree, he was blowing smoke when he talked about the risks involved with transformation.

As wonderful as it is to have broken free of thoughts and beliefs that were strangling me, I still must remind myself not to move too far and too fast. I'm counting on Bill for guidance, but it's ultimately my responsibility. It's kind of funny. My everyday life goes swimmingly. It's only when things are going really well or poorly that I have to watch it. I will be fine as long as I can maintain the discipline to be here now. There's another somewhat surprising aspect. When I stop to take the time to completely immerse myself in the present, whatever I'm experiencing opens up to me in an entirely new and different way.

Rick's Journal

August 2

So far, I've done reasonably well in maintaining my balance despite all that Bill has thrown at me. In fact, I'm rather proud of myself. I know. I know. In writing or even thinking that, I'm opening the door for my ego. Fortunately, I believe I'm sufficiently aware of what I'm doing and can mitigate the risk. The reason I feel good about my part is simple. I've expanded my boundaries beyond belief, quite literally. In the process, I haven't completely lost my grounding in the way Linda did. I'm not saying that I haven't come close because the fact is I have. And who knows what Bill will throw at me next?

As long as I'm indulging in how impressed I am with myself, I might as well continue. This whole therapy thing is more natural to Linda. She is much more inclined in that direction with what she reads and watches on TV. If you ever see me watching "Real Housewives," you might as well take me out and shoot me.

But now, look at me. I'm right in the dad-blasted middle of something I would have ridiculed not long ago. What's more. I'm enjoying the heck out of it. I realize how much others and I have cheated ourselves by closing off possibilities simply because they didn't fit stereotyped ideas of what should interest them. Next thing you know, I'll be talking to my law partners about feelings. Strike that. Sometimes I get carried away.

Am I happy? You bet. Do I feel secure in that happiness? Well, that's a little trickier. At least I know now that I'm far from being alone in the jungle of life. That's not to say that Linda hasn't always been there. But now we have a safari guide. So far, he seems to know the terrain and the threats that might be out there. It's a good thing since I'm discovering dangers beyond anything I had ever imagined.

Twelfth Meeting

Linda's look of consternation returned as she began listening to the recording. "I was already frustrated with you because you were so fussy with how I used words. I think this is where it came to a head."

"Yep," I responded. "And I somehow manage to irritate you even further. Now, why would I have gone and done that?"

"Looking back, there are many things that seem obvious now. Previously, they just seemed to be designed to torture me. When you told me you were always right, it almost put me over the top. I was starting to trust you when you pulled that on me. I kind of know now, but I'm still not totally sure what you were up to."

"I've talked about working on multiple levels and allowing you to gain insights accordingly. My most obvious purpose was to confuse and weaken your ego. If I said something that made sense in the usual scheme of things, your ego would have felt comfortable, and you wouldn't have budged."

"I get that for sure. That's not to say I liked it, but I can now see it as necessary. But what else was going on?"

"Think back to the situation. I wanted you to continue to grow and blossom, but not beneath my shadow."

"Right, that's when I began to accept my power! It wasn't easy because I still wanted to depend on you. It would have been so much more comfortable. But you pushed me into it by making a joke of things. How could I lean on a man who turns in circles and spanks himself on my command?"

"As we continue to unravel that seemingly straightforward session, what was another lesson?"

"I remember rummaging around your office looking for a mystic book. I didn't want to have to depend on you for answers because you could be a son of a bitch. At the same time, our interactions had raised questions that begged for answers. I, in other words, would have felt greatly relieved if I could have found a book to explain what you were doing."

"Instead, you found something much better. Care to explain?"

"In your charming way," she said with a strange combination of a smile and a jeer, "You allowed me to discover that the answers were right in front of me. If I had continued to look in safe and familiar places, I would have found answers that were safe and familiar. But I would have learned nothing. I had to learn to trust myself so I could be open to genuine knowledge.

"To find information that is real, it's necessary to look beyond the pillars of safety which will placate, but not really inform. It's so different from what I was accustomed to doing: going to the same people and places I trusted and getting the same answers. But somehow, I was never satisfied with what they told me."

"And one further thing," I added. "We began experimenting with 'as if' during that session. It's a wonderful tool. It lifts you beyond what you think of as the limits of reality. In doing so, you can begin to play with the world. You discover that you can make it whatever you want. If you want to be a fighter pilot, enter into that space. Make it real for you. Walk around as if you own that role. Want to be a princess? Try it on. As you grow in awareness, you also re-develop an incredibly valuable talent that was socialized out of you. You discover that you can once again play make-believe."

Rick commented, "As an adult, I've always felt sort of cheated. When I used to play cops and robbers as a kid, I was right there on the scene. I don't think it could have been much more real if it had been going on."

"There's a reason that may not seem so obvious to you now as an adult. You created a separate reality when you were a child. You were totally immersed in it. There were no concerns about what other people might think, and you felt no need to conform to a social reality. You weren't reflecting on yourself, and you weren't questioning what was going on. The price we pay for accepting the shared consensus is enormous.

"Now I've got another big one for you. You might remember one of the books I mentioned previously. It contains a comment about whenever two or more people are gathered in my name. Any idea what it was referring to?"

"My gosh!" Linda's mouth was shaped like a large O. "Boy, do I get it! I would have totally missed it if you hadn't brought it up just now."

Rick seemed perplexed. "I think I may have missed something along the way."

Linda explained, "When the three of us are together, we are capable of anything. If we want to hold hands and fly to the top of Mount Everest, we can. Do you doubt it?"

"Well, when you put it that way, it makes sense. With our beliefs, we can do anything we want. It doesn't matter if other people notice because it's totally true within our agreed reality. Through our joined beliefs, we have the power to break through the constraints of ordinary reality.

Something just occurred to me. That's how many revolutionary changes get their start. It's necessary to get a handful of people willing to adopt a different belief system and then hold to it in the face of contradictory evidence. It happens in events ranging from scientific breakthroughs to government overthrows. When people band together under the banner of a belief that is strong enough to withstand the inevitable resistance and even disdain from the public, change can and does happen."

"I will add one caveat. As video games become more realistic, the lines are blurred for our children. While parents may not want to admit it, they feel threatened as their children overvalue an alien reality. And, in fact, I can see a point where that danger might become real since their kids don't have the grounding in the everyday world that you are developing."

Linda added, "You had told me about entering a client's space. I've been practicing that skill with friends. It's amazing how much I'm able to get into their heads. And I'm starting to really get that psychic thing as well. The more I become attuned to their reality and out of my own box, the more I can predict what they are going to do or say. I have to be careful not to reveal too much because there's nothing to be gained by freaking them out."

"I couldn't agree more. It goes back to the idea of responsibility. If you were much smarter, stronger, or better looking than someone else, what would you have to gain by trying to demonstrate it to them? Once again, a caution about the ego is in order. As you progress in awareness, never think that it makes you superior. In a way, it's even a burden. It's not easy when you know you can provide the answers but realize that it's much better to allow a person to learn for themselves."

"And another thing just came to me," Linda commented. "Using 'as if' helps me remember that it's all just a game. My life on this planet is part of a process. It's an endpoint only if I allow it to be. In developing my awareness, I have a greater purpose in mind. The resulting sense of direction allows me a tremendous safety net as I face the inevitable frustrations and disappointments of everyday life."

Rick was anxious to join in. "This discussion has been surprisingly helpful. When it's time for me to present in court, I don't have to question myself or dwell on my insecurities. Instead, I can enter the space of being a highly competent trial lawyer. I can even imagine projecting that image so that others feel it subliminally. What's great is that the more I do it, the more real it will become."

"I like where you're going but need to throw in an important tidbit. If you change the way you present yourself, you will face challenges. Remember, people like the familiar. When they see you, they're used to the Rick they've known. If you assume a more powerful persona, they will be taken aback. They will question you. But if you use your awareness to hold the space, they will soon accept the new you."

"Due to the importance of using 'as if,' it's worth considering how it might work in a variety of situations. You've probably heard the idea of dressing for the job you aspire to and not the job you have. As an extension of that practical advice, act as if you were already in the place you hope to achieve. I will also add something further. By holding yourself as if you were in a superior position in the job hierarchy, you will easily avoid the petty squabbles and office intrigues that make people miserable and their work insufferable."

This time, Rick nodded vigorously. "I've been in too many offices where people come to dislike and distrust one another. Since so much of our time is spent in the workplace, our lives can become intolerable. When someone comes to me with petty gossip, I won't berate or engage with them. Instead, I will act as if I were an effective supervisor. I will do my best to redirect them toward their job but in a positive and constructive manner.

"Work can be monotonous and boring. Unsurprisingly, people glom onto anything that makes it seem more interesting. But in too many workplaces, people begin to live for gossip. Ultimately, everyone suffers as the workplace becomes tense and dysfunctional."

"I agree with everything you said. But there's a critical component that you must keep in mind. If your response to your coworkers is tainted by ego, you will come across as judgmental or arrogant. Good leaders and such people are rare and have a natural talent for taking the high road without demeaning others. You've probably never heard it said this way, but they have a knack for balancing a strong ego with a sense of essence. In other words, the outstanding ones serve a higher goal or purpose without losing sight of their subordinates. They project, at least to a degree, that their egos encompass those of their followers. As a result, others release their own egos and allow them to take charge.

"Back to what you were saying, gossip is laden with ego. People who indulge in it realize deep down that it's a filthy habit and, by engaging in it, they are sullying themselves. The challenge is to lead them in a better direction without making them feel bad. You might think of the goal as inspiring others, but in a manner that doesn't smack of ego."

Linda's Journal

August 10

It was fun listening to the session in which he played with me by saying he knew all the answers and then saying he knew none, only to lead to a gratifying ending. He could have found a less humiliating way of going about it, but then he humbled himself as well when he spanked himself. In the end, I owned my power! That has to be the culmination of the long and winding tale of my obsequiousness. Now, I really, really don't have to lean on anyone else. Listening to it again indeed strengthens what I learned in the first place. It's unbelievable. I got what appears to be such a simple message on another level.

As an extra bonus, I will no longer depend on others for answers. The truth is right in front of me. Well, I've got to admit that I sometimes still think of Bill as representing the truth. As much as I trust him, and I do, I won't allow myself to be reliant on him or anyone else. After all these years of being the good little girl, saying that is quite a mouthful. But I mean it. It's interesting, in retrospect, to see how the people I care about molded me according to their own beliefs.

The great thing is that I can still love the people in my life. In fact, I can love them more since I now see myself on an equal footing with them. I've gained a new understanding concerning self-respect. It's not about ego. It is about knowing when it's appropriate to stand up for myself and my opinion. I've tried doing that in the past with unfortunate results. I think it was because of my insecurity. There's a huge difference between standing up for myself and standing against someone else who has challenged me. Assertiveness must come naturally. Otherwise, it comes across as aggressiveness or defensiveness.

Rick's Journal

August 11

It was amazing to listen to Bill as he played with Linda's head. I can just imagine the look on her face when he said that he was always right and followed it up by saying that he was always wrong. I'm glad that she was able to own her power. I hope that she doesn't go overboard with that idea when dealing with me. I'm all for feminism and all that. Except, to be honest, I don't want it to hit too close to home.

I knew something was missing from my life now that I'm all grown up. I just couldn't put my finger on it. I used to be a genuine badass when I played as a kid. I became so wrapped up in my imaginary games that I wouldn't even hear my mother calling me in for supper. I'm not totally back there yet, but I can visualize being able to play 'as if' again as I free myself from the constricting beliefs that I had allowed to capture and define me.

I've already started trying on the identity of a powerful trial attorney. To be honest with myself, I wasn't quite committed to it. I've had a few stumbles. I can now see that I've got to completely let go so that I can be there. If there are any doubts on my part, it will fall apart at the slightest challenge. And there will be challenges. The last thing my fellow attorneys want to see is a competent and forceful opponent. Even the ones in my firm are likely to be jealous. That's where the added lesson about dealing with coworkers comes into play.

I'm just beginning to appreciate the power of beliefs. I've gone through my life with little self-examination. I just assumed that the things I believed represented the truth. I now understand how people who are able to step beyond their ordinary vision of the world can do extraordinary or, just as likely, terrible things. What a responsibility that ability entails! I'm glad that Bill learned his lesson early and has resisted any urge to change the world.

Thirteenth Meeting

Linda began by commenting, "I'm finding myself to be in a bit of a conundrum as I seek to reconcile what I'm learning from you with what my professors are saying."

Rick agreed. "While I have no doubt that we find ourselves in the ultimate AP course as we're working with you, it can make it hard to communicate with our colleagues. I'm finding it necessary to watch myself so that I don't come across like I'm speaking another language. But that's the easy part of it. The real challenge is interacting with them like I'm the old Rick when I see everything differently. The other lawyers try to ignore it, but it's obvious that I look at the world in a totally new and somewhat foreign way."

As Linda thought about it, she seemed increasingly disturbed. "I want to learn and develop my skills as a psychotherapist. Instead, I'm stuck listening to these blow-hard professors talk about totally irrelevant and arcane matters. You won't believe this, but one of my profs bragged about a woman having a spontaneous orgasm during a session with him!"

"Linda, I almost wish I didn't believe you. The field of psychology has a way of attracting students who are not exactly mainstream. When they earn an advanced degree, they enjoy the power and mystique that comes with it. As they thrive in the cloistered walls of academia, they have little impetus to normalize.

"Let's keep it our little secret, but some are not the best-adjusted human beings. Still, they are the gatekeepers. It might help to keep in mind that they are very, very smart people. As you know, becoming accepted into graduate school in psychology is extremely difficult. The acceptance rate is very low. What's more, your professors have survived the academic rigors to get to where they are. They deserve your respect, and you will get much more from your experience if you provide it."

She looked down and seemed uncomfortable before continuing. "Rick, I'm going to tell you about something, and I hope you won't become upset. It's just a part of growing up female."

Suddenly, Rick was noticeably more alert and attentive. "I'm listening."

"A couple of the profs occasionally stare at me in a way that makes me uncomfortable. They haven't said or done anything inappropriate. It's just that look at me a little too long. Women are highly attuned to that sort of thing. It's a matter of survival for us as individuals and for the species."

I laughed. "Thanks for throwing that last part in there. Naturally, they would want to look at you. It's the price of being eye candy. There are worse reasons for catching their attention. And you're right. Women, and I'm speaking in generalities, sometimes want more than anything to be looked at. It's a critical part of the mating game.

"But regarding women's reaction to being eyed, it's a matter of timing. Even more importantly, it's who is doing the looking. Men don't have the advantage of knowing what's in their heads. The proverbial dirty old man, who everyone thinks of as disgusting, has the same interests as the young studs. It's not their fault that women are repulsed by their attention. I should mention that there is another reason that you may have overlooked."

"I'll bite."

"Linda, you are familiar with the place of knowing. People sense your knowing even when they don't realize it. There is a look in your eyes that wasn't there before. It's impossible to describe, but I'll give it a shot. You have a depth like there is some inner wisdom that is unshakeable. In looking at you, they see more than the expected other person who is returning their gaze. Instead, they find themselves staring into a deep and limitless pool. If people simply glance at you or if you hide it, they won't recognize it. But if you remove the filters and allow them to see you, they can't ignore it."

"You know, you're right. I had begun to take it for granted, but I catch people's eye at unexpected times. It then feels like we have a sudden, intense connection. Typically, they smile. But at other times, it seems like they want to get away. I think it's because they don't understand what just happened. They feel a thrill, just as I do, but it confuses and even scares them. I think they somehow realize that I've seen into places in themselves that they have never dared to face."

I unexpectedly changed the subject by disclosing, "My wife said something the other day that surprised me. She said her hope was that our prospective children would be average. Like many fathers, I had dreamed of having a child who would be a great athlete or an academic superstar."

Rick was totally with me and had no problem shifting gears. "We haven't decided yet about children. But, for me, the idea of cheering on the star quarterback would be a motivating factor."

Like it or not, I had to agree with him. "I guess I am a sexist because, time and time again, I conclude that women have it put together better than we do. I'll admit that after I gave the matter some thought, I had to acknowledge that my wife had a point. If your child is outstanding, for reasons, whether positive or negative, their life is going to be a lot more complicated. I would love them regardless and would just as soon spare them the drama."

Our conversation had taken an unexpected turn since I had thrown in a random thought. Nevertheless, Linda seemed relieved to have brought her concerns about academia out into the open. Having expressed her frustration, she was ready to get back to our work. "As I think about it, my professors are simply products of the system. I don't have to particularly like them. At the same time, I can't fault them for playing the game effectively. I respect their success in getting to where they are. It's another reminder to use perspective."

I was pleased with her easy transition. "That leads to the next concept I introduced: high indifference. You care tremendously about your education. You obviously want to learn all you can. And yet you realize your teachers are limited in what they can offer. It's easy to indulge in feelings of annoyance or disappointment. But you're fortunate to have benefitted from our work. You know, quite literally, how to rise above such petty and counterproductive thoughts and feelings."

"You're right. I can care more about the limitations of the system because, in another sense, I genuinely don't care. I can see holistically how it developed and how it self-perpetuates. It's not good or bad. It's simply another 'isness.' I could get mad and drop out. Quite obviously, that wouldn't improve things. Or I could play the game and do all I can to maximize my opportunities. But I must confess that it still bothers me. You have taught me so much that is totally foreign to what I'm learning in school. Sometimes, it seems like I signed up for an advanced math class and ended up in Basket Weaving 101."

I advised, "As useless as it can seem at times, I think you will find that your professors do have things to offer. They have had experiences as psychologists, and you can benefit vicariously from what they have gone through. There is a significant knowledge base concerning human behavior. You might as well tap into it and learn what you can. Let's return once more to the idea of being in the world but not of the world. If you're thinking of it from a higher vantage point, you will have no problem accepting the limitations of the ordinary reality."

"Thanks, I needed that reminder. It's like so many of these novel concepts. When I first really got them, I was amazed. And then, they started to fade away. But events in my life bring them back, and they become increasingly salient and powerful. My gosh, what have I gotten myself into?"

I grinned as I said, "You're saying that now. Just wait a couple of months and see what you think."

Rick's protective instinct kicked in as he said, "Just show us a little mercy along the way if you don't mind."

"It's a reasonable request. But, sorry. This process is ruthless. Once you begin on the path, you have to follow it. Believe it or not, I'm doing my best to be gentle. But you'll still have to experience some metaphorical cuts and bruises. I could tell you to forget all that and look toward the end goal. But that would be antithetical to what we are doing. Remember, it's a process. It's something to be cherished every step of the way."

"You're absolutely right," Linda said in agreement. "How many people throughout time would have killed for this opportunity? Of course, that doesn't mean that I don't sometimes want to kill you," she said with a thinly disguised grin.

I wanted to hug her, and so I did. "We're on a path that others have traversed many times through the ages. Our frustrations and fears are nothing new. In saying that, I don't want to minimize either the risks or the thrills involved. Where we started, just as well as where we might end up, is unique. The discoveries along the way are ours alone. What an incredible gift it is for me to share the journey with two people I genuinely love."

Linda wiped her eyes as Rick uttered a loud harrumph in an all-too-obvious attempt to mask his feelings.

Linda hugged me. To my surprise and delight, Rick joined in.

Linda's Journal

August 18

It really felt good to express my frustrations about school. I didn't even begin to describe my professors. Come to think of it, I think they would provide excellent fodder for a sitcom. Maybe thinking of it that way will make it more tolerable. I'll have to admit, though, that they are smart. Sometimes, I feel intimidated by just how intelligent they are. Then, I remember the distinction between understanding and knowledge. They have mainlined a tremendous amount of information into their brains and managed to file it in a way that allows it to be accessible. I'll give them credit. But what counts is the degree to which they can use it. As with us all, personality quirks often serve to glitch the input-output mechanism.

But enough about them. Let's face it. Based on my own choice, I'm becoming one of them. Hold up for just a second. That came out wrong. I'm siphoning information from them and doing the grunt work to gain the needed credentials. If I disrespect them, I'm only hurting myself. That doesn't mean I have to bow down to them, but there is no reason not to provide them with deference and respect based on their achievements.

Bill confirmed something vital that I already knew. I've heard that the eyes are the windows to the soul. No truer words were ever spoken. When I take off the filters, people are blown away. I've learned to modulate the degree to which I allow people to see me. At the right time and with the right person, it's truly marvelous. I love the connections I'm able to establish. That doesn't mean I'm forming long-term friendships, and that's okay. I don't have the time.

But I'm now seeing my fellow human beings as a smorgasbord. When and if my life settles down, the universe of people will be open for me to choose from. What a great way to think about the possibilities for establishing deep and meaningful relationships!

Rick's Journal

August 19

As I told Bill, I'm going through an adjustment. I liken it to the metanoia idea I remember hearing on one of the recordings. I compare it to taking a deck of cards and shuffling it. I feel like my way of looking at the world has been picked up, twisted, and jostled around. I do not doubt that things are better now than I'm settling on the other side. But that doesn't mean that it's not confusing to me. It's got to be even more puzzling to those who know me since they're finding that the person they thought they knew has, more or less, disappeared.

Bill has taken a sledgehammer to so many ways in which I was accustomed to looking at life. His idea of preferring an average child is a great example. It's a shock to the system. After all, doesn't everyone dream of their child being extraordinary? But the quandary forces me to examine where I view this from — through my lens or theirs? Would my future child find genuine happiness at the lonely high end of the bell curve? Is it about me or my child? What's certain, though, is my unwavering love for them, irrespective of where they stand on the spectrum of achievement. That, in itself, is what truly matters.

Not long ago, I would have been on the warpath after hearing what Linda said about her professors eyeing her. Once again, perspective comes to the rescue. As I think about it, how many times have I felt proud to walk into a room with my beautiful wife on my arm? If the issue of attracting attention confuses me, I can only imagine how it must be for her.

It's funny how women spend so much time with their makeup, hair, and dress. What are they trying to achieve? Even when they're happily married, they seem to want to be noticed by other men. Or is it that they want other women to be jealous? I think I'm getting in way over my head with my speculations.

At the end of the session, Linda hugged Bill. I still can't believe it. Rather than feeling jealous and possessive, I pushed my ego aside and joined in the fun. As I see it, my ego wants to hold on while I want to let go. I think it means that I'm now identifying more with essence.

Hallelujah! By allowing myself to get in on the fun, I could see not only embracing the people I love but essence itself. What a great lesson!

Fourteenth Meeting

I began, "As much as I would like to continue basking in our love for each other, we have work to do. The world we live in has not yet achieved oneness. Since it is our fate to live amongst the chaos and competition, we must adapt and adjust. It would be wonderful if we could all join hands for the common good, but humankind has not evolved to that level. The failure to recognize that basic fact has, historically, led to constant political struggles and even warfare."

Linda agreed, "I wish we could all just get along. So many charismatic politicians have promised to lead us in a positive direction only to have let us down."

"And why do you think that is?"

"Ego," Rick popped in. "They may initially have good intentions, but the ways of the world catch up with them. They become enmeshed in power struggles. They were forced to form coalitions with competing interests to become elected or appointed. Unfortunately, no matter how noble they may want to be, they end up wading in the muck. It's like the saying about herding cats. There are simply too many egos wanting to go their own way."

"I'll agree with you, Rick. What would you say our role should be in the midst of the inevitable conflicts?"

Linda volunteered, "I think it goes back to that serenity prayer from AA about knowing what you can change and accepting what you can't. We can play the game of being political rabble-rousers if we want to make that choice. But doing so requires all the entanglements that come with it. Alternatively, we can decide to live in awareness. Taking that route would invite others to rise above petty squabbles. If we set the right example by living from Self rather than ego, we might even inspire people to show more empathy and concern for the needs of others."

"Just be sure you don't confuse being egoless with being selfless. As Linda said, it's important to remember the idea of living through rather than from your ego. Since you're still living in this world, you must take care of your needs. Ideally, you would do so while keeping others in mind. If you're not overly tied to your ego, you will find it easy to be responsive to those around you because you won't be so wrapped up in yourselves. As you move into essence, you will naturally become attuned to the direction of humanity as a whole."

"Now I see where you're going with this," Linda said enthusiastically as we listened to the recording. "It fits in with your warning about power. As we grow in awareness, we begin to find that we can do things we hadn't thought possible. There is then a natural temptation to use our special abilities. We first must learn to avoid doing so in the service of our egos. But then, a more subtle temptation tries to sneak up on us. We can easily fool ourselves by thinking that whatever we're doing is okay if we use our awareness to benefit someone else, or even humankind in general."

"You've nailed it, Linda. That's the greater and more subtle trap. Our egos are sneaky. They are tied to this world and want us to stay here. What better way to do so than to convince us that we're helping others."

"I get what you're saying. I instinctively want to help. In a way, I've always known that it's kind of selfish. I feel better when I do things for my friends and neighbors. Thinking about it reminds me of times I watched someone I cared about as they opened a gift I'd carefully selected. It's all about them, but it's also all about me. As I now understand it, my gift allows me and the recipient to move into essence together."

"Agreed. And there is a possible trapdoor. What if they don't like the gift? Do you then move even more toward ego/separateness?"

"Good point," she acknowledged. "I've had that happen. I was incredibly excited about a necklace I bought for a good friend. Then I felt let down, and even a little bit miffed, when she didn't seem to like it. I hate to admit it, but our friendship has suffered since then."

"So, here's a reminder. It's great to throw ourselves into things just as our egos demand. Fortunately, high indifference allows us great latitude in doing so. But you must retain the attitude that allows you to keep your balance regardless of the outcome."

Rick wanted to participate and asked, "I've always been interested in politics. How do you apply your thinking to problems like world hunger?"

I responded, "Castaneda introduced the term, 'controlled folly.' Through its use, he said that he could throw himself without reservation into things he elected to think were important. He was able to do so because another part of him realized that they were of no significance in the greater scheme of things."

Linda rubbed her chin as she thought, "I think I've got it. He could involve himself so fully because he knew it was just a game. It's a variation of high indifference. He cared deeply, but on another level, he didn't care. He could see the world as being a perfect manifestation and felt no need to change the divine plan. That knowledge freed him to become totally involved in whatever he chose while, at the same time, he almost laughed at himself for being so foolish. Many of these concepts transcend centuries and cultures."

"Makes sense," Rick piped in. "I see homelessness, poverty, and drug abuse all around. It's horrible, and I feel for the people who are in distress. I know that I can't make a significant difference in their situations, but I also think it's not an excuse for just sitting idle." He then chuckled to himself. "And it gives me a new way of looking at my obsession with football. I know it makes no difference in the long run if my team wins. At the same time, I absorb myself in each play like my life depends on it. I now see it as a metaphor for the greater play of life itself."

I concurred. "I can't imagine standing by and watching someone suffer unnecessarily. I'm saying that if there is something concrete that I can do to make someone feel better, I will do it. But it's tricky. Does that mean I would give money to a street beggar? Actually, I would not because I wouldn't trust how that money would be spent. I respect people who dedicate themselves to dealing with issues like hunger on either an individual or a global scale. My approach is quite different. I believe I can best contribute to humanity by dealing with my own evolution."

Linda was horrified. "Bill, if I didn't love you, I might have to slap you again. How horribly selfish."

I threw up my hands in mock self-defense. "I totally agree. On the surface, it sounds terrible. But think about it. I'm all in favor of people who do things for others. In doing so, I believe they enrich themselves and the people they are helping. I enjoy participating in such endeavors. But even as I do, I'm very aware of the insignificant impact I'm having. If you consider the issue using perspective, you can see the much greater benefit you can provide if you can nudge people in a manner that promotes our natural evolution towards God/essence. "

"You're getting a bit abstract again," Linda complained.

"You don't have to be on a conscious path to awareness to think about making the world a better place. Every time you interact with someone, you have the opportunity to make their lives a little brighter. When you pass by a stranger and your eyes meet, allow yourself a brief smile. If they reciprocate, or even if they turn away in surprise, you will have done something positive for humanity. At the extreme, if you're able to access levels of awareness that serve as a clarion call to angels, you will provide humankind with a serious bump in the right direction. Either way, the warning remains. Keep your ego on the sidelines."

She commented, "I see what you're saying. For the most part, I agree with it. Still, part of me feels a more direct responsibility."

"You're part of humanity. Naturally, you want to improve the world for your fellow humans. I'm totally with you. Just make conscious decisions. If your priority is ending world hunger, go for it. I'll even chip in a few bucks. You don't even have to be realistic about your expectations. Suffering is real, yet we haven't even come close to defining reality. On a personal level, I feel good when I've done something to help another person. I'm grateful any time I have the opportunity to do so. I'm also aware of the limitations I have as an individual. In the end, I choose not to tilt at windmills."

Linda said, "I certainly see what you're saying. If I allow myself to get caught up in all the tragedies in the world, I will feel miserable, helpless, and inadequate. I've also struggled with the way we treat animals. At times, I've flirted with becoming a vegetarian."

"I hear you. I've had similar thoughts and even spent a couple of years as a strict vegetarian. I still haven't come to a complete inner resolution, but I have a way of rationalizing the matter."

"Oh, great guru," Linda said in a mocking, sarcastic tone that belied her obvious curiosity, "Please share the pearls of your wisdom."

"Slaps can go both ways," I warned in a facetiously menacing manner. "But I will tell you what I have come up with as a resolution that causes me the least distress. On a biological level, humans are simply animals. We're part of the food chain. We're not, at least at this point, sufficiently evolved to eschew eating. We begin this world as omnivores, which is tremendously advantageous for our long-term survival. The chemistry of our bodies requires a considerable amount of protein. The most efficient way of staying alive and healthy involves eating animals. It's not pretty. I've never visited a slaughterhouse and pray that I never will."

It was obvious that Linda was still struggling with this troublesome issue. "I get the whole survival thing, but I can't stand the way that some people treat animals. As an example that's close to my heart, too many people abuse dogs. Humankind, if we can even use that term in good faith since we're not particularly kind, has bred dogs to be loyal to us even when we mistreat them. I can't tell you how angry and upset I get when I hear about people beating and starving their pets."

"I can only tell you to use the magic word. As a reminder, it starts with a 'p' and has three syllables ending in 'life.' It's truly one of our most valuable word tools, and it's incredibly easy to forget about it as we get caught up in the world we live in. I share your affection for dogs. What an enormous gift they provide.

"I think there is a sort of generalized karma for our species. If we brutalize helpless animals, there is a price to pay in terms of reversing our spiritual evolution. I see it as my responsibility to counter the negative by respecting all animals. Even if we deal with them as food crops, a term that makes me shudder, it's up to us to treat them 'humanely.' I feel sort of like I'm talking in circles. I'll have to admit that this whole topic brings me down. My natural tendency is to live more in the heavens with one foot lightly touching the earth."

Rick almost mocked me as he said, "You're not slipping away from us that easily, sucker. You made a deal with us, and I'm here to make sure you don't go skipping off into the ozone."

Linda's Journal

August 25

Our last session was more philosophical, which is okay with me. It's good to take a break from the metaphysical atom bombs that Bill scatters along the way. At the same time, I can see that he is preparing us. If we grow in power to the extent he suggests, we don't want to be blasting the world with our good intentions.

He made us think about a topic that I generally try to avoid. It just hurts too much to see the suffering in the world. I find myself feeling caught. If I stop to consider it, I feel compelled to act. At the same time, my rational brain tells me that I can't really make a difference. I start going round and around and can't find a resolution until I find a way to distract myself. I know that sounds terrible, but I doubt that I'm the only person to find themselves in that dilemma.

It's good that this journal is intended for my eyes only. What would happen if others started doubting their charitable efforts? That would, indeed, be horrible. We need to keep the wheels of the world turning until we reach the point where we're prepared to stop the train. And our ultimate destination is nowhere close to being in sight.

Another strange thought just occurred to me. Bill was talking about the state of the world and how tempting it is to bemoan the tragedies that we bring on ourselves through war and other stupidities. And here's what gets me. The fact is that in our current state of spiritual evolution, we want those horrible things. Yep, you got me right. Why do you think people watch police and 911 shows? Though most of us are loath to admit it, we want at least a touch of drama in our lives.

Rick's Journal

August 27

I've long been a fan of politics, so I found our last session particularly thought-provoking. Bill provided us with what, at least to me, was a totally novel way of considering the massive blunders that our leaders make. We say we don't want war, and then we elect people who lead us right into it. And then what do we do? We re-elect them in the name of patriotism. I hate to say it, but there is a parallel to sports. We become almost bloodthirsty in rooting for a group of people who form a team, typically for no better reason than convenience. It really makes no sense.

And yet, it does. In our current state, we thrive on conflict. No one wants to admit it. We all talk about seeking peace and ending hunger. But we want to be entertained. There is nothing more boring than watching people sitting around and getting along. And if everyone is financially stable, where is the need to get ahead? As much as it pains me to say, I've even known people who get off on the problems of others because it makes their troubles seem less significant.

I'm glad he threw in that tidbit about the difference between egoless and selfless. It seems trivial at first glance, but it's anything but. The distinction is subtle, but I can see where he was going. In our efforts to do for others, we certainly don't want to lose the most crucial aspect of who we are: our Selves. On the other hand, it's okay to temporarily free ourselves from our egos as we perform charitable acts. Of course, as Bill intimated, there is probably no greater temptation than to allow our sneaky egos to take pride in how beneficent we are.

I like the idea of working on myself as a way to improve the world, but I certainly recognize that it can be a cop-out. I'm glad that I have Bill and Linda. Neither of them would hesitate to slap me right out of my shoes if I started losing perspective. Even in saying that, I don't want to pawn the responsibility off on anyone else. It's up to me to keep my eyes open and watch for my tendency to make lazy excuses for myself.

As I think about it, I expected our sessions to be focused on me and Linda as a couple. I wonder where Bill is going with this apparent diversion into politics and suffering. He doesn't engage in idle chatter. I'm sure there is an underlying message concerning our relationship. The best I can figure is that he's encouraging us to develop a worldview, allowing us sufficient latitude to grow together. I'm guessing that he wants us to avoid becoming enmeshed in the petty grievances of the world around us. I'm sure there is more to it, and I will wait for it to be revealed.

Fifteenth Meeting

I began, "It feels a bit odd listening to the current recording because there are so many gaps. Just so Rick understands, it's because we traveled to higher spaces and had no need for words. We will revisit those spaces as we get closer to transformation, but let's continue with reality as we know it."

"I'm relieved you said that," Linda said as she relaxed in her chair. "Speaking of higher spaces, I continue to be disturbed by that weird energy thing you did with me earlier when I lost it. I know that we've talked about it and that I'm not supposed to understand it, but that doesn't mean that it doesn't scare the wits out of me. If I didn't trust you..."

"Totally understood and accepted. If it helps, I don't really get it either. But it's just a space. And being able to pull that sort of power out of your back pocket can come in handy. You were off in the unknown, and I had to do something dramatic to bring you back. If I hadn't had the means to do so, there was a real risk that I would have gotten lost in a psychotic space. Let's revisit the incident that provoked it."

"That's a part of my life that I would just as soon forget. There was so much angst, so much anger, so many regrets."

"And so many lessons," I added.

"I hope you don't mind if I curse you a little more before we dig further into it," Linda said with a humorless laugh. "I tend to avoid subjects and people who bring me pain. I know I've asked you this before, but do I have to keep reliving it?"

"You'll love my answer. Of course not. We can just hold the wagons, and you can return to your 'normal' life."

"Again, I feel like you're mocking me. You know that I can't do that. Moreover, I can't cheat Rick out of what we're doing. I want more than anything for us to discover the kind of marriage you described."

"Linda," I counseled, "It should be much easier to go back over what happened at this point. The threats that Barb posed are no longer hovering over you. We now have the liberty to examine all the spaces she provoked dispassionately. It's definitely one of the many gifts she left you."

Linda released a deep sigh. "I know deep down that you're right. In some ways, the painful times in our lives offer us more opportunity for lessons than the good times."

"Looking at it that way, isn't it interesting that people expend so much energy avoiding people and things that make them uncomfortable? I'm certainly not suggesting that you deliberately expose yourself to things you dislike. What I am saying is that life presents such situations to you automatically. If you enter them with an attitude of openness and grace rather than resistance, you might be surprised to discover that there is something to gain."

Her sarcasm was evident and even a bit sardonic as she protested, "That sounds well and good in theory, but it almost cost me my husband."

"Now that you're removed from the situation, I hope you can see that it did almost the opposite. I think I can be objective rather than critical when I say that you didn't have a husband before she entered the picture. Barb stirred the pot and provided the fuel to revitalize a stagnant marriage."

"There you go, being right again," she protested. "That's not one of my favorite parts of you. Since you know how I feel about you deep down, I feel free to tell you what I like and don't like."

"Sounds like that honesty thing. You know how much I value it as long as it's in the true spirit of the word. I even appreciated it when you turned on me during that session, accusing me of stripping you of your natural defense by taking away your self-definition of jealousy."

For the first time since we had resumed our meetings, Linda appeared to be flustered. "I'm not going to deny or defend what I did. Not that I could anyway since it's right there on the recording. But at the time, I felt like you had misled me. I had always believed that I could somehow ward off other women who might intrude on our marriage by being jealous. I was determined to hold tightly to that shield until you ripped it from me."

"And now?"

"I see jealousy as sort of like guilt. It's an emotion/thought process that produces nothing but neurotic reactions and is more likely to damage than enhance relationships. At the time, I didn't totally get the lesson about identifying myself in limiting ways by using the word 'is.' You weren't saying that I should be blind. I misinterpreted the lesson and allowed myself to become oblivious to the obvious. I felt so free in losing my identification with jealousy that I went to the opposite extreme. I ignored what was right in front of my face."

I cautioned, "I hope that you can say that without self-condemnation. It was a necessary, if somewhat unpleasant, clarification of an important lesson. Once again, words can help us, or they can paralyze us. Only by gaining the ability, as well as the discipline, to stand over them can we know the difference. You're still learning, as am I. Lessons, as much as we may hate them at the time, tend to continue to present us with opportunities."

"I know I have a habit of giving you a hard time. I trust that you know it's because I care."

"Absolutely. It goes back to the misconception that the opposite of love is hate. If you hate someone, let them go. Releasing your emotional attachment to them is, in a sense, the ultimate revenge. In doing so, however, I don't particularly recommend looking at it in the context of retribution because it still implies a degree of attachment. There goes that tricky ego thing again."

"I wanted so much to do just that with Barb while we were battling for Rick's heart, mind, and body, but you wouldn't let me. I'm so glad you encouraged me to deal with her through my head rather than my heart. The evolution I experienced in seeing her as an enemy, then a teacher, and ultimately as an externalization of my ego was breathtaking. In the process, I was able to release her absolutely."

"Just to be clear, I'm not in the business of letting or not letting people do things. I simply guided you in a direction that I thought would allow you to gain the benefit from an unpleasant reality that manifested. The insights that followed were yours. Interestingly, Barb almost sucked you in again by coming to you and asking for counseling."

"Reality is a bitch," she remarked with an understandable touch of sarcasm. "She almost got me again. I don't say that as a way of being critical of Barb. In retrospect, I'm truly grateful for all the opportunities for learning that she provided. It's fascinating that after all we had been through, she allowed me a chance to clean up another attachment. I now realize that my desire to help can be a trap in itself. As I learned that lesson, I could ultimately support her without being attached to how she responded."

"It's interesting to view what happened in the context of our previous discussion about charity. Do you remember the story about the Boy Scouts who helped an older woman across the street? As it happened, she didn't really want to cross the street. She got run over on the way back to where she started.

Linda's laugh was brief but genuine. "I can see how important it is to recognize when we are helping people due to our own needs versus helping people who genuinely want and need our help. To truly recognize the difference, we must remove our egos from the picture."

"Clarity is important. Insight can be helpful as well. But they are both potential traps. You can become stuck in either, believing you've accomplished something significant. If you do nothing with the realization, you've made absolutely no progress. It's one of the limitations of traditional therapy. And it's certainly one of the challenges you will face as a therapist."

"Maybe I should stop the insidious torture of this whole graduate school idea and just keep notes on what you're saying."

"Like the rest of us," I warned, "You're looking for the easy way out. "You're being presented with an amazing number of opportunities for learning at school. You're working with bright people who have mastered an enormous field of learning. You can also develop camaraderie with dedicated fellow students who share your interests and your struggles. It's among the best life has to offer. Rather than questioning it or looking for an easy out, embrace it."

"Thank you. Once again, I needed a reminder. It's that darn perspective thing. Maybe I need to wear a rubber band around my wrist to keep popping myself."

"Not at all," I advised. You would be missing the beauty of perspective. It's only when you've lost it and then regained it that you can truly appreciate and benefit from it."

Linda' Journal

September 4

Hearing the silent stretches within the recording, where our conversations once lived, was a remarkable experience. They propelled me back to those moments aloft with Bill, soaring through skies that one could scarcely dream of. Yet, these memories resist the confinement of language; they're not a narrative to recount but a state of existence to re-inhabit.

I've touched the edges of what felt like spiritual rapture at specific points in my past, moments of profound bliss and connection. But those instances, as breathtaking as they were, belong to their own category. They differ entirely from my flights with Bill - each extraordinary yet distinct in the essence of the experience they provided.

Let me see if I can explain it to myself. With Bill, I felt unbound. We were the masters of the universe in the ultimate sense that we were the universe. Rather than worshipping some higher power, we were simply uniting with that power. That sounds egotistical, which is the last thing I want to portray. As a clarification, we weren't feeling superior or apart. We simply were. As I think back, there was a common theme in my previous and more recent experiences. They all involved essence. Ever heard the phrase, "Let go and let God?" Well, I'm here to tell you that there is something to it.

I know that Bill is hesitant to tip-toe into religious waters. He sometimes alludes to religious thought but wants to keep religion in the background. I really considered the matter and concluded that he doesn't want religious preconceptions with all the likely associated baggage to sully our new experiences. He previously made it clear that he is not against religion per se. As always, he is trying to keep everything we're doing as clean as possible.

It's encouraging that I wasn't as thrown this time when he brought up my crazy episode. It's still not fun when he reminds me, but it does have the effect of desensitizing what happened. It's becoming apparent that by resisting, I've been holding on to it. If I'm to become clean, I need to reach the point where nothing grabs me in a way that prevents me from letting go.

Of course, the fun part of the session was observing our interaction as my natural feistiness started to peek out. Bill has never tried to portray himself as superior in any way, but that doesn't mean that I haven't found him intimidating. At least in my experience, you don't meet a demigod every day. I don't want to bring him down in size, though that's more of my natural tendency. Instead, I want to rise to his level. I'm so glad these notes are private. Anyone reading them would have to conclude that I'm getting nuttier and nuttier. I can't imagine what my minister would say.

Rick's Journal

September 5

Previously, I would have been envious of listening to the gaps in the session as Linda and Bill traveled to paradise and beyond. Okay, you got me. I still am. But there's also some rather unexpected, good news. I wasn't nearly so much troubled as I was uplifted. I felt myself traveling right alongside them. I can't even tell you how excited I am at the prospect of what is to come. My usual skepticism has flown the coop along with everything else. I'm ready for wherever Bill leads us. I'm naturally guarded in dealing with others, so that's a huge statement.

I'm so lucky to be able to benefit vicariously as I'm listening to Linda's sessions. It's almost like cheating since I don't have to risk any disclosures from my own checkered past. Of course, that's just my ego talking. I think that, in doing it the way we are, I'm going to be sufficiently free from ego to withstand the mortification likely to come. I realize that the recordings in which I discussed my interactions with Barb are still out there. When it's time, I will simply have to, as Bill says, walk through it.

I'm always seeking to derive lessons from what Bill tells us. I especially liked the way he talked about negative experiences. While it would be ridiculous to seek them out, the bad things that inevitably happen might contain gifts. It's up to me to flow with them while maintaining an open mind that allows me to learn.

Sixteenth Meeting

"You may have wondered why I spent so much time on the topic of charities."

They both seemed somewhat perplexed. Rick finally said, "I thought it was because of the moral dilemma we face. I can't turn around without someone asking for money."

Linda agreed. "It seems like every time I turn on the TV, I see a starving or sick child. It tugs at my heartstrings. It's tough because I can't just send out checks in every direction. I've also learned that one donation only leads to an avalanche of requests for more."

"Speaking of strings, I'm now going to tie it up in a nice little bow for you. I will never ask you to keep a secret. Doing so never leads to anything positive. All the same, it would probably not be a good idea to share what I'm about to say with the rest of the world."

"Well, you've certainly set the stage. Are you going to tell us or not?" Linda demanded.

"Interestingly, much of what I have to say is repetitive. Genuine knowledge seems to have that characteristic. We're constantly exposed to it in different forms. Some of it we miss because we simply aren't looking in the right direction. But you could shout the greatest truths from a mountaintop, and the most likely outcome would involve a call to 911."

"Enough, already," exclaimed an exasperated Linda. "Just tell us."

"What I have to say does merit a buildup, especially since I've said it before. Now I think you're in a place to really get it. If you remember, I once pulled the rug out from under you by saying that God is not good."

"Yep," Linda said in response. "That was a real zinger. I still thought you were at least half crazy at that time, so I took it with a grain of salt. It took me a little longer before I realized that you're full-on crazy."

Ignoring her awkward attempt at humor, I sat back and allowed the energy to develop between us. "Now take a look from this perspective."

"Wow!" they said in unison. "The whole charity thing is more or less a misdirection. We torture ourselves with notions of what we must do in order to be a good person. And that's appropriate in our ordinary lives.

But at a transcendental level, it's laughable. We don't need to try to be this or that. We already are."

"I hope you're seeing how the things we're discussing tie together. There is a common thread, whether we're talking about jealousy or charity."

Linda thought about it for a minute before the light bulb came on. "It's one of the first things you told me about. Like so much of what you've revealed, I have to keep getting it on different levels. The 'is of identity' is sneaky. Once again, it goes back to a conjugation of the verb 'to be.' We misuse it frequently and unconsciously. In doing so, we trap ourselves over and over again."

"What happens if you stop thinking of yourself as good, noble, righteous, or anything else?"

It was Rick's turn to light up. "Freedom. As I'm contemplating the notion, I feel incredibly light and carefree. It's like a huge load has been lifted. I remember our previous discussions on the topic. It made sense before, but not in the way I'm getting it now. I no longer feel the pressure to live up to something impossible. I can donate as much as I want, but guilt doesn't have to affect my decisions. I will give because it feels good to do so rather than giving to minimize feeling bad. Neither giving nor not giving defines me as a person."

While it wasn't necessary, I thought it was time to remind them of the purpose of our current sessions. "I want you to begin seeing everything in the context of 'being' together. Take away the words and simply contemplate being. We want to go beyond space and time or any other limitations you might impose. It's a thrill to do so individually. But doing it in tandem will have an exponential effect." As I was speaking, I began raising the energy.

"Brother!" Linda remarked. "I can sense us holding hands together as we traverse the universe. As we do so, we wave to our egos in the far distance. I'm using the word sense rather than see because the experience has nothing to do with our limited sensory organs."

Rick beamed as he reached for her hand. "I feel connected to you in a way I never even dreamed possible."

After a couple of beautiful moments, I broke them back to earth with a comment. "We're getting closer, but we're not there yet. I trust that this experience will keep you moving. By the way, I checked in on your progress with marital therapy. So far, all I'm getting is green lights. You guys are doing the work with her as well as with me. Congrats."

Rick seemed pleased. "I thought marital therapy would be a waste of time. I've resisted it in the past. But the sessions have helped us work through issues that I didn't even realize there were issues. I'm glad you bifurcated the work. That way, we can focus on the ethereal with you while getting down in the mud with our marital therapist."

"Speaking of getting dirty," I reflected, "let's talk about the childish pranks we hear on the recording. The story about slipping Ex-Lax to Barb before the SAT exams was over the top. Entertaining, I'll admit. But don't you think it was needlessly cruel?"

I was glad that Linda didn't hesitate to take ownership. "Tricking Barb into eating a brownie laced with laxatives was, I'll have to agree, a bit much. When you're in high school, matters that later seem foolish feel like life or death. I felt that Barb was out to undermine and ostracize me. I thought I would lose my place in the social hierarchy if I didn't do something dramatic. At that point, there was no thought of an existence beyond high school."

I chuckled. "You managed to do something so dramatic that the aftereffects of what you created continued into your adult life. Practical jokes are hilarious at the time. Unfortunately, the humor is based on humiliating and isolating another person. As funny as the jokes can seem, they are destructive. Moreover, these actions often carry consequences, typically rebounding in unexpected ways. Few realize that their primary effect is to magnify the individual's ego through a harsh, destructive method that isolates more than it educates."

Linda stiffened slightly. "I hope you're not lecturing me. It's a sensitive topic. I'm pretty sure I learned my lesson."

"You're incredibly lucky. It turned out to be a lesson that kept on giving. I think it's worth a review. Would you mind?"

"Looking back, I recognize that a stroke of luck played its part in my success. However, the dedication I put in and the invaluable guidance you provided truly made the difference. Though I may not have fully appreciated your influence at the time, it was a significant factor in navigating those challenges. I certainly needed the reminder you provided about perspective."

"But you did the work. As much of a struggle as it was, you could back off sufficiently to see her as your teacher. Rather than limiting your thoughts of her to consider her a threat or a competitor, you were able to see her from a higher level. Developing the ability to make that transition is critical in learning to deal with and benefit from life lessons through awareness. And the beautiful thing is that you didn't stop there."

"You're absolutely right. It was quite an internal battle to accept her as my teacher. Once I had made that leap, I was able to enter into full-blown ob-op. Amazingly, I saw, though not in the usual sense, her role in the cosmic play. I'm glad that you asked me to relive it once more. It helps me to clean up my attachment. I'm still learning about this 'seeing' thing. But that was one of my most powerful experiences. I agree with your attempt to describe it. Seeing has a visual element, but it's much more accurate to consider it as a knowing or a realization."

"And even after you 'saw' her, she still represented a real-time problem. But you began to put your emotions on the shelf. You were able to begin problem-solving in a way that strengthened your relationship with Rick."

Rick chimed in. "My God. Now, it makes sense. I was blown away that you handled the whole thing without throwing pots and pans at me. I just knew it was going to be the death of our marriage. Moreover, I didn't expect it to sink slowly. I was waiting anxiously for the fireworks to begin. I knew that you had grown through your sessions. I just had no idea how much you had progressed."

Ever the teacher, I said, "It's a good reminder of advice you hear in different forms. It's not so much what life gives you as it is what you make of it. It also relates to the ego's desire to always want what it doesn't have. Having things doesn't make us happy for more than a minute. Possession does not equal satisfaction. When I think about owning a mansion, you know the next thought that comes to mind? Who's going to take care of it?

It's worthwhile to have goals and strive for them. You have to keep in the back of your mind that it's all a game. On another level, it's about more than simply reaching your goals. The pot of gold at the end of the rainbow is illusory. Searching for it can be a lot of fun as long as you remember that crucial fact."

Linda's Journal

September 11

If it weren't for the incredible value of our meetings, I would have stopped them long ago. It's basically the only luxury I allow myself due to demands on my time. It's reached the point that sleep fits into the luxury category.

But boy, is it worth it. After a couple of relatively safe and intellectual sessions, he took us on the trip of a lifetime. It's gratifying that Bill is now including us both on these rides to infinity. It was incredible to be able to share the experience with Rick. Other than the strangling time constraints, my path through life couldn't be more perfect.

Bill, being Bill, doesn't just gift us flying lessons. He always has a purpose in mind. He landed a punch with this one. Even though I've had success in freeing myself from the yoke of others' opinions, I haven't been able to completely shed an underlying, pervasive sense of guilt and failure. I hadn't been able to put my finger on it until Bill pinpointed it with his discussion of giving.

Now, it's clear that I will never be able to do enough to be a perfect person, much less to alleviate the problems of the world. I can continue to help in a way that feels right for me. But I don't need to impress anyone, including myself, with my generosity. I can see it in terms of the cosmic egg that keeps us swimming along the inner boundaries of the shell but unable to punch our way out. Well, I just had my eureka, and it feels like a major layer of sadness just peeled away.

It's incredible how much Bill covers in each session. While it seems repetitive at times, it is anything but. There hasn't been a single time when I haven't learned something new when we've reviewed a lesson. I've made a decision and hope I don't regret it. I realize that Bill tends to build important things up for a reason. But sometimes, I feel like shoving my hand down his throat and pulling it out of him. Okay, that's a little overly dramatic. I intended to write that I'm going to take a more demanding role in ensuring we get everything possible in the limited time available.

Rick's Journal

September 13

Whew! Linda has had more of these trips to the vast unknown than I have. What a tremendous experience! And to share it with the woman I love with all my heart. I can't believe what I've been missing all my life. I could feel bad for all the people who don't have the opportunity, but then I would fall back into the sinkhole of my own expectations.

Now, I know I can do what resonates with me and feel good about it. I'm enjoying an incredible freedom and lightness of spirit. I now realize and accept that I'm not defined by my inadequacies in solving the problems of the world. It goes back to the lesson concerning responsibility that I heard in Linda's recording. Since the word means ability to respond, I can look at my position in the universe objectively. I will do what I reasonably can to make the world a better place, but I'm not going to get down on myself when the impact of my efforts proves to be insignificant.

I think it's another example of how we trap ourselves into a sense of futility with our words. I just hope Bill hurries up with his earlier promise to fix the English language. It would be nice if he could find the time to clean up a few more languages along the way, but he needs to start by taking care of matters close to home.

I was both shocked and amused to hear about the laxative-laced brownies. Linda is full of surprises. It's amazing that I was married to her for so many years and never really got to know her. I'm licking my lips when I think of the possibilities when we can finally spend time together. Marital therapy is worthwhile, but much of our sessions are spent going over past grievances and previous ways of miscommunicating. I'm glad we're doing it. I just wish we had the time to implement the new things we're learning.

It's relatively trivial amid all we're going through, but I still thought his comments concerning practical jokes were notable. I don't know how it is with girls, but cruel jokes are pretty well routine with guys. While I was in college, there was an innocuous guy who fit the description of a nerd. My classmates started innocently enough by filling half of the hair tonic bottle he used daily with urine. I even participated in some of their raucous, alcohol-fueled plans as they talked about taking it to another level.

Fortunately, some part of me stayed out of it when they kidnapped him and dropped him off in the middle of nowhere with no clothes or shoes. I don't think that the perpetrators thought about how it would feel if it happened to them. I did, so I didn't. As I reflect on it, I was rather cowardly in not intervening. I'm just glad that I only have to grow up once.

Seventeenth Meeting

I began by observing, "I really hit a nerve when I emphasized the importance of dealing straight on with Barb after she had come between you. You knew you needed to hear what I was saying, but your ego wanted no part. You became interlocked with anger and stalked out of my office, canceling any future appointments."

Rather sheepishly, Linda acknowledged, "It wasn't one of my prouder moments. I wanted to pretend I could make it go away. Of course, you wouldn't let me. It's amazing how many women deal with their husbands' affairs by pretending they aren't happening. Part of me didn't want to rock the boat. Another part of me wanted to go in with guns blazing. My ego grabbed hold, convincing me to turn my anger toward you."

"And it must have been a relief, albeit temporary, to do so. Your ego had been wanting to chuck me overboard for some time. It seemed like the best opportunity to make its move. As I've told you, the path to knowledge offers many twists and turns. What it doesn't offer is a way back."

"Somehow, I don't remember your telling me about the last part," Linda said in a half-hearted attempt at humor. "I can accept that now. At the time, I was in purgatory. I couldn't go forward, and I certainly couldn't go back to you. Then reality, in the form of Barb, hit me square in the jaw. I knew from high school that she was a worthy adversary, but I certainly wasn't prepared for what she did."

"And her timing wasn't coincidental," I observed. "She sensed that you were in a precarious position. Remember, you had some a cosmic connection with her. She went for the jugular by showing Rick purported evidence that you were in the porn industry."

"I can almost laugh about it now. At the time, I felt like my world had ended. How unbelievably mean!"

"Now that you have some distance from the incident, allow me to make the same comment concerning the laxative episode. Once again, what goes around comes around. Without getting too much into

Eastern religions, I do have to agree that there are karmic cycles. The merry-go-round continues until we finally come to our senses and find a way to jump off. We have to lose our minds to find our Selves."

"If you had talked to me that way once I finally convinced myself to see you again, I would have turned around and walked right back out the door. I was nowhere close to accepting my role in the whole mess. At the same time, I was so beaten down that I probably would have just let you swing away at me."

"Linda, please tell me you've never really thought of me in that way."

With a sly grin, she said, "Well, maybe. You do sometimes act in a way that brings to mind the hind end of a horse. But no. I'll admit I always sense that you have my best interests in mind. And you certainly came through when you helped me back off sufficiently to see the whole mess objectively. I finally gained some traction in what turned out to be an all-out war with Barb."

Rick was understandably reluctant to get involved at this point. But he did have to throw in a rueful comment. "I hate that I was so stupid. I know that 'shoulds' are worthless, but I can't help wanting to kick myself for being so slow to see that Barb had set her up. How in the world could I have ever thought that Linda was a whore?"

"First of all, I totally agree that there is no place in this world for the word 'should.' It's a harmful word tool. I think of it as a 2-edged saw-tooth blade with no handle. No matter how you try to grab onto it, it only causes harm. Going back to the whole karma thing, it's interesting how it backfired on Barb. She led you into a state of confusion similar to what Linda was experiencing. After you each individually found a resolution, you were able to come together in a new beginning.

"You really can do magic, can't you?" Linda commented. "I would have said there was absolutely no way there could have been a positive outcome. You helped me find an answer when I couldn't imagine one existed."

"Well," I admitted, "that is the function of magic. But I must add one qualification. In all modesty, it was the two of you who created the elixir."

"Looking back at my earlier sessions, I'm glad you gave me a heads-up that our work was nearing an end. I was excited that you felt I had made so much progress. But more so, I was terrified. I didn't think I was ready to fly solo. I guess you weren't surprised by my reaction."

"As I told you, I've traveled many of the same roads. I've also encountered similar dead ends. You had been through tremendous emotional and cognitive turmoil. Your attempt to retreat into spirituality as we were ending was almost predictable."

"How do you know when to let go? Beyond that, how do you know when to turn on the juice and when to let it off? I have a long way to go in approaching this whole enlightenment idea."

"Your questions are natural. And you can probably guess my response. It's all a matter of knowing. I'm no genius. But if you'll indulge me for a moment, I'll get a little spooky. At one point, you mentioned a concern about loneliness as you traversed the path. The thing is that when you reach a certain level of awareness, you join the company of other souls. I don't have to consciously think of what and when to say. Any words that I might use to describe it would be grossly inadequate. Let's just say there are more than just the three of us on this trip."

"Thanks a lot, Bill," she said sarcastically. Whenever I feel like I'm getting my bearings, you throw in another major wrinkle. Now I feel even more excited but also more than a little bit scared."

"Excellent!" I responded with genuine enthusiasm. "The immensity of this journey is starting to unfold. There are facts that I'm now able to introduce that won't cause you to high tail it out of here. The things that I'm now and will be telling you are absolutely absurd in the ordinary world. But as you begin to experience them, they are undeniable."

Linda sighed. "I guess it's time I quit fighting you. I mean, you do know I love you. But that has nothing to do with it. Every time I start to get my feet on the ground, you make the floor collapse underneath me. Strangely, I like it. Well, truth be told, I don't exactly like it. But when I can stand up again, it's on decidedly higher ground. I love being able to see myself and my world from the heavens. At the same time, I know I've not yet earned my place there as a permanent resident. There's considerable rent to be paid to be worthy of that slot."

"Which brings us back once more to a recurring lesson. We are involved in a process. There both is and isn't a goal in mind. What matters is right here and right now. To the extent that you can compress your awareness into the totality of this instant, you will have approached 'Oneness.' The awesome fact is that you now realize that infinity is at your doorstep."

With a slight grimace, Linda said, "No more complaining. I'm determined. You're going to keep saying things that make my jaw drop. I'm just going to take it in stride. Who am I kidding? You'll keep scaring the bejeezus out of me while simultaneously enthralling me."

Linda's Journal

September 19

How long has it been since I stalked out of Bill's office and vowed never to return? I think it was 5 minutes ago or maybe 50 years. That's just how distorted my sense of time has become. Of course, I now realize my anger toward Bill was displaced. I couldn't tolerate the situation I found myself in as Barb was moving in on my husband. My rage had to go somewhere, and Bill was right there in front of me. He was, after all, the easily identifiable culprit in the changes I had undergone.

As it turned out, Bill was the one who brought me back to earth. That's strange to say since he's usually the one who has a habit of catapulting me to parts unknown. I've got to hand it to Barb. She made a compelling case when she accused me of having a hidden career. But, come on! Me, a prostitute? It's distressing that Rick fell for it, but he was off balance at the time. I had no idea that Barb was such a master manipulator.

It's fascinating to think of the role my ego played when I made the show of telling Bill just what I thought of him at the time. Previously, I had been doing so well, and my ego had been fading into the background. However, with the help of Barb, my ego did its best to reclaim me. And it nearly did, especially when I felt my world was crumbling.

"My body did its part to weaken me as well with that horrible GI bug. Dragging myself back to Bill's office was a significant and critical achievement. If I hadn't done so, I guess I would be watching on the sidelines as Rick and Barb managed a clandestine affair. What a disgusting thought!

Bill didn't seem surprised or shocked at the turn of events. I really cheated myself by canceling my sessions with him at the time. He had a point about the parallel with raising children. What mother of a teenage daughter has not had their cherished daughter walk out, slamming the door in the process.

Looking at it more positively, it was the beginning of the end of that phase of my relationship with Bill. He was preparing me to fly on my own. I wonder how many mothers consider their daughters' tantrums a necessary, though unpleasant, attempt to shed the dependency of childhood. Well, I might as well consider the upside. Once I get my psychology license, there will be no shortage of business.

Rick's Journal

September 20

I remember all too well what a horrible time we went through. Linda couldn't eat or sleep. She became a habitual bathroom dweller. Instead of immediately coming to her defense, I believed Barb when she accused Linda of being a prostitute. I'm pretty effective as a debater against other people, but there's no way I'll ever be able to convince myself that I handled that situation appropriately.

My first instinct should always have been to support and defend Linda. It doesn't matter that Barb was working her spell on me. If I hadn't already been half out the door, I would have seen through her machinations. As much as I would like to, I can't go back and change what I did. The only thing I can do is pledge to be a better husband. I think Linda would agree that I'm well on that road. Self-recrimination will do neither of us any good.

Not surprisingly, Bill provided a positive spin to that terrible time. Not long ago, I would have laughed at the idea of losing your mind to find yourself. Now it makes perfect sense, at least in the way everything we're doing does. He did get a little spooky, as he tends to do, in saying there were more than the three of us present. It's hard to believe, but I could resonate with the idea of infinity lying at our doorstep. If Bill is crazy, a possibility that can't be totally discounted, I'm happily going there right along with him.

Eighteenth Meeting

"Ever heard of synchronicity?" I began. "It's beyond marvelous that Linda entered graduate school while we're in the midst of our process. What great timing. Maybe the universe does have a plan."

She smiled in agreement. "It's awesome, horrible, and perfect. Just a year ago, I could never have imagined all that had happened. Since I've sworn off resisting you, I guess all that's left is to join Rick in thanking you. I can't promise I won't have a periodic urge to slap you, but I'm determined to keep it to myself."

"Whew," I said with mock relief. "I thought I was going to have to schedule a standing appointment at the emergency room. But seriously, your decision to embrace acceptance is major. Why fight the inevitable? As you think of it, was it ever really me that you were fighting?"

"Don't get me started again," Linda joked. "You just never let up."

"Somewhat ironically, you're going to ultimately realize that I am, more or less, incidental to the process."

"Don't you **even** think about disappearing on me," she protested. "You've already kicked me out once. I understand your reasoning, but don't try to pull that again."

"Allow me to repeat what I said before about love. It does not allow attachments. It simply is."

"What about me?" Rick protested.

"That's the thing. The goal is not for Linda to form an attachment to either one of us. Instead, she will join you as one."

Her obviously relieved husband was able to lean back in his chair. "I'm so glad you cleared that up. I was sincere about saying that I love you. I could even feel good when Linda told you the same thing. I don't want to sound petty or selfish, but there's no room in a marriage for an extra person."

"I couldn't agree more. Certainly, friendships are fine. They can enrich a relationship. But as I told Linda, it's critical always to keep your priorities in order."

"Speaking of that," Linda commented, "I've had some trouble with what you said about your spouse coming before your children in terms of priorities. I'm not saying that you're necessarily wrong. It's just that it's different from what I've always heard."

"I'm not surprised, and I'm glad you mentioned it. Maternal instinct is a powerful and necessary force. It's so strong that it can screw up a marriage."

"But how can it be wrong to prioritize your children?"

"Linda, I think you may be making one of those leaps in illogic. Let me back up. Marriage serves as a foundation, albeit sometimes a shaky one. It's the binding force that allows for the development of a family. When a child arrives, parental attention naturally and appropriately is focused on the child's needs. However, it can easily go wrong."

"How so?"

"An infant is demanding but also accepting. Despite their tantrums and seemingly endless crying, they are easy to love unconditionally. Spouses are another matter. They have a fully developed ego, and dealing with them requires energy, which is likely to be in short supply. It can easily become a habit to dote on the child at the expense of the relationship."

"I'm still not exactly seeing the problem."

"Families are the building block of a child's development. If the marriage isn't solid, the child has no terra firma from which to develop. All too easily, the marital partners can begin doubting their commitment to one another. If fault lines develop, the child becomes confused. For a developing child, the reality is black and white. Parental ambiguity and ambivalence lead to feelings of anxiety with potentially lasting ill effects."

"If my child needed me and, no offense, Rick was demanding attention, how should I handle the conflict?"

"Your question is somewhat abstract, and context would be necessary to provide an adequate answer. But, in general terms, young children cannot meet their own needs. It's only natural to first deal with them. That doesn't mean you would prioritize your relationship with them over your marriage. If you establish bedrock in your marriage, doing so would not provide a challenge. Rick wouldn't feel in the least threatened if you took care of your child first."

"I don't mean to be a pain, but let's say the house is on fire. Do I save my child or Rick?"

"Well, you are starting to be sort of a pain," I jokingly replied. "Isn't the answer obvious? If your child needed assistance, you would provide it. You have a partnership with Rick; all things being equal, you would trust him to manage his survival. In doing so, you wouldn't be placing the child above Rick in your list of priorities. You would simply be making a rational decision."

"It kind of goes against what I've been led to believe, but I can see your point. I've seen too many mothers get so wrapped up in their children's lives that they forget about what's important. It's not only the marriage that suffers but also their children. Helicopter moms are well-meaning, but the effects on their kids can be unhealthy. What's more, the attention the child receives can lead to an overly strong ego as the kid comes to believe that their needs are all that matters."

Because prioritizing relationships is a critical and often ignored issue, I wanted to ensure they got it. "As you and Rick had been drifting aimlessly through your marriage, you began to shift more time and attention to your parents."

"Of course, they were always there for me. Rick wasn't."

"Totally understood. It's natural to share your energies with people who reciprocate. There's also a potential danger."

"You might as well go ahead and elaborate."

"Thanks for the invitation," I said, afterward hoping I wasn't sounding snide. "We're now directly addressing one of the great challenges of life and relationships. Typically, people don't spend most of their time with their spouses. Whether in work or friendships, they often interact more with other people. It can be incredibly easy to forget priorities when someone else provides the attention we naturally desire."

"But we have to spend time with other people."

"And now you're getting to the crux of the matter. Marital vows need to be blind, just like faith. They cannot allow for other possibilities. When you enter into a belief system as you do in a marriage, you must necessarily abandon alternatives. Other opportunities must simply disappear. That doesn't mean that you can't notice that another person is attractive or interesting. But the association with that observation and the possibility of any deeper relationship must be completely severed."

Not surprisingly, Rick was somewhat dubious. "I disagreed with Linda about having a female friend before. She didn't demand that I quit seeing Barb, but she made her position clear. At the time, I thought she was being ridiculous. I hate to admit it, but I now see she had a point. I hadn't achieved the commitment you described, so I was playing with fire."

"As we end our review of Linda's sessions, I want to make sure both of you are on board with what I am saying. The type of marriage we are moving toward involves another leap of faith. It's a giant step into the unknown. There can be no room for ambiguity. You won't be able to disentangle from each other any more than you can remove a part of yourselves."

They looked at each other and smiled as the room lit up. It was obvious that we had accomplished a major step.

Linda's Journal

September 25

I'm relieved that I've survived listening to my recordings. Can you believe it? I'm almost sad…or at least nostalgic. Every minute of those sessions was precious to me and valuable in leading me to the person I now am. Of course, I'm in no way declaring that I'm finished. I'm obviously still very much a work in progress. I've got to say, though, that my life and consciousness have been truly and thoroughly transformed.

I realize I'm now putting Rick first concerning the priority of relationship issues. It was by no means easy. It's been drilled into me since childhood that mothers put their kids first. Once again, Bill convinced me. It's not the first time he's shown me that things I've heard all my life are not necessarily true. I said that I wouldn't slap him again, but I wish he would let me be right every once in a while.

Now that my recordings are done, I can look back without the anxiety I had going in. It was all so beautiful. The confluence of events that led me and Rick to where we are today is astounding. Even though Rick is still not much more than a stranger due to our demanding schedules, he means everything to me. Strange to say, but our relationship is blossoming even though I hardly have the chance to speak to him.

Rick's Journal

September 24

As much as I hate to admit it, I felt great relief when Bill clarified the nature of his relationships with Linda and me. Despite all the changes I've gone through, I still feel possessive. Maybe that's something we need to work on. Or maybe that urge will dissipate as I learn to trust our relationship completely. If I were ever to feel jealous or insecure, it's obvious who the culprit would be. And yet Bill has done an incredible job of staying clean with us. I won't admit it to anyone else, but I genuinely do love that guy.

There's just one more tiny little thing. I'm next. I'm almost surprised that I'm not more anxious about the prospect of reviewing my sessions. I think it's because now I can sit back and consider everything that has happened with a genuinely new perspective. My trust in Linda has grown immensely. I believe that our marriage can withstand any of the things that are about to be revealed.

It just occurred to me. Rather than looking at the review as a threat, I'm going to open myself up to seeing it as an opportunity. As Linda listens to my revelations concerning my interactions with Barb, we can re-evaluate everything about our marriage. Instead of looking at Barb negatively, I'm hopeful that we will both be listening with an ear to how she was our mutual teacher. Boy, is that a new perspective.

I was really headed down the wrong path with the idea that I could maintain a Platonic relationship with Barb. It's not that I don't think that men and women can be friends. But we are all too capable of fooling ourselves. It's so easy to rationalize a lunch or tennis date as totally innocent, even as we set ourselves up for trouble. Sure, it sounds fine to visit an old friend. At least, that's what I told myself. I think I could handle a similar situation now. But then I remember how easy it is to think I know better than I do. I somehow bet I'm not the first, and certainly not the only, man who "accidentally" fell into a similar trap.

Review of Rick's Sessions
First Meeting

I began by saying, "Congratulations, Rick. It's your turn."

"As much as I appreciate the attention, how about we just pass and keep focusing on Linda."

Her reaction was immediate and enthusiastic. "No way you're getting out of this, Buster. I showed you mine. Now I get to see yours."

I intervened by saying, "Linda, let's give him a break. None of this was his idea. Remember, he's a professional pugilist. For him to come in and lower his guard, knowing that a punch was likely on the way, was a huge act of courage. It's also a strong indication of how he feels about you."

Linda became timid. Of all her expressions, this was a new one for me. "Albeit reluctantly," she finally muttered, "I'll have to agree. We went back and forth about my meetings with you early on, and his attitude was generally querulous and even contentious. After he saw me during my craziness, I never thought he would put faith in you. I'm almost surprised he didn't try to sue you somewhere along the way."

"A risk of the profession," I concurred. "As a future therapist, you might as well be aware that promoting real change also provokes real consequences. I'm sure you have studied Carl Rogers. His approach, known as client-centered therapy, involved reflective listening. If you want to stay safe, just listen and repeat the client's words, adding a more positive spin. It's an important weapon to have in your arsenal. However, by itself, it won't win you any battles with the ego."

She nodded, "I'm genuinely grateful for any wisdom or tips involving psychotherapy. But let's put Rick back on the hot seat."

I chuckled, "Better watch it, Linda. Your empathy is showing."

Rick demonstrated his chivalrous side by volunteering, "You guys are welcome to have fun at my expense. I've certainly enjoyed listening to what happened between the two of you. Though in truth, enjoyed is probably not the best word."

"Okay, back to business. Let's begin by recognizing that a major motivating factor in your interest in seeing me was to learn more about what happened in Linda's sessions."

"I'll have to agree with that conclusion. I wasn't sure how much I wanted to get into discussing my issues, and I thought a reconnaissance mission was in order."

I said, "It would have been easy to let slip some minor details about my interactions with Linda, but I held fast. I'm curious about your reaction to my insistence on respecting confidentiality."

Rick was ready with his response. "More than anything else, your standing firm on that issue told me that you were a professional. What's more, I came to realize that you were a man I could trust. And, for me, that's saying a lot."

Turning my gaze toward Linda, I said, "I hope you're hearing what he's saying. It's so easy for counselors to take shortcuts and reveal seemingly innocuous details about their clients. People notice. The consequences lead to a loss of trust. Such breaches create a sense of informality and allow an impression that the process is not to be taken seriously. It can be tempting to treat your clients as friends. Considerable discipline is necessary to remember and maintain the nature of the relationship."

Rick smirked, "I guess you must be speaking from experience."

"Yep," I surprised him by readily agreeing with his conclusion. "But, as you can see, it's much less stressful for us to reflect on other matters. Let's get back to it. What was it like for you to let down your barriers with me?"

"Well, it didn't happen all at once. I had been torturing myself concerning the time I had spent with Barb, the infamous 'other woman.' I decided to admit to some of what had happened in order to see what you would do with it. I was not at all happy when you broached the topic of feelings. At the same time, I was relieved that you soon switched to a problem-solving approach, which I found to be much more syntonic with my way of looking at the world."

"Feelings are messy. Men typically claim to be uninterested in talking about them. The ghastly truth is that men have them just as much as women. If only we were as rational as we would like to think, peace would guide the planets, and love would steer the stars. Coincidentally, divorce would be nearly nonexistent."

Rick persisted, "I don't think it was really about feelings. It was just guilt. Other than the churning in my stomach and the obsessive thoughts, I don't really think it was a feeling thing."

Linda couldn't hold back at that point. "What in the hell do you think feelings are?"

I nodded in agreement. "We still need to get past the macho thing. I appreciate that it's been bred into you, especially from your time playing football. There is also an aspect of bravado in court battles. As we discussed previously, it can be useful to access the place of dominance and power as long as you don't get lost in it.

"It's equally important to accept and even cherish what has traditionally been considered your feminine side. The goal is for each of you individually to begin this process as complete human beings who subsequently come together to make an exponentially greater whole. You may have noticed that I've been working with you individually more than as a couple throughout this process."

Linda interjected, "I object to your sexist statement. Aren't we past the point of stereotyping people?"

"Linda," I responded, "biology is what it is. The last thing I want is to become enmeshed in discussing modern politics. Can we agree that men are generally born to develop more muscle mass? Evolution, divine creation, or both fortuitously led to a natural division of labor in which men have historically defended their families and women nurtured them. I'm not making an argument that we should perpetuate sexist attitudes. In fact, I encourage you to embrace your masculine side.

"I'm sort of glad this topic came up. As a society, we put way too much emphasis on highlighting our differences. In that way, we lose sight of the fact that we're all the same deep down. Whether it's

LBGTQIA+ or whatever variation you can come up with, people are people."

With an accepting smile, Linda agreed, "I went through the women's lib thing in the past. It served a purpose, but I'm no longer bothered and certainly not threatened by the difference between the sexes. More importantly, I hear you saying I should feel good about my own brand of strength and power."

"Within certain limits," I cautioned, "as defined by ego functions. But yes, I agree with your inference. I love the idea of us all being born equal. But in no time, differences appear, both phylogenetically and socio-economically. It's up to each of us to make the best of the circumstances we're given."

I redirected our discussion, "Let's get back to the recording. Rick, there was a vital lesson in our first session. Tell me how it affected you when I asked you to remember when you didn't get your way as a young child."

Rick appeared thoughtful as he reflected, "It sounds silly that something so trivial from so many years ago could have had such an effect on my life. I had my heart set on getting a pony for Christmas. When, instead, I got a toy truck, I was shattered. My parents, wisely as it turned out, didn't fall for my temper tantrums or tears. If they had, I would have missed out on learning something that has since greatly influenced my life. Learning to accept, rather than resist, what life offered me has been of tremendous benefit in navigating roadblocks and disappointments I've experienced.

"It's funny. Until recently, I didn't realize how much it led to my being who I am today. If my parents had given in, or if I had been successful in wearing them down and getting my way, I could have become an oppositional child. I now get that loving a child is the easy part. Good parenting requires setting limits."

"If you're interested," I volunteered, I will tell you about one of my related experiences next time we meet."

Linda was gleeful. "It's about time! Do we really have to wait?"

Linda's Journal

October 1

It was finally time for Rick to face the music. I guess that I shouldn't be surprised that he tried to wriggle out of it! I'm looking forward to hearing his true confessions, almost as I dreaded his hearing mine. There was a time, not long ago, when I would have made that comment vindictively. I still remember my combative instinct. It's just that I feel so differently about him now. If he feels wounded by anything we hear on the recordings, I will feel hurt as well.

I had probably better watch myself. I remember what happened when I quit being jealous. I certainly don't want to give the impression of condoning his misbehavior. I'm still not completely over his interactions with Barb. Remembering how I came on to Bill makes it a little easier to swallow. But that was me, and I thought I knew what I was doing. Now we're talking about Rick, and I never imagined he would do something so stupid. I guess I need to sit back now and see what the recordings reveal.

At the very least, I'm proud of him for making the appointment. I know it was far from easy for him. He never really made fun of me for seeing a psychologist, but I could tell that the thought was in the back of his mind. I can now see how he unknowingly made changes right along with me. Going through the transformation process is impossible without the inner turmoil and ongoing revelations affecting your life partner. His willingness to stand with me through all the nuttiness I went through says a lot about him and his commitment to our marriage.

Rick's Journal

October 1

I was extremely reluctant to step into Bill's office the first time I saw him. Surprisingly, our first session was great. As I'm thinking about it, I've likely been overly concerned about listening to the recordings of my sessions. I don't remember all the details I disclosed about my time with Barb, but I no longer fear that my stupidity will doom our marriage. At least, I'm telling myself that.

If it weren't for my tremendous curiosity about what was happening with Linda, I would never have made that first appointment. I foolishly thought that I would make sure that I stayed in control. As it turned out, we were playing on his turf, and he knew all the rules. It would have been a quick session if he had lorded it over me. As much as I wanted him to reveal what he knew about Linda, he held firm. My frustration quickly dissipated as I began to respect his professionalism.

Bill started right in talking about feelings. Of course, that made me want to leave. In truth, it wasn't so bad. I now realize that the troublesome thoughts that sometimes engulf me are rooted in negative emotions. It was so easy for an unhealthy thought to trigger unpleasant physiological changes that then justified a doomsday scenario. I purposefully wrote that in the past tense. I can say much more honestly that it is no longer so easy for that to happen. What a tremendous difference that a slight change in wording makes.

That childhood incident with the toy truck was somehow tucked away in the back of my mind. I gave it no significance, and yet I had never forgotten it. It's amazing that something so seemingly trivial from when you're only four years old can determine the direction of your life. I've thought about it a lot since it came up during the session. While I don't remember the details, I somehow recall a sense of having decided to enjoy what was in front of me.

I'm so blessed to have embraced essence at such a young age, which is what I wouldn't give to be able to share that lesson with other youngsters. I must credit my parents as well. It would have been tempting for them to tell me to shut up and then later relented in the face of my repeated complaints and temper outbursts. I would bet anything that Bill and Linda have a term for that.

155

Second Meeting

Before we started, I couldn't help but notice Linda's look of anxious anticipation. I began, "As I've told you, this adventure is something totally new to me. Believe me; I'm learning right along with you. As you've probably already noticed, I held the space of mastery during most of our earlier talks. I purposefully want now to be myself as an ordinary person, especially so I can own my questionable role in my early interactions with Linda. Along the way, I've debated just how much of my regular self I should reveal.

Not unexpectedly, Linda squealed, "Stop debating and spill the beans."

Rick concurred by nodding, so I proceeded. "My hesitation stems from 2 factors. First, I want to make sure we keep the focus on you. Second, I don't want to, in any way, contaminate your experience by talking about my 'stuff.'"

"But I will tell you about an experience since it relates to Rick's lesson. If it seems appropriate, I will tell you more about my life later. You will find that, for a quiet, introverted guy, I have been blessed to have enjoyed an extremely enriched life. Some of that is due to my choice to become a psychologist, something Linda can look forward to. That profession can lead to incredible opportunities or, just as easily, a job where you do nothing but wait for a pension. To me, the latter option is incredibly sad, but a surprising number of psychologists opt for it."

Linda snorted, "Do we have to wait for the National Anthem to finish playing before you get started?"

"Very funny, Linda. As you will see, Rick's experience is quite reminiscent of an event early in my career. When I was president of a professional school..."

Linda couldn't help interrupting. "You were what? You mentioned an involvement with a professional school. I had no idea that you were in charge of it. I thought you were a psychologist."

"As you may recall, I don't like being tied to roles. I'm not nearly as buttoned up as you might think. I've done many things that would surprise you. In any case, that position allowed me to host seminars with nationally known figures. During that time, I got to know Dr. Harold Greenwald. He had the distinction of being the only person whose doctoral dissertation was made into a major motion picture. Given that it was about prostitutes, I guess it's not overly surprising that it gained such infamy. In any case, he wrote a book called <u>Direct Decision Therapy</u>.

Linda inquired, "Is it available today?"

"Linda, is there anything you can't buy on Amazon? In a seminar he facilitated, he asked if anyone in the audience could recall an early childhood experience during which they made a decision that later defined the rest of their lives. Numerous hands went up before he selected an Asian woman. The audience was mortified to hear that she had been sold into sexual slavery when she was 4 or 5 years old. She said that she distinctly remembered that she made a conscious decision at that time not to allow that horror to define her.

"The members of the audience were entranced as she related her story. She revealed that she could have lived the rest of her life in shame but made the choice to accept what life had offered her. As strange as it may sound, she decided to make serving others her mission in life. Her positive and giving attitude led to a later opportunity to move to this country, where she became an RN. She said that she was still dedicated to serving but was incredibly grateful to now have the opportunity to do it in a different way."

Linda understandably looked shocked. "What a horrible and yet beautiful story. Now that you've started, I can't wait to hear more about your adventures."

"Linda," I chastened. "Don't tell me you're not anxious to hear more about the fun Rick had with Barb."

As soon as I said it, I knew I had crossed the line. Rick was understandably pissed, "I can't believe you disrespected me like that. I shared one of the most difficult times in my life, and you joke about it."

"Point taken," I readily admitted. "I was doubting myself for providing personal information, which I never do, and inappropriately made light of a very delicate matter. My most sincere apologies for violating your trust."

Fortunately, Rick grinned. "We've shared a lot of give and take. I've taken many risks with you, and I'm glad you're willing to do the same with me."

"Let's get back to what we were doing," I directed hastily. "During this second recording, you felt on top of the world. Care to tell us about that?"

"Well, it's a little awkward now, but nothing as bad as what I learned listening to the recording with you and my wife. I've never been known for my way with the ladies. The truth is, I reveled in the attention I was getting from Barb. I was irritated and disappointed when you wanted to bring me down to earth."

"Rick, I can't blame you for enjoying your newfound popularity. But, as Linda discovered, if you allow yourself to bounce too far based on the actions and opinions of others, you're going to lose yourself. It's important to find your bedrock and live from there. In saying that, I'm not advising you to ignore how others react. But don't act solely on what they might think. And that discussion led into the next lesson."

"And thank you for that one, Bill. In telling me about losing my self-importance, you prepared me for what was to come. I can see now that you were teaching me about perspective as you did with Linda but in a totally different manner. It wasn't easy for me to give up wallowing in Barb's attention and admiration, but I was getting too caught up in it. Along the way, I was losing Linda, which is exactly what Barb intended. I'm still shocked at the way she targeted me. I had absolutely no idea that she was trying to split up our marriage."

Rick then surprised us all by smacking himself on the head. "Damn, I can't believe I was so stupid!"

"Rick," I counseled, "Remember the lesson about self-recrimination? You can chew on the past or decide to live in the present."

Linda wasn't quite so forgiving. "How could you have gotten yourself involved with her? Don't you know that I've always loved you? What about our marital vows?"

Rick's hang-dog expression said it all. I brought things back by reminding them of the importance of living a clean life. "We've all done things we're not proud of. We don't always get a chance for do-overs. Now, you both have the opportunity to let go of things that happened and begin again from a different place."

With some residual bitterness, Linda said, "You know, it's easy to say but not quite so easy to do. But when I return to my special place, I can completely see and accept what you're saying. I certainly don't condone what Rick was doing, thinking, and feeling, but I can accept it as part of his path."

"I've talked to both of you about the necessity of mental discipline. You've both experienced what reality offers when you don't maintain it. As you begin this journey, life doesn't get less complicated or the choices less tempting. If you allow yourself to pursue a shiny object, beware of what's likely to happen if you try to pick it up.

"The fact that you can now more easily grasp what you want through using awareness makes it doubly challenging. But you will find that if you get whatever you thought you wanted, it will likely come back and bite you in your nether parts. The ultimate goal is not out there somewhere. You can still have fun with the reality. In fact, you can enjoy it much more if you remember who you really are. You need to keep in mind your inner witness, or what I have labeled the observer-operator, that allows you to remain in, but not of the world."

Rick appeared to focus internally as he muttered, "Boy, this is a lot of work."

"It can be a challenge, especially initially. But as you learn the lessons, seeing and acting in the world from a higher awareness becomes a habit. In a way, it's even tougher then, however, because the consequences of your actions become greatly magnified."

Linda's Journal

October 8

Bill was right. I was pretty keyed up. It was a good, if not entirely welcome, reminder to return to the present. I was allowing myself to get caught up in anticipation of where we were headed.

I kind of like Bill when he's being more of himself. No, let me take that back. He's an onery SOB, or at least he can be. It seems like I'm constantly having to drag information out of him. If he's ready to act like a regular person, like he says, maybe he should just act like a regular person.

Boy, did he ever get me excited when he talked about the possibilities I might enjoy in my potential role as a psychologist! It's been my dream for so long, but it always seemed out of reach. And then he gave us another shocker. He had been president of a professional school. He's right about one thing. I sure can't tie him to any single role.

Once more, I proved I'm not yet where I want to be. I found myself judging Rick for his behavior with Barb. But come on, I'm still human. That seems to be a pretty big lump for anyone to swallow. Rick has been amazing in his tolerance of my earlier misbehavior. If he can be the bigger man, then so can I.

Rick's Journal

October 10

I guess Bill meant it when he said that he would be more like a regular person. He really surprised me when he made that flippant comment to Linda about listening to the fun I had with Barb. If anyone else had said it, there would have been consequences. It's a sign of the respect that I have for him that I was able to get past it so easily. If he's willing to be human with us, I guess I should be willing to accept him as a human.

It's funny how I ended up having to go through my own version of being overly concerned about the opinions of others. It was certainly interesting, though more than a little bit awkward, as I listened to myself bragging on the recording. I loved the idea of Linda and Barb both being hot for me. Even so, I knew better. I didn't particularly appreciate being called on it, but I needed it and deserved it.

It was reminiscent of my football days. If I caught the touchdown pass, everyone would love me. Unfortunately, sometimes, it went in the other direction. People are fickle, and their opinions change with the wind. I had to find a way to keep myself on an even keel.

I'm still reaping the benefits from recalling the childhood experience in which I didn't get the pony I had hoped for. It totally fits with what Bill was saying about Direct Decision Therapy. If I had continued with my tantrum or if my parents had relented, I could easily have gone on to become a spoiled brat. I'm not saying that I've always been easy to get along with when things didn't go my way. On the other hand, I feel good about my ability to release my disappointment when necessary.

Looking back, I think that decision, while not totally conscious, provided a pivotal moment in my development. I guess learning that the world doesn't change to meet your expectations is something everyone has to go through as part of the growing-up process. In my case, I'm fortunate to have rediscovered a specific example that marks the space for me. Since it's so clear, I can readily draw from it when needed. I wonder how many other people can recall such childhood decisions. I'm guessing that many kids didn't make the best choices and then spent their adult lives dealing with the consequences.

Third Meeting

"Before we get back to the recordings, I've got to ask if you can help with something," Rick requested.

"Sure. Tell me what's going on."

"I hate to ask because I don't want us to get off track, but I'm having a lot of trouble getting to sleep lately. I have a big trial coming up and want to be at my best."

"Rick, I appreciate what you're telling me. I've been gradually increasing the energy in preparation for the next transformation, but I want to give your body time to adapt, and I may have been moving too quickly. Right now, we are dealing with a much higher level of energy than at any time during our individual work."

Linda had to object. "Bill, you sneaky rascal. I suspected you were letting us get too comfortable. I've been feeling differently and didn't really know why. Sometimes, I feel like there's electricity running through my body. Other times, I feel like I'm made of light. Generally, I enjoy it, but it can still be a bit spooky."

"So now you can better understand why I've been heavy on explanations. We're getting closer to the airy-fairy stuff, but I don't want to go too fast. Let's get back to Rick's more immediate situation. I'm sure you know about the myriad relaxation techniques available. They do work, but for the most part, people don't use them."

"Why is that?"

"Rather than my answering, let's see if you can figure it out."

Rick thought briefly before his face lit up. "Of course. Relaxation means letting go. That's the last thing the good old ego wants to do."

"In line with that simple fact, I'll tell you something else that you might find useful. When you drift off to sleep, your rational mind must release its hold along the way. If you're thinking about things that have happened or might happen, you're still thinking. Sleep doesn't involve rational thought. One thing you might do if you caught in your worries is to fool yourself by thinking irrationally."

With a wrinkled brow, Rick asked, "How does that work?"

"As soon as you catch yourself latching on to a thought or worry, fool your mind by changing it to something nonsensical. For example, if you start thinking about a client who yelled at you, visualize him as a purple clown floating around the room. If you have a thought about an upcoming trial, change it to a musical theater production with the judge and jury singing and dancing. Just don't dally too long with any of your irrational escapades. Allow your mind to drift until it's ready to let go. Of course, the most dangerous thought is, 'I may never get to sleep, and I've got a big day tomorrow.'"

"You're right with that one. How do I handle it?"

"Change your focus. You might begin by doing deep muscle relaxation. Tense each part of your body sequentially for several seconds and then release with a deep exhalation. Notice the difference between when your muscles are tense and when they are totally relaxed. Allow yourself to enjoy the change from tension to relaxation.

"I especially recommend doing self-hypnosis. For example, imagine your body as being extremely heavy and feel yourself sinking into the bed. At the same time, think of strings pulling you upward so that you're both heavy and light simultaneously. By engaging in two discordant thoughts, you can disconnect your conscious mind.

"Our bodies have their own cycles. I'm sure you've noticed that sometimes you're more hyped than usual. It's not necessary to fight it. Think of it as your body's natural expression of energy. If you find yourself tossing and turning, get out of bed until your body tells you it's ready to let go. You might get a little less sleep time, but what you get will be much more rejuvenating."

Rick responded, sounding a bit dubious. "Some of what you say makes sense. Other things tend to be a bit far out. I thought you were crazy before. Thanks for confirming it."

"Well, Rick, it's gratifying to know I've met your expectations. But seriously, if you do what I recommend, you will notice your brain attempting to regain its hold. When it happens, remember to stick with the nonsense until it releases and allows you to sleep.

"Believe me, what I suggest is more effective than counting sheep. Taking it a little further, following my recommendations will be of benefit overall in loosening the hold of your rational mind. That's a necessary step in preparing you for direct experience. I know that we tend to think of rationality as supreme. As you are learning, it simply isn't."

"I ask a simple question, and you throw in something totally new. What the hell do you mean by direct experiencing?"

"I don't want to jump the gun on you, but I'll go ahead and give you an idea. As you prepare for God's awareness, for lack of a better term, you must begin shedding your ordinary sensory and cognitive filters. If you attempt to directly experience the 'isness' while still maintaining your ordinary sense of reality, your filters and you, along with them, will be incinerated."

With a nervous laugh, Rick commented, "You sure like to keep us on our toes, don't you?"

Linda objected to Rick's diversion. "You've already skated on dealing with our marital problems by shipping us off to see Elizabeth, not that she isn't great. But now you're helping Rick with his individual issues. How about pitching in on one of mine."

"I'm so glad that you guys are working with Elizabeth. I've heard nothing but good things about her; she is more qualified to work with marital issues. As you may have noticed, I gravitate more toward the abstract."

Linda couldn't suppress a laugh. "Really, Bill. I had no idea. If I needed to replace a light bulb, you'd probably be the last person I would call."

"Fair enough. Those threads can be tricky. I wouldn't want to screw it in wrong and cause a fire. But you said you had a personal issue. I'll give it my best shot."

"I've run into a concern that's very new for me. I don't like to admit it, but I'm starting to gain a little weight. It's never been a problem before, and it's bothering me."

I scratched my head in puzzlement. "Congratulations, Linda. You've come up with something totally unique. Since I've never heard of anyone worried about their weight, I can only provide you with some thoughts. But seriously, anything I tell you will be programmatic. I want to be judicious and avoid sounding directive in what I have to say. Again, it's not my area, but I'm willing to share some fairly benign ideas."

"Well, it's not a huge issue, but I respect your opinion and would appreciate your guidance."

"I will begin by clarifying that I am not about to give you a personal opinion about your weight. I say that for a simple reason. I'm not suicidal. It's a personal issue. If you feel that you need to lose a few pounds, I respect your decision. If that's the case, the first thing to recognize is that eating is a habit, albeit a necessary one. Assuming you have your usual thirst for knowledge, I may as well give you my take on habits."

I continued in professorial mode. "Undesired habits typically begin when we do something that makes us feel better, at least momentarily. It can be eating, taking an alcoholic drink, thinking about something that's nagging at us, or even scratching an itch. Some actions help us relax by temporarily bringing us to homeostasis; in other words, they make bad feelings go away. Alternatively, our actions may provide stimulation in a way that causes a release of 'happy' neurotransmitters. The problem begins only when and if those behaviors take on a life of their own and interfere in the rest of our lives."

Rick volunteered, "I hope you're not going to tell us that we can't scratch. I have eczema, and sometimes the only relief I feel comes from scratching."

"For one thing, it's a matter of degree. Do you scratch until you're bloody? Or do you find yourself scratching even when you don't realize you're doing it? It's at that point that an internal battle begins.

You know you would be better off stopping a behavior but find it increasingly difficult to do so."

Rick agreed. "I've even gotten to the point of wearing gloves. Sometimes, I ask Linda to remind me when she sees me scratching. It's frustrating. If I resist it, I can't think of anything but how much I want to scratch."

"I think you've come up with a great example. If you obsess about how much you want to relieve your discomfort by indulging in the act, you're going to become miserable. What could you do instead?"

"As I think of it, I'm less prone to scratch when I'm busy. If I get engaged in some activity, it takes my mind off of it. If I'm doing something that requires me to use my hands, it's even better."

"That's a good way of dealing with it. You're being active, which keeps you in the present. You're also engaging in a competing behavior. "That's a good beginning. That strategy can help in dealing with chronic pain and many other unpleasantries that lead us to counterproductive behaviors."

"But it always comes back," he objected.

"We have come to believe that we can control all the negatives in our lives. We've been conditioned to think there must be a quick and easy solution for any discomfort. Some things just are. The healthiest thing you can do is accept them rather than resist them. By breathing into whatever you are feeling and experiencing it without evaluating it as good or bad, you can better come to terms with it.

"Think of the itching, for example, as part of your being. Strange as it may seem, imagine it as your friend. Visualize it. Does it have a color, texture, or even a personality? Rather than fighting it, flow with it. Consider the itching as stimulation rather than something awful that you must get rid of. It's sending you a message to do things to better care for your skin. It's an autoinflammatory response that tells you that your body is fighting itself and it's time to find inner harmony."

"I'm glad you're giving me some direction. I'm much more open to that sort of strange way of looking at it now than I would have been when I first met you."

"Here's another way of considering it. If we see a 3-legged dog, our first impulse is to feel bad for him. But do you think the dog sits around thinking about the lost leg? His reality is that he has three legs. It just is. In the same way, you are prone to having skin inflammation. It's part of the life you have been given. Maybe I shouldn't give this away, but to the extent that you accept it, you may find it disappearing."

"Should I make curing it my goal?"

"Certainly not," I cautioned. "That would be the opposite of becoming one with it. Instead, I recommend you step back and look at the internal storm you experience as you struggle with scratching. Just as we are seeking external harmony between you and Linda, it's important to find inner harmony. That doesn't mean that issues won't arise. But it does provide you with the opportunity to recognize and resolve them with grace.

There is a genuine parallel to the efforts required in dealing with internal and external discomfort. If you find yourself scratching, just notice what you are doing and remove the judgment. It's going to happen at times. Scratching an itch is reflexive and natural. It only becomes a problem if you continue to scratch and begin to fight yourself about it.

Linda's Journal

October 17

It's kind of funny. Bill acknowledged his tendency toward the abstract only to follow it up by giving us practical advice. One thing is for sure. I can never predict him. Rick got his answers, but you can be sure I will get mine. I'm glad that I put it that way. It's an excellent reminder that Rick and I are becoming one. It's silly for me to be jealous just because he's getting the attention.

I'm relieved Bill came clean with us about how he's been increasing his energy during our sessions. I just never know what he has up his sleeve. I don't think he ever intentionally tries to deceive us. I just think he takes his time in revealing what he's up to. I guess I should take him at his word. It doesn't serve any purpose for him to explain things before we're ready to hear them. My natural objection is to think that he's treating us like children. The fact is that we are. We have no idea what to expect in this crazy version of reality that he's leading us into.

I hadn't talked to anyone, including Rick, about my increasing concerns about my weight. I know that some weight gain is common with aging. I'm just not ready to let go of my identity. I'm embarrassed even to write this, but I've long considered myself attractive. People have often complimented me on my appearance. I guess I fell into the trap of being attached to a fickle and transient identity.

I've often wondered about older women who spend inordinate time on their hair and make-up. Who are they trying to fool with their expensive dresses and thick makeup? When I step back, I recognize they've fallen into the same trap. They just can't let go of the idea of being pretty. There is no point in judging them. Society places such a value on how we look, especially for women, that it's hard to shift how we view ourselves. In some cultures, older people are valued for their knowledge and experience. Try explaining that to the men who have trophy wives.

Rick's Journal

October 17

I'm glad to know that my sleep problems may be related to Bill's turning up the juice. At least, there is a plus side to his efforts. During the day, I've been zinging with energy. I must be in a good mood since my office staff has commented about how cheery I've been. It's good to know that there are some real-world benefits to all this craziness. If someone had told me a year ago that I would be listening to some dude spouting such weirdness, I would have laughed in their face.

You know, I have resisted practicing all the ways I know to relax. Especially when I have a lot going on; I just don't want to let go. I do think that, as Bill says, it's my ego. It's never so much in charge as when I'm keyed up. At those times, it seems like everything gets on my nerves. It becomes all about me. Why would my ego want to release its hold?

It was great to get some down-to-earth advice from Bill. Sometimes, I feel like it's necessary to summon him back from the clouds where he is at home. He had to throw in a zinger even when providing information about sleep problems. What is this whole direct experiencing thing? I never know what's coming next.

My struggle with eczema has been a big and entirely unwelcome part of my life for the last few years. It's almost sinful how much relief I get from scratching. And yet, there is such a price to pay. It's not just the additional damage to my skin. It's also the self-punitiveness that accompanies it. I think to myself that I should be stronger. Then I am for a few minutes only to find myself going right back at it.

It's just another example of my tendency to feel guilty. If I think about it positively, it provides me with another vehicle for learning and letting go. I've started the visualization he suggested. Amazingly, it's beginning to take effect. Rather than fighting the itching or trying to ignore it, I embrace it. It sounds unbelievable, sure, but that's nothing new. I've started taking the time to permit myself to feel inner harmony. I especially like the idea of extending it to our marriage.

Fourth Meeting

`Linda began, "I'm sympathetic concerning Rick's issue, and I know it's his turn. But I was starting to wonder if you had forgotten about me."

"That's hardly likely," I said with a grin. "What I'm getting at is the parallels between many of our counterproductive behaviors. We humans regularly set goals only to end up sabotaging them. In your case, it's a matter of losing a few pounds. Here's the way it typically works. You change your eating habits and start to see some progress. Then you step on the scales and feel disgusted when you discover your weight has increased."

"Yeah, that's what gets me. I'll be following a diet and doing well. Then it seems like my body turns against me."

"It's one of the cruel aspects of biology. There is no direct, or at least immediate, relationship between food intake, level of activity, and weight. Sometimes, it will seem like your body has a mind of its own. Here's the key. If you allow yourself to become discouraged when that happens, you will likely feel like giving up. You may then return to your old eating habits with predictable results."

"It's even worse than that. When I get completely disgusted with myself, I binge."

"Now we can start to see the similarity with alcoholism and any number of unfortunate behaviors. Our egos want to be in control. If they feel that they are winning the battle, everything is humpy dumpty. When things don't go their way, our egos can become self-destructive. They aren't rational. That doesn't mean that they are bad. In fact, they insist that they are rational. And that's part of the problem. When an ego starts to realize that it's spinning out of control, it can lead us to do things that have horrible results."

"Hmm. That's an interesting take on a puzzling problem." Linda started to become excited. "Maybe I can start to use that insight in dealing with my clients. Your way of describing things opens new avenues of thinking for me. The challenge will be in transforming the abstract ideas into information that my clients will find useful. I'm glad that you've taken the time to expand on your thoughts because undesired habits are so ubiquitous. By giving me a framework that I can use to help my clients conceptualize their experiences, I think I will be able to better guide them without necessarily involving them directly in transformation."

"Well, Linda, I certainly don't want you to feel cheated. Even though it's Rick's turn, I might as well throw in some other tidbits concerning dieting. There is an obvious reason that it's so hard for people in our society to control their weight. If you live in an underdeveloped country, you often feel hungry because food isn't available. In your case, if you're hungry, all you need to do is open the refrigerator. When your body signals that it wants food, you have a quick and easy answer at your fingertips. You don't even have to be hungry. You could simply be bored or in the mood for a quick sugar fix. It's easy for food to become a habitual, short-term answer for any negative mood."

"Well, I've tried using practical self-control measures that don't directly involve self-control, like keeping candy where I can't see it."

"Makes sense. If it's not in your visual field, it's less likely to trigger a desire to indulge. While I agree with your strategy, it only serves to feed, forgive my terminology, an ongoing internal battle. In other words, you are entering a world where too many people live."

"I'm almost afraid to ask, but exactly where is that world?"

"You've already stepped into it. Children don't know about it, but adults try to drag them into it. You're so immersed in it that you are unaware that it exists."

"Damn it! I hate to admit it, but I habitually engage in internal battles. It's so easy to judge myself. I've gotten better at it, but I still catch myself thinking things like, 'Should I eat that scrumptious chocolate sundae?' If I give in, I get mad at myself afterward. But it sure feels good going down."

Somewhat facetiously, I said, "You'll be glad to hear that you no longer have to put limits on your eating. You can indulge in whatever you like."

"Okay, you've got me again wondering whether to slap you or hug you. If you're making fun of me, I'll go with the former."

"Since neither of us is currently able to transcend the limits of biology, let's find a better way to look at it. Life continually offers us lessons. We can get mad about it or frustrated about it. But fortunately, we also have the option of benefiting from our frailties."

"I've been very successful with the angry and frustrating aspect of self-control. I can't wait to hear the good news you're promising."

"It's not as great as you may hope, but it is quite positive. We are lucky to live in a world where physical discomfort is uncommon. Consequently, we think of it as an enemy and do all we can to avoid it. We've become a 'take a pill' society. As it happens, we don't have to endure the misery that Indian yogis endure in order to learn the lesson."

Linda was now sufficiently comfortable with me to be openly mocking. I liked it. "Oh, great one, please shower us with your wisdom from above."

Maintaining the spirit, I responded, "Oh, ye insignificant peasant, I will generously provide you with a dung heap of my spoils in which you may wallow."

"Don't forget. The slapping option is still readily available. What's more, I have a very large husband to back me up. Don't get too cocky."

"Message accepted. So, here's the thing. The key lies in how you interpret your internal signals. Your body provides you with cues. It's up to you to decide what to do with them. If you experience acute pain, you'd better do something about it. A feeling of nagging hunger is a different matter. Any time that you can ignore it or simply think of it as an unnecessary signal, you're winning the battle. You can then rack one up for the good guys. It's important that you emphasize those occasions rather than the times that you give in to the urge. By accepting that you are an imperfect human being and focusing on your positive efforts, you will feel increasingly at peace with yourself."

"I'm not sure I like where you're going with this. I didn't sign up to feel miserable. As it happens, I like to eat."

I chuckled, "Do you notice how we keep repeating the same lessons under different circumstances? If you want to feel comfortable with your weight gain, visit a counselor. They might, at least, help you with the guilt as your weight see-saws."

"I think you're saying that when my tummy rumbles, I have a choice. I can interpret it as a hunger 'pain,' or I can think of it as a sign that I'm making progress. If I'm smart, I can absorb myself in other activities rather than sitting around thinking about being hungry. Giving it a positive spin, I can also think of burning calories instead of storing them."

"Good for you," I applauded. "This diversion into weight control serves a dual purpose in that it is also an effective way to address your interest in psychotherapy. As a newly developing therapist, I would like to open doors for you to discover novel ways of approaching your clients' issues. You don't have to 'fix' everyone or propel them to unknown levels of awareness. Recognize your role and perform it as effectively as possible. Just to be clear, you touched on another aspect of habits that must be emphasized."

They both looked at me expectantly. "Habits aren't easy to change. To do so, we have to be ready to experience discomfort. Despite what you have likely seen on TV, losing weight is not painless. You must be prepared to feel hunger pains and listen to your stomach growling.

Linda agreed, saying, "I absolutely hate that part. I've tried doing healthy snacking, but that doesn't seem to help."

"As you may have already figured out, I don't always stick with conventional ways of thinking. I believe that, for some people, healthy snacking can be a mistake."

Linda looked at me rather strangely. "How so?"

"When you snack, it gives you temporary relief. At the same time, you are signaling to your body that it's time to eat. You start salivating, and various hormonal changes occur as your body prepares for a meal. It can be a form of self-torture. If you want to lose weight,

I suggest that you avoid the various ways of teasing your body and, instead, accept that you are making genuine changes in your attitude towards food and eating. Here's a novel revelation. You can't have your cake and eat it too.

"But there's good news. As you accept the change in eating habits, your stomach will shrink. Your interoceptors will reduce the number of hunger signals they transmit. Eating will become less of an issue. To the extent that you stick with your decision to change your lifestyle, you will discover that you are eating to live rather than living to eat.

"And as a bonus, I'll throw in an extra little tidbit. Scientists are finally beginning to gain some insight into the gastrointestinal biome. We're finding that it's filled with the same chemicals that allow your brain to function optimally or, alternatively, go haywire. There is an intimate connection between your gut and your brain. Anyone who habitually overeats is playing with fire. I'm not making a judgment in any sense. I'm just informing you that there is an additional consequence for your eating habits."

"Oh my gosh! You're screwing with all the ideas I've learned about dieting. But, as you said, you don't really know that much about the subject. I could keep following what the experts say. In doing so, I could be comfortable maintaining the cycle of my episodic indulgence followed by guilt. What a great plan," she concluded with a heavy dose of sarcasm.

"Obviously, what I'm suggesting is not for everyone. Most people don't want to shake themselves out of their misery. As I've said more than once, it's comfortable. It's like an old pair of shoes you can't seem to throw away. They may stink a little, but they're familiar. Putting on new shoes can feel awkward, so why not stick to what you know?"

"Message received. Isn't much of what you're saying a form of cognitive behavior therapy?"

"No doubt, and I'm glad you're beginning to collate lessons. I am, after all, a psychologist, and I have a genuine love for the field. I'm a proponent of cognitive behavior therapy, but it doesn't provide all the answers. For one, it's hard for people to remember to catch themselves when they fall back into habitual ways of thinking. Additionally, the emphasis on changing thoughts is inadequate unless the accompanying emotions are also brought into play. Sad to say, there is an even more important limitation. And you no longer have an excuse for falling for it."

"I'm way ahead of you. I now know how to rise above thoughts and the accompanying feelings. It is up to me. Dang it! Before I met you, I could get away with my cycle of overeating and self-recrimination. You've taken that away from me, and I can't even slap you anymore."

"I know that you aren't really serious, and here's the beauty of what I'm saying. As you begin to transcend unpleasant habits, you quiet the internal storm. In the process, you begin to develop the habit of living as your Self rather than your ego. As a bonus, your body will settle into its natural state. Your weight will stabilize, and the hunger pains will diminish. Developing stability with your weight, just as with scratching, can serve as a vehicle toward your ultimate goal. Do you remember when you overcame your resistance and accepted Barb as your teacher? Notice the parallel. The things and people we most hate can become invaluable. It's all up to you."

Linda's Journal

October 24

Well, I asked for it. I guess I should be okay with getting it. I wish that Bill could have done his presto thing and made the whole weight issue disappear. Deep down, I know that he's right. I will be better off looking at the dieting issue as a means for developing self-discipline and reducing my preoccupation with physical wants. As I think of it, practically everything in my life represents that opportunity.

I'm going to shift my way of thinking. No, let me rephrase that. I **am** shifting my way of thinking. Food is not my friend. Neither is it my enemy. It's something that I truly need for survival, and there's nothing wrong with enjoying it along the way. I'm no longer food-centric. When it's time to eat, I will do so. I will also tune in to my internal signals and stop when I'm seated. Even when I slip, I will use it to practice self-acceptance.

I've decided on my first step. For years, I've had a snack at 3:00 p.m. Starting today, I will skip it. I'm looking forward to hearing my stomach growling. My body expects food at that time. I will train it to a different schedule. After a few days or maybe even weeks, I trust that my body will become attuned to a new way of doing things. It will give me a chance to prove the inner strength that I know I have in me.

Now that I think about it, I'm going to stay aware of what I'm doing throughout the day. I will look at my automatic routines and decide which ones work for me and which could be improved or eliminated. I now have the ingredients - awareness, discipline, and motivation.

It helps that I can fit this unsavory (unfortunate word choice) idea into my interest in psychotherapy. I think that some form of internal struggle with various types of unhealthy habits is pretty well universal. I'm licking my chops (I've got to clean up my language) when I think about all the clients out there. It's obvious from my writing that food can easily permeate our thinking and subtly influence our behavior.

Of course, I want to remember to keep my ego on the sidelines. I love that I can relate what Bill says to what I'm learning about cognitive behavior therapy.

Rick's Journal

October 24

While growing up, everyone praised me for gaining weight. I remember stepping on the scales and feeling pleased when I'd added a couple of pounds. At the dinner table, I was constantly encouraged to take another helping.

Well, times have changed. My doctor looked at my numbers and frowned. It's not that his happiness is my greatest concern. I just wish I didn't have to care about his opinion. Linda still looks incredible. I'm glad she brought the subject up because I'm the one who could benefit from a more rational approach to eating.

I'm not going to should all over myself. Instead, I'm changing my attitude toward food. From this instant forward, it's going to be a matter of peaceful co-existence. I will continue to enjoy eating, but I'm dropping out of the Clean Your Plate club.

It's all about habits. It took me a lifetime to develop the habit of overeating. I'm not going to starve myself. Instead, I'm going to adopt a more common-sense approach to eating. I guess you could call my plan conscious eating. When I'm eating, I will enjoy it to the fullest. When I decide that it's time to pull away, I will self-reward for my positive behavior. I have goals in mind that have nothing to do with food. My priorities have changed. I will no longer spend my mornings in anticipation of lunch.

Fifth Meeting

I began, "I realize that I allowed us to drift. But as I said in the beginning, I want you to experience the process in a context allowing you to gain the maximum benefit. It's my great and awesome responsibility to share a gift with you that few have ever imagined. The preparation may seem tedious at times, but I'm confident you will find it more than worthwhile as we proceed."

Linda didn't hesitate. "Are you kidding me? In your wildest dreams, did you ever imagine that we don't appreciate what we're learning?"

Rick stepped in. "Truth is, I'm more of a cut-to-the-chase kind of guy. At the same time, I wouldn't want to lose a minute of what I'm learning. I can tell that I'm evolving personally, just as is my relationship with Linda. I'm becoming a more complete person, and our marriage is blossoming. By all means, take the time you need, and feel free to explore any side streets that pop up along the way."

It was obvious that Rick was right in his observation concerning his evolution. His attitude and demeanor had changed, and he truly was all in. We were getting close.

Then Rick added, "In the spirit of honesty, something from our earlier conversation has been nagging at me. I think it's because I've been taught about the need for tithing since childhood. I'm starting to think you don't believe it's necessary."

"I'm glad you brought that up. And you're absolutely right about honesty. If you had kept silent about your concern, you would have also held back on your investment in our relationship. A word for doing so is separateness. It's the polar opposite of what we are moving toward. I appreciate your conflict concerning the act of giving. You might remember that, in the Bible, Jesus saw someone toiling in the fields on Sunday. His disciple stood next to him and was horrified to see a man working on a holy day and pointed it out. What did Jesus say?"

"Boy, you're taking me back to Sunday school lessons from years ago. As I think about it, I realize I never really thought about it. Oh! The light bulb finally went on. If he is violating the commandment about not working on the Sabbath, he is sinning. But if he truly knows what he is doing in the higher sense of the word, he is not making a mistake. In the latter case, he can step above the ordinary rules that keep the wheels of the world turning."

"I'm glad you asked for additional clarification because it can be a dangerous game. It's quite easy for an ego to convince someone they don't have to play by the rules. It's an obvious trap and has the potential to lead to societal breakdowns. Unless you are truly living in essence with decisions emanating from your Self, it's best to move in harmony with the world in which you live. The church plays an important role in communal relationships. It is important to support it financially if you're living cooperatively with others in society."

"Do I get another turn?" Linda pitched in anxiously. "I want to listen to the recording where Rick talked about Barb, but I'm torn. I also want to absorb all I can from you about psychotherapy before you show us the door."

I laughed. "You don't have to worry about my showing you the door. I have a bouncer who takes care of such unpleasantries."

Linda drew back her hand almost involuntarily. "Okay, Dr. Jokester. But please understand how precious these minutes are to me."

"Nuff said. I respect you and don't mean to make light of your concerns. Please accept, as part of my personality that I'm now sharing with you, that I'm a natural comedian. I tend to see the world at a slight angle compared to 'normal' people. I often laugh prematurely at jokes because I anticipate the punchline before it's delivered. Consequently, my sense of humor doesn't always come across as intended."

Linda blushed slightly. "I didn't mean to criticize, but you seemed to be taking lightly a matter that is extremely serious to me."

"As with Rick, I'm deeply appreciative that you trusted me sufficiently to mention it. If we do nothing but play nice, we won't really get to know each other. It's great fun to be all lovey-dovey, but there is much more to each of us than that. To find true intimacy, we must share parts of ourselves that we don't ordinarily reveal.

"Many couples have a great time during their honeymoon. Once it's over and reality sets in, the marriage quickly becomes rocky. You don't have to show all your warts too soon. At the same time, it's a mistake, and even in a sense dishonest, to try to maintain an illusion for too long."

"I love the way you manage to embed lessons within lessons. I hesitate to confront people. But when I take that chance with you, I come away feeling better. As a bonus, I feel that we're able to clear the air between us."

"I trust that you're working to do the same during your marital counseling. I've talked to Elizabeth to make sure we're on the same page. She's a little puzzled by some of the things you are sharing from our sessions, but she is genuinely thrilled by the way in which the two of you are growing in your relationship."

Linda glowed on hearing the report. "As good as that makes me feel, I don't want to get stuck in ego. It's funny. The more I'm identifying with Rick, the easier it is for me to get caught in our joint as opposed to my individual ego."

"Good observation. The joint ego you mentioned can be a trap as well. How many couples invest themselves in presenting to the world as having the perfect marriage? It's especially challenging when they've invested a small fortune in a story-book wedding. When things start to go wrong, as they inevitably do, the partners have nowhere to turn except against each other. Any admission would be a chink in their carefully constructed image and serve as a betrayal of the illusion they have created. It can easily lead to a dissolution of the relationship."

Rick got a kick out of my remark. "No problem like that here. I screwed up and nearly had an affair. You might also remember that half the town thought that Linda was a prostitute. And then I got arrested for cocaine possession. I don't think anyone is going to say we are putting up a false front. The only self-image I care about now involves honesty. The only people I truly care about recognizing that are you and Linda."

"I've got to admit," I admitted, "I love our diversions. I start to respond to one question and end up talking about something entirely different. We are then able to clean up leftover, but important, baggage while moving closer and closer to our goal. This is really fun!"

Linda matched my enthusiasm by saying, "I couldn't agree more. Just to make sure I'm following, it wouldn't hurt to have a little reminder of what our goal is."

"Good point," I acknowledged. "In the course of our earlier sessions, I mentioned the possibility of discovering a marriage beyond anything you had ever imagined. You both readily embraced that plan. Along the way, you expressed interest in developing knowledge while growing in awareness. But, I'll admit, I was the one to define the goal. You just jumped on board. It seems appropriate to ask you both your thoughts at this point."

I was pleased that Rick took a moment to reflect before responding. "When you mentioned the possibility of strengthening our marriage, I was naturally excited. At the time, however, I had no way of knowing the extent of what you were proposing. My thinking was simply that it sounded like a good idea, and why not go for it?

"Now that I realize just how profound the commitment is, I'm glad to have a chance to re-examine my decision. It's pretty much like deciding all over again. At least from my end, I'm happy to say that I'm more excited and enthusiastic than ever. Let's do it."

For her part, Linda showed no signs of hesitation. "Who am I to poop on a party? You've given me/us the opportunity of a myriad of lifetimes. Do you think there's any chance I would take a pass?"

I was pleased but certainly not surprised by their responses. "I feel it necessary to throw in one last reminder. We're dealing with something much greater than just the three of us. You don't go knocking on the doors of heaven without giving it some thought. If there isn't adequate preparation and purity of Self/Selves, you can't be sure of who might answer."

In spite of some obvious trepidation, Linda finally managed, "You do have a flair for the dramatic, don't you?"

Linda's Journal

November 1

I almost went into panic mode when Bill talked about reaching our goal. It's not that I don't want that very thing. The problem is I want to keep sucking on the teat of knowledge. Okay, that sounded a little crude. Still, I'm very intent on getting every morsel from our sessions. Why do I keep using food terms?

It's funny that he was almost apologetic for allowing our discussions to wander. To tell the truth, I've done everything I could think of to nudge him in different directions. It's like he represents a mountain of knowledge, and I want to climb right up there with him.

I had the tiniest of confrontations with Bill. This time, I wasn't just teasing as I had done before. I guess I shouldn't have been surprised to find I could be totally honest with him without damaging our relationship. It feels so good to be clean with him, Rick, and myself. I truly have nothing to hide. It's like that naked thing from our earlier sessions.

I couldn't have been more serious about the internal conflict I'm experiencing as we are approaching the end of our road. In saying that, I'm ecstatic about what lies before us but want to cry like a baby when I think about our sessions coming to an end. I can't wait to hear more about the recordings during which Rick discussed his time with Barb. On the other hand, I'm even more excited about the opportunity to learn from a master psychotherapist. Bill is incredibly willing to share. I just wish that I had the time to formulate all the questions I would like to ask. Years from now, I know that I'm going to have regrets about that.

Rick's   Journal
November 1

After all the time we spent talking about charity and giving, I think I've reached an inner resolution. I hadn't realized how much that issue had troubled me. Mostly subliminally, I had been caught up in a worldview that involved hopelessness and inevitable failure. I thought, deep down, I could never do enough. It's a great relief to accept the world as it is, along with my role in it. It really is okay to do what I can and then feel good about it. There's no reason to think there is something or someone out there who is constantly judging my inadequacies. Why should I do it to myself?

While it's, in some ways, antithetical to the harsh realities involved with my profession, I love Bill's emphasis on honesty. I'm looking constructively at the inconsistency between my ideals and what I must do to make a living. I look forward to the challenge of being, and my colleagues would laugh if they read this, an honest lawyer. Because the foundation of our legal system is adversarial, it will be a tricky and ambitious undertaking. Most importantly, I don't want to let my clients down.

It may sound like a cop-out, but I'm going to begin the identity shift by thinking of myself as living in the spirit of honesty. In doing so, I don't have to reveal everything I know. After all, the legal system is basically a game. I will still play to win. I will be straightforward while representing the interests of my clients.

I expect some nicks along the way, but I truly believe it's possible to establish a persona of genuineness that jurors will come to recognize. If clients really believe in their case, they will want an attorney who will represent them in a forthright manner. Am I dreaming? I guess I'll just wait to see how the world responds to my noble intentions. I guess there's always a balancing act between how we want to be and the feedback we receive from reality.

Sixth Meeting

I was both surprised and pleased to learn of Elizabeth's request for a meeting between the four of us. I wanted to learn more about her approach to marital therapy. I also wanted to get a real sense of the progress Rick and Linda were making on the nitty-gritty of their marriage.

Elizabeth began, "I really appreciate the chance to meet you, Bill. I've heard some marvelous things about your work with this wonderful couple. I will, however, admit that some of the information that they have revealed makes me a bit uncomfortable. I felt it was my ethical responsibility to my clients to learn more. I don't, in any way, think they're being drawn into a cult or anything like that, but I am quite curious about what your efforts entail."

Linda got an obvious charge from her introduction. In line with our earlier banter, she said, "You're right. Better lock him up. He's leading us straight to crazy town."

Elizabeth was obviously shocked, though she did reasonably well in maintaining her objective demeanor. She was a professional and not prone to overreacting. "Linda," she admonished, "You're obviously quite taken with him. The progress you have described is amazing. Is your humor originating from a sense we're getting too close to home? Now that Bill is here, you have the opportunity to tell me more about your interactions. But there is also the risk that I might disapprove in some way."

A chastened Linda shuffled her feet before responding. "My gosh, are all you shrinks so astute? You nailed it. I'm incredibly invested in the work we have done with Bill. The possibility that another professional might make light of it or not condone it terrifies me."

Elizabeth's warmth was evident as she responded, "Remember, Linda. Judgment is not part of my job description. I'm thrilled with the things I've seen with both you and Rick. I just want to make sure Bill and I can balance our mutual efforts."

Rick was obviously relieved. "Marital counseling is like a foreign land to me. Then we throw in our work with Bill, and I feel like I'm on a different planet. If it turned out that the two of you were working at cross purposes, you might as well sign me up for the funny farm."

I interjected, "I'll be glad to explain some of my work, but I would like to get an overview of the progress with their marriage. I have the luxury of sailing right past the inevitable dirty laundry of relationships. But that doesn't mean I have the right to totally ignore it. Hope you don't mind that I've shipped it off to you."

Elizabeth enjoyed a quiet but pleasant laugh. "Not at all, Bill. I'm thrilled to work with these guys. In fact, it's been a genuine highlight of my career. I don't want them getting the big head, but they've worked through issues like power struggles and resentments with almost no resistance. In fact, their atypically harmonious approach to the usual areas of conflict was almost a source of concern. What are you doing that facilitates their ease in dealing with the inevitable conflicts of married life?"

I responded readily, "Credit where credit is due. I guess there is a relatively simple explanation. We've re-prioritized matters that would ordinarily create friction. To provide a concrete reference, a tailback doesn't worry about how many yards he's gained if he scores a touchdown. For Linda and Rick, their eyes are focused on something much more important than who forgot to buy tissue."

"I'm quite grateful you came in," she exclaimed unexpectedly. "I would love for you to share your secret. It might cut down quite a bit on my practice, but it would be incredibly gratifying."

"As disappointing as it may seem, there is no secret. The work we're enjoying is the product of thousands of years of knowledge. Because people get caught up in unnecessary power struggles, they ignore it. Linda and Rick are re-prioritizing."

With a frown on her face, Elizabeth protested, "Don't even try to tell me it's that simple."

"You're right," I acknowledged. "I didn't mention the missing ingredient. There is an energy that sets things in motion. It allows a person to recognize and benefit from the wisdom of the ages."

Elizabeth's puzzlement was clear. "Rick and Linda have pretty well steered clear of the specifics of your work. It sounds like you're getting to the crux of it. What is this mysterious energy you mention?"

"Here's the thing. I can easily talk about it. But it would be as pointless as trying to tell a blind man what the color purple looks like."

"Can you at least tell me the source of this mysterious energy?" Her tone was noticeably dubious.

"The energy is ubiquitous. It's a matter of recognizing it, cultivating it, and directing it. A simplistic way of describing it would be to call it light. It's the very force that underlies life itself."

As is common on the rare occasions when I attempt to explain my work to the uninitiated, her doubts and confusion were only growing. "Elizabeth, I have a strong, positive feeling about you, and I can tell you are thoroughly grounded. With, and only with, your explicit permission, I will offer you a direct sense of what I'm talking about."

She seemed excited but also uneasy. "I'm not up for being hypnotized. Do you have some sort of magic wand? I hope what I'm saying is not offensive. My interest is sincere, but I really have no interest in parlor tricks."

"Understood and accepted. If both you and Linda agree, I will ask her to show you. I've never asked her to do so before, but I believe that she has achieved a state of development that will allow her to share her energy with my supervision while remaining egoless."

Linda seemed surprised to the point of being taken aback. "What the hell, Bill! You've never told me that I might have that ability, much less given me permission to use it."

"I certainly agree. You're soon going to be sharing it directly with Rick as you mutually allow your energy to grow. I think it's time to do it in small measure with another person whom you trust."

For her part, Elizabeth was still wondering what to make of the whole matter. She more or less thought we were just playing a game. Nevertheless, her curiosity was evident. "I'm pretty strong-minded. I would really like to learn about this energy thing, but I have my doubts."

I reassured her by saying, "There is really no need for concern. I'm sure that you have confidence in Linda. I'm not suggesting anything that would shake your sense of reality. Instead, I'm offering you the opportunity to satisfy your curiosity. In the process, you will be exposed to possibilities that you may have never considered."

"Okay," she said with some trepidation. "Sign me up. What do I need to do to get ready?"

Linda seemed equally perplexed. "Exactly what do you want me to do?"

"First of all, clear your mind of all doubts and questions. Go to your special place. Leave your words behind and just be. Then, turn to Elizabeth and 'see' her. Take in her inner beauty and sense the person she truly is."

Linda's glow was obvious to me and to Rick as well. It took only a few seconds before Elizabeth looked at us in amazement and exclaimed, "Wow! I can't believe it. I saw myself and Linda as well in a way I had never imagined could exist. We were so beautiful. The immensity and perfection of the universe was right before my eyes."

She was excited. Linda was equally as ecstatic. "I didn't know I could do that. And I guess you're now going to tell me that there are rules."

"You know me too well. You can't imagine the consequences if you go blasting people without knowing their readiness. Elizabeth has been working with you for some time. She's been exposed to your energy in a less direct manner and was ready for more of the full-frontal approach."

Elizabeth was wide-eyed and yet had a look of absolute serenity. "What a gift! You've given me a totally new and exciting view of the possibilities of life. I'll never forget it. Now that I've had a taste, you can guess what I'm going to ask."

I had anticipated her question. "Please complete your work with this beautiful couple. You will likely benefit as much or more from the time you spend together as they do. After their transformation, I will be expecting your call."

Elizabeth looked at me with wonder as she continued to glow. "Before you go, I think there is one other concern that I should express in the context of our mutual efforts. In spite of all the great work that they have done, there have been times when they've broken the prime directive of marital relationships."

I looked at her in surprise. "I think I may have missed something along the way in my education. Do I need to take myself along with them to the woodshed?"

She indulgently said, "I don't think it's quite that serious. But the rule is sacrosanct."

"Now I'm the one being held in suspense. And I'm no more patient than Linda."

"Okay, here it is. I know that both Linda and Rick have been under lots of pressure from numerous sources. But the character of their everyday communication is of vital importance. The rule is simple. At a bare minimum, at least 50% of the statements they make to each other must be positive. Otherwise, relationships turn sour. Who wants to be around another if what they're likely to experience is going to be unpleasant."

I was sincerely grateful for her input. "In our sessions, Linda and Rick typically communicate directly with me. I haven't had the opportunity to observe how they interact with each other. The feedback you just provided is invaluable. I will certainly use it in working with my other clients as well. I will also watch my interactions with my recent wife to make sure that we stay the course of our marriage.

Linda's Journal

November 8

I was giddy about the idea of Bill and Elizabeth meeting. It's a bit embarrassing, but I was out of control. I couldn't just flow with the wonder of our session. I had to make a stupid comment. Well, one of the things I've made progress on is self-forgiveness. I guess it's okay to talk like a jackass every once in a while. Fortunately, everyone seemed to recover quickly.

Just when I think Bill can't surprise me any more than he has, he up and does it again. I couldn't be more excited! It was the most palpable experience I've had in sharing my new energy. And to do it with someone I greatly respect! It just doesn't get any better. Once again, I automatically start thinking about what I might do as a therapist. It's probably a good thing Bill keeps reminding me to stay in the now.

My ego wants to get off on my newfound power. I'm simply not going to go there. Instead, I want to think about the beauty I found when I looked into Elizabeth's eyes. My gosh, she's an incredible person. Bill talked about counselors getting burned out. That's certainly not the case with her. I looked right into her soul. She cares. I get weepy just thinking about the immensity of the experience.

Rick's Journal

November 9

Our meeting with Bill and Elizabeth was everything I'd hoped for and more. I can't believe how lucky I am to have these wonderful people in my life. What did I ever do to deserve all this?

Interestingly, the very question I asked myself reflects back on my ego. The great experiences in life, just as the bad ones, can provide an unexpected opportunity for learning. It's easy to see how people get into trouble by feeling sorry for themselves. When they're feeling grateful, the temptation is much more subtle. Interestingly, I can view the entire issue dispassionately. My good old witness is kicking in.

It's way past time that we got Bill involved in our down-to-earth work in relationship building. It's great fun to learn all these new concepts and fly around the universe with him. But at the end of the day, we still have to work out who is going to turn out the light when we go to bed. Mind you, I'm not complaining. It's like having the best of both worlds in working with Bill and Elizabeth. And her respect for Bill was almost tangible. It further validates everything we've been doing.

It wasn't that long ago that my life centered around financial worries. I don't think it would be a stretch to say my priorities have shifted. Now I'm walking around feeling ten feet tall. I'm getting calls from new clients, and I sense that my colleagues are treating me with a new respect. It's funny. I think at least a small part of it is that I don't care in the same way. Don't get me wrong. I care a helluva lot. As it turns out, ob-op is much more than just a novel idea.

Seventh Meeting

Rick seemed relieved as we began. "In listening to the recording, I'm painfully reminded of all the idiotic mistakes I made in dealing with Barb. But compared to everything else I've learned through these meetings, my bumbling attempts to counter her advances seem trivial."

"Anything but," I surprised him by saying. "Barb was a genuine catalyst. You couldn't have asked for a more effective spur to your awakening. She also allowed you to truly explore important concepts, such as trust, commitment, and honesty."

With a dejected look, he admitted, "Well, I guess I pretty much failed in all those areas."

"Yup," I once again surprised him by agreeing. "And look at the end result. Now, you truly know those concepts in a way few people ever have. Take, for example, honesty. I would guess you generally tried to be honest with Linda in the past. But even with your best efforts, you would have been holding back part of yourself. Do you agree?"

"I hadn't really thought about it, but you're right. Way in the back of my mind, I was hiding doubts and wondering how she might take any information I volunteered."

"Don't you think most people have the same reservations? I hope you're now able to see that Barb represented much more of a gift than a curse. She stirred things in both of you that forced you to confront your Selves. It was far from a comfortable process, but you know what I say about comfort."

"But I don't know if Linda will ever be truly able to trust me after what I did," he protested.

"I guess we need to turn to the source to find out."

Linda shrugged uncomfortably. "Rick, if you're hoping that I'm going to tell you that I'm okay with everything, you're going to be disappointed. I hate to my core that you, more or less, fell for her attempts at seduction and can only hope that you didn't totally forget about me at the time."

With a half-smile, Rick was able to say, "At least I can say that you were always in the back of my mind. Except for maybe one time when I allowed alcohol and physiology to grab hold of me."

"Cop out!" Linda nearly screamed. "Just what part of your mind did I occupy during your dalliances?"

"You got me," Rick admitted almost gladly. "I screwed up royally, and boy, did I punish myself afterward. I'm just glad that Bill was able to help get me turned around."

"Now I'm mad at both of you," Linda protested. "You deserved to wallow in guilt after betraying our marriage. He had no right to give you a pass."

"Have you decided just what price he needs to pay?" I inquired innocently.

"Well, I guess I would just settle with his being a good husband from now on. But I'm not finished with you either. You're the one who told him not to be guilty."

"Not exactly," I said as a gentle reminder. "You've already made that sort of accusation once. It didn't stick. You, along with everyone else who shares our language, have a thoroughly ingrained, unhealthy way of using conjugations of the word 'to be.' I would never tell anyone not to be guilty. The only thing I would consider saying is to tell him 'to be' without including a limiting and inevitably fallacious ending. To my mind, Linda simply is. Same for Rick."

She had gotten wound up, and it wasn't easy for her to back off. With obvious reluctance, she admitted, "Okay, I did make some jumps in logic. When I found out what was going on with Rick and Barb, I wanted someone to blame. You were an obvious target, but you're hard to get hold of. Reason and logic were not top of mind when I got mad at you."

Rick had been sitting meekly, obviously not wanting to share in our tension-filled interaction. The smug grin that had been growing on his face disappeared quickly when the spotlight turned to him, and he was forced to take part. "Whose idea was it to listen to these recordings anyway?"

"You're not going to skate on this one, Buster."

I thought it best to intervene by saying, "There is nothing to be gained by continuing to stomp on him. If you can't forgive him, I understand. Just get a divorce so we can move on with our lives."

Linda was beginning to catch on to my ways. "You're doing it again, aren't you? You decided to circumvent my ego by agreeing with me. Boy, do you infuriate me, even when I know you're doing it for my own good? Knowing that almost makes it worse."

"I'm glad we had another shot at the 'is of identity.' Its importance can't be underestimated. But there's certainly nothing to be gained by continuing to pummel your husband."

Rick was suddenly eager to jump back in. "Bill, did I ever tell you that you're my best friend?"

I knew that Bill would love to draw me into taking sides. Instead, I said, "I'm not condoning or forgiving anything. I'm simply saying, lesson learned. If it hasn't been, we're back to square one."

Rick was more than ready to endorse my conclusion. "Bill, I'm so glad for our work. I can't even imagine making that mistake again from my current level of awareness. It's almost like Linda and I have returned to the Garden of Eden. But this time, I'm not going to be fooled into taking a bite of the apple. Linda and I simply 'are' from this point forward."

"Linda," I inquired. "I want you to genuinely think about whether you can now trust him. Way too many women have been fooled by repentant husbands. I've seen more repeated cycles of abuse followed by remorse and then forgiveness than I care to think about. You have a choice of accepting that he is now in a different place. Alternatively, you can continue to torture both him and you by continuing to question. Ordinarily, I wouldn't even ask about your willingness to trust him. I would lean toward the assumption there is simply a repetitive pattern. What it now comes down to is your readiness to accept that he has genuinely changed the core of his identity."

Linda's smile lit up the room. "Abso-friggin'-lutely. I was sort of funnin' with you guys before. Now, when I look at him, I 'see' him. In a very real sense, he's a different person. I guess it might be more accurate to say I see a beautiful, luminous being encapsulated in Rick's body. In saying that, I certainly don't mean to minimize the reality that this big old lug is my husband in the world as we know it. Bottom line, I love the whole package, body and soul."

"Now we're really getting somewhere." I then followed up my statement with a bit of unnecessary melodrama. "And now the end is nigh."

"I think I like where you're going with this, but I can never be totally sure with you," Rick commented with a hint of trepidation. "Just to be sure, you're not about to execute us, are you?"

I humored him by saying, "What an interesting thought. However, that would take all the fun out of it. But, quite seriously, I can see that you're both getting it. You're moving past the silly games that consume most couples. I think you're ready to move to the final preparation for supra-self-transformation. How about you?"

In response, Linda stood, smiled broadly, and applauded.

Linda's Journal

November15

We finally started getting to the meat, and there's another food term of Rick's interactions with Barb. As much as I had tried to prepare myself, I just couldn't hold back. But, come on. What wife who truly cared about her marriage could? I allowed old programs to take hold, and all I could think about was blame. My barely modulated rage even carried over to Bill. It wasn't as easy to justify since he came along after the fact, but it hardly mattered at the time.

As unbelievable as it seems, the unpleasant encounter was more than worth it. It's not exactly reasonable, but I felt like I had to release some of my anger concerning Rick's stupidity. I'm now feeling more like myself and can see the perfection in the whole scenario. I was able to release doubts and feelings that had been taunting me and just wouldn't let go.

I know it's getting repetitive, but Bill was right. We needed to play out this scene in its most naked form. Rick and I both had unresolved feelings that would have kept us at least a tiny bit apart if we hadn't expressed them.

Now, there's not the slightest doubt in my mind. I have no sympathy for cheating husbands, and I have little respect for wives who take them back. At least, I have a much greater understanding of the dynamics. Did I ever mention that I can't wait to become a therapist?

Rick's Journal

November 15

I've been dreading it for months, and it certainly wasn't any fun. Now I'm so glad we went through it. I could have hidden it all from Linda, and she might not have been any the wiser. However, I know that our relationship would have hit a dead end if I had denied her that critical bit of information. I would have started the ball rolling toward hiding other things from her. True intimacy does not allow room for secrets.

Angry confrontations are much more entertaining to watch on TV than to experience. It was like experiencing a catharsis that needed to happen. She needed to express it, and I needed to feel her anger. It's only now that I feel like my dalliances with Linda have been wiped clean. I'm so glad Linda shares my sense of resolution.

I'm guessing most couples enter relationships with a conviction of fidelity and honesty. It takes little to start chipping away at their ideals. If you innocently run into an old girlfriend on the street, do you tell your wife? If you know it's going to start an argument you can't win, isn't it better to let sleeping dogs lie? After all, wasn't it just a stroke of fate? When it happens again, and she suggests grabbing a cup of coffee, what could be more innocent? And so the story goes.

I never know what Bill is going to pull on us next. His Shakespearian end to our last session was intriguing. Are we really close to being ready for the next step? I think surviving our last session was a major accomplishment, and I'm ready to experience this glorious bonding with Linda. At the same time, I can't help but share Linda's opinion that there is so much more for us to learn.

Eighth Meeting

"During this phase, I'm planning to provide you with additional information to help in negotiating life following the upcoming transformation. Since Linda likes for me to reveal uncomfortable information about my dull, boring life, I'll even give you a personal glimpse into how I got to where I am."

"Now you're talking!" Linda exclaimed, rubbing her hands together in anticipation.

"Please recognize that it won't be easy for me. I've gone through my own share of struggles, along with occasional minor triumphs. I'm just as mortal as anyone else and have more than my share of limitations. I've overcome numerous temptations and fallen for many more."

"Yeah, yeah. We've heard all that. You're only human. Believe me, you have been quite convincing on that score." Linda made no attempt to disguise her sarcasm or her impatience.

I swallowed before continuing. "I've always felt sort of different. In that way, I guess I'm pretty much like everyone else. But unlike most others, I decided to delve deeply into existential questions. I wanted the same material successes as others but knew that nothing in this world would ultimately be satisfying."

They were obviously listening intently, so I continued. "I'm going to skip right past the highs and lows of adolescence. You're both, quite obviously, familiar with your own. I was always an idealist. I was attracted to religion. I had moments of ecstasy as I caught a glimpse of essence while singing Christian songs and felt the thrill of religious bliss during wilderness experiences at church camp. But the mundane realities of services and the petty actions of church members repelled me."

"I hear you," Rick added. "I've been there as well. But it's important for me to keep up the image. A lot of my referrals have come from attending church. I kind of feel two-faced about it because that's not what religion is supposed to be for. But it's reality. As with many things, you do what you must to survive."

I nodded. "You're obviously more tolerant of the game than I. I give you credit. I'm not a good follower. Conformity has never been my friend. I sought to create my own way and believe me; I've paid the requisite dues.

"After a difficult time in my life, I hoped to find solace in the world of ideas. I entered a graduate program in Philosophy but found it unrewarding. It involved more of an intellectual exercise than a search for truth."

"What did you do next?" Linda asked.

"As I've made clear, I didn't have any greater success in finding answers during my time in the Clinical Psychology program. But there were at least fellow students who shared my aspirations. During that time, I embraced some of the tenets, or at least the ideals, of Eastern religions. Since I'm being unabashedly personal in my revelations, I'll tell you another one. I gave celibacy a shot. As it turns out, there are no warnings in the religious texts about the likely consequence."

"Other than being incredibly horny, what was the problem?" Rick asked.

"Prostatitis. It turns out that denying biological urges is fine in theory, but the practice has an important drawback. Unfortunately, my urinary tract didn't share my lofty aspirations. I did at least benefit from the self-discipline required, as well as the inward redirection of the associated energy. At the same time, I learned that it's important to be in tune with my body. We have a physical being for a reason, though it's not always readily obvious. I was glad that my body told me not to try to rush too quickly in my dash for the heavens."

"I'm sure that many girls were grateful for that lesson," Linda said, giggling like a teenager.

"You're being way too kind. I think the female members of the species did quite well in my absence. But to the point, one of the ways that I dealt with my denial of physical needs was meditation."

"I've wondered why you've never recommended that we do that sort of thing," Rick commented.

"Just for clarification, very few people actually meditate. Meditation does not mean simply repeating a mantra or thinking about your breathing. The true meaning of meditation is complete, one-pointed concentration. When that perfect concentration is centered on God, it's called Samadhi. Yoga, tai chi, and even Christian rituals serve as ways to prepare for meditation.

"I do think that the practice of what people refer to as meditation is useful as a tool. It allows a person to reach a deep state of relaxation and promotes an internal focus. I did it twice a day by subvocalizing a Sanskrit word that, at least in theory, promoted an internal vibration that was intended to become harmonious with and thus open one of the chakras or centers of energy."

Linda stated the obvious. "It must not have worked well for you."

"I'm impatient. Additionally, I found myself becoming increasingly disillusioned with the supposed gurus that I both read about and even encountered personally. I eventually concluded that meditation wasn't central to my journey. On the bright side, it did help me come up with my formulation of the ego and its role, both positive and negative, in our lives."

"How did you get that from studying gurus?"

"I found that most, though not necessarily all, had deep spiritual convictions. They had made considerable progress in following the path to awareness. But they got caught in the trap of their own success. As you might imagine, it's incredibly gratifying to have people sitting at your feet. When you act like you don't care about money, the dollars start coming your way.

"Then there's the most seductive trap of all. There are many, many female followers who are more than willing to give their bodies as well as their souls to anyone promising enlightenment. The gurus ended up surrendering to their egos as the temptations overwhelmed their previous sense of dedication. Some even gave in to the point of open debauchery."

Linda took a minute to process what I was saying. "I'm comparing it to my experience with you. You were straightforward about financial matters and made no unrealistic promises. In fact, you encouraged me to set goals for myself and then surprised me by offering unexpected opportunities. You did, quite effectively, seduce me. But you didn't follow through. I'm still not entirely sure why you didn't, but I'm so glad that things turned out as they did."

"Allow me to second that conclusion wholeheartedly," Rick volunteered.

"As much as I would like to close the book on that chapter, we did both learn important lessons. While I didn't try to give you the impression that I had some sort of God-like powers, I did present as a psychologist. Everything about the setup with my office and diplomas on the wall led you to give me considerable credibility. I appeared to have the answers you were seeking. Like the aforementioned gurus, I turned out to have feet of clay. Before I met you, I didn't come close to realizing the extent of it. Our egos can really be treacherous bastards."

"The reason for your disillusionment with gurus is obvious. Did you give up on them entirely?"

"I learned about one man who seemed to have transcended mortal temptations. From everything I've read and learned about him, he was able to remain in his mortal body while living in a celestial state. The term for that achievement is 'bodhisattva.' In Eastern literature, that word is reserved for one who has achieved nirvana but decides to continue living in his or her physical body out of compassion for those of us who continue to suffer."

Rick jumped in, "Who is this dude? I've got to learn about him."

"His name was Paramahansa Yogananda. He was an incredibly prolific writer. His best-known book was *Autobiography of a Yogi* (1946). He also wrote extensive lesson plans for those who chose to follow his path. I attended several services at a temple of the religion he founded, which is known as Self Realization Fellowship. Interestingly, placed on the altar were pictures of him along with Jesus and other leaders of the great world religions. I took my parents, who are devoted Methodists, to a service. To their credit, they didn't totally freak out. But that's not to say they approved. I can only imagine their conversations afterward. I'm pretty sure they never mentioned it to anyone back home."

"What were the services like?" Linda inquired.

"Everyone in attendance was quiet and worshipful. There was little to no conversation before or after the service. There were periods of meditation and a talk by the leader. I'm not sure that you would call him a preacher because the things he said didn't sound like any of the endless sermons I heard growing up. Allow me to correct myself. It would be more accurate to say sermons that I was exposed to since I rarely listened."

"You called it a religion, but you're not a big fan of organized religions. Care to explain?"

"I used that term for lack of a better one. The fact is, I'm now a long way off from that time in my life. I hope I can provide you with more accurate information. Self Realization Fellowship, or SRF as it's called, is quite different. Yogananda inspired the 'religion,' but he never sought followers. People were inspired by him and his writings, but I never heard of anyone worshipping him."

"You're saying that you're now a long way off. What happened?"

"I'll explain next time we meet."

Linda's Journal

November 22

You'd think that Bill was Jack the Ripper, the way he's so guarded about his past. I sometimes wonder if there's something horrible that he's hiding from us. Ordinarily, I would come to that conclusion. In this instance, it just doesn't quite fit. I think he really is struggling, like he said, with the deviation from his usual professional role.

It's interesting that he shares my personality quirk. If he weren't so damn fascinating, there's no way I would have sat and talked with him for so many hours. I like to keep things moving and don't like to be held in suspense. I've always known that I tend to be impatient. Goodness knows that Rick has told me about it often enough. It's just never seemed so real to me. I want to know everything Bill can teach me right now. My need for speed does make sense because he's already let us know that he's going to be flaking out on us before long.

I find his history with gurus to be fascinating. He was driven by an inner passion that is rare. Of course, I've contemplated existential questions myself, but never that seriously. The fact is that they have always scared me. When I've stopped to think about death, I have quickly stopped thinking about death. I'll bet that I'm not unique on that score.

Rick's Journal

November 23

You just never know what direction Bill is going to take us in. All this talk about gurus is foreign to me. Do those guys who claim to have no interest in sex and money really get seduced by the very things that they say they disdain? Well, I guess it's understandable. Especially now that I know more about the ego. It's like the more you try to transcend it, the cleverer it becomes in finding a backdoor.

It's funny how lessons that I blew off as a child start coming back to me. I can't remember the exact reference, but one had to do with only paupers being allowed into heaven. It's astounding how I let the wisdom of the ages just blow right by me. You don't know what you don't know until you know. Pretty crazy, huh?

Linda and I are incredibly lucky, although it's been made very clear that we're not special in any way. We're able to vicariously benefit from all of Bill's struggles. We don't even have to spend hours meditating. That's not to say this process has been totally pain-free. It's been anything but. I cringe when I think about Linda's listening to my time with Barb. And then there's her sexual interlude with Bill. I'm growing to appreciate the word, disillusioned. Everything I see and hear is, in a sense, an illusion. It's all transitory. Luckily, I'm finally confident that what we're moving toward is real in the ultimate sense.

Ninth Meeting

"In answer to your previous question, I found SRF to be largely syntonic with my values and ideals. But it wasn't my path for the long run."

"But if it worked for you, why would you leave it?"

"First of all, I must admit I wasn't the best of meditators. During my internship, I did my best to put in the requisite 20 minutes twice a day. The problem was I couldn't stay awake. I believe I received a modest benefit from my efforts, but it just wasn't a good fit. I have friends who meditate for hours at a time. I admire them. I'm just not set up physiologically to stay awake for that long without external stimulation."

Linda pondered what I had said before commenting. "I'm glad that you're exposing more of your human side. I like you better when you aren't so darned perfect."

"Then I look forward to your liking me more and more as you continue to get to know me."

Rick was also curious. "If you're such a fan of SRF, what happened?"

"First of all, I failed. After a year of faithful meditation, you're eligible for initiation into a higher form of practice. Because I couldn't stay awake, I wasn't granted initiation at the next level."

"What a disappointment that must have been after all your efforts."

"It was, and yet it wasn't. As I may have said previously, the universe provides. When you're ready, the right teacher appears. I continued with my increasingly erratic attempts at meditation. Then, unexpectedly, I got a call from an attorney. He represented a company called Potential Research Foundation and was looking for a psychologist to spearhead it."

They both agreed, "It sounds fascinating. We're anxious to hear more."

"The first person I met was their psychophysiologist. He was a man who was too smart to live in this world and, for the most part, he didn't. He spent hours sitting in the tub, sipping beer, and playing a complex Chinese game called Go by himself. Are you sure you want me to continue?"

"If you don't, I'm going to go back on my word about not slapping you."

"Okay, you win. He was fascinated by the ability of species lower on the phylogenetic scale to replicate themselves. As I'm sure you know, if you cut an earthworm in two, the halves simply regenerate. Something similar happens if you cut off the tail of a salamander. It just grows back. As species become more complex, that ability is lost.

Rick piped in, "That's Biology 101. There's really nothing you can do about it at this point in our knowledge of the science."

"That's just the thing. We were dealing with potential. Our hope was to surpass that biological barrier."

Linda had a bit of a smirk. "You just decided to play God. I know you're a great magician, but it sounds like your egos were getting a bit bloated."

"I get your point. The theoretical side of our operation was a bit ambitious. The real-world aspect, however, produced awesome results."

"Okay, I've got to ask. What did you do that was so fantastic?"

"Actually, I didn't do much," I admitted. "But I haven't yet described the man who was the other part of the equation. When I was first introduced to him, I was told that he was basically a technician. I thought he would assist with relaxation techniques and provide basic instructions for dealing with chronic pain, which was our primary area of clinical focus. Boy, was I wrong!"

Linda rubbed her hands together. "You're finally getting to the good part. There must have been a flash of lightning or something equally as stupendous."

"I hate to disappoint, but nothing dramatic happened. I was mildly impressed by him, probably a little more than I expected. At the same time, my early reaction was limited by my prejudice."

"I'm almost scared to ask, but was he Black?"

I chuckled. "No, nothing like that. He was a rather tall man with signs of premature graying in his beard. His deep, bass voice had an unusual bit of a rumble to it. But, without question, his most salient feature was his eyes. He could penetrate you with a mere gaze. It wasn't totally obvious at first because he was protecting me and showing me only one layer at a time. And as I intimated, I was expecting a mere mortal, so that's what I saw. After all, I had this fancy education. His only degree was from a local community college. My eyes saw what they were programmed to see…a technician."

Rick was curious. "Since he was relatively uneducated, how did the two of you work together?"

"I've got to admit. We sort of didn't. As I discovered the extent of his skill and power, I took a back seat. I had never seen anyone who could perform miracles. You sure you want me to keep going?"

At that, Linda stood up and cocked her hand back in a teasing but still blatantly threatening manner.

"Okay, I think I get the message. Please understand that I'm not used to talking about this. As a matter of fact, you're the first people I've talked to about it in any detail."

Linda continued standing with her hands on her hips. "And if you don't continue," she said in a playfully menacing tone, "We will likely be the last."

"Message accepted," I responded meekly. "As I mentioned, he was extremely powerful. He could cause people to do things they wouldn't ordinarily do with just a look. His voice could have been a weapon, though he didn't use it in that way. When he spoke, your body could feel what he was saying."

Rick asked somewhat hesitatingly, "So he was like a god or something?"

"It wasn't quite like that. It took several months before he showed me his true Self. In retrospect, I'm grateful that he had the wisdom not to overwhelm me. If he had revealed too much too fast, I'm not sure I would have stuck around."

"Did he teach you about the ego and the other things you've talked about?" Linda asked.

"My conceptualization concerning the ego and the Self is pretty simplistic. But at least I guess I can take credit for it. I learned many of the other concepts that I've introduced from him. Interestingly, Linda, my experience paralleled yours as you've worked with me. The things I gleaned from him were totally different from what I had gained from my professors. He taught by example. He never lectured. I learned simply by working with him or, more accurately, watching him work."

Rick was puzzled. "I'm trying to put all this together. You talked about making physical changes and doing miracles. What did you actually accomplish?"

"Good question. And that's the challenge of manifesting knowledge in the ordinary reality. The rather idealistic goal of the Potential Research Foundation was to enable people to reach and remain in a state of awareness sufficient to allow for re-creation or transmorphism. We wanted to do the impossible. We hoped to surpass the limits of known science."

"You were an unrealistic bunch, I've got to say."

"You couldn't be more right. Our goal was overly ambitious, just as are the goals of most of those who achieve great breakthroughs. The reality doesn't give way easily. There are a couple of built-in safeguards. I can't say who or what devised them, but it's safe to say. It was a force much greater than I."

"Will you elaborate on the limits?"

The first is the battleground between the ego and Self, which we have covered extensively. As you know, when the ego gets carried away, the Self combines with the external reality to bring the person back down to earth. And I'm sure that you remember that there is no parachute for the return trip. The other basically involves other people."

"You're going to have to explain that one."

"Let's say you perform a miracle. The first instinct of observers is to try to explain it away. In doing so, they can stay safe within the bounds of their familiar reality. If they are unable to do so, they find themselves in a quandary. They must reconcile the new reality with their old. It makes them uncomfortable. So, guess what they're most likely to do?"

"I got that one," Rick volunteered. "Denial. If they can't explain it away, they try to act like it never existed. And if that doesn't work, they blame the perpetrator or attempt to discredit him in some way."

"Score one for the Rickster," I joked. "We were hired to run a pilot program for a major city designed to reduce excessive sick leave abuse. The results were impressive. However, a bureaucratic decision was made not to continue the program because the politicians didn't understand how it worked. In the meantime, we also worked with individuals suffering from chronic pain. Those results were astounding. But again, the physicians couldn't believe it. For the most part, I think they concluded that their patients must have been nut jobs or simply faking to begin with."

"As long as I'm spilling my guts, I'll even mention another vignette. As president of a professional school, I sponsored an event at the Coliseum in Phoenix featuring Uri Geller. You may have heard of his fame from bending spoons psychically. When I picked him up at the airport, the first thing he told me was that he had to have children at the event. He said that, for him to be successful, he required the presence of children since they don't have fixed belief systems that would unintentionally subvert his efforts. So we put out a PSA offering free attendance for kids and filled the stadium.

I can promise you that he was incredible. I witnessed a close-up as he did astounding things. One of my students was a 300-pound Olympic weightlifter. Uri lifted him easily off the ground using two fingers. He got watches to work that had no internal parts. The Amazing Randi showed up in an unsuccessful attempt to disprove everything he did. Randi followed him around the country, trying to prove that what he did wasn't magic."

"Wow, thanks for sharing. Where did things go from there?"

"After my final transformation, my teacher said that he had taught me everything he knew. It was up to me to integrate the knowledge with my previous and ongoing experiences. He basically set me free with a stipulation that I somehow managed to forget."

Linda's eyes lit up. "I think I remember what it was. You weren't supposed to perform a transformation for at least a year. He told you it was important to allow 365 days to transpire in order to have gained sufficient knowledge to lead another person through that step."

"You're right. But there was an associated qualification. It seemed absurd at the time because I couldn't imagine it happening. But it did."

"I think I've got that one as well. He asked you to agree not to ever have followers."

"Move to the head of the class. I led a seminar about the concepts involved with transformation. Not surprisingly, the students expressed an interest in experiencing it. I somehow rationalized and denied my way into acquiescing. It didn't take long until people from all walks of life wanted to be students. People were ready to dedicate their lives to teaching. I was overwhelmed by their demands but subsequently even more blown away by my stupidity. I experienced flights into the stratosphere and could barely find my way back to earth."

Linda was understanding and sympathetic. "It sounds like what I went through, only ten times worse."

"It was the first and only time in my life that I've felt crazy. I mean, I had my experiences with hallucinogenic drugs and all that, but those trips were nothing compared to what I was going through at that time."

"What!" they exclaimed in unison. "You never told us you were a druggie."

"I don't think I ever was. I thought of myself as an explorer in consciousness. I didn't take drugs to get high. I took them to learn. During my early adulthood, I took mescaline, LSD, and psilocybin several times. I tripped, but what I brought back from those risky and foolhardy endeavors was basically worthless."

"I'm glad you learned your lesson and stopped when you did," Linda said with apparent relief.

"I'm no superhero. I did once have the opportunity to take LSD after my transformation. I wanted to see how it would affect me with my new, vastly expanded awareness."

"Oh, my gosh! What happened?"

"The funny thing is, not much, other than the rushes I felt in my stomach. My thinking was unaffected. The hallucinogenic effects of the drug were no longer unfamiliar since I had visited those spaces in my journeys through awareness. It did little to nothing for me."

"Maybe you just got a bad dose," Rick suggested.

"Unlikely, since I had to drive the guy who took it with me to the emergency room. He couldn't stop his frightening hallucinations."

"What other surprises do you have in store for us?" Linda was caught between curiosity and a sense of mortification."

"Thanks for validating my resistance to talking about my personal experiences," I commented sarcastically. "While I look back on the decisions I made as having provided me with incredible gifts, I think it wise to spare you any further memories for the time being."

For once, Linda seemed satisfied with my decision.

Linda's Journal

December 1

Another thing that Bill said has come back to haunt me. I had been obsessed with learning more about him. Now that I have, I'm understanding his caution about getting what I wished for. Bill has been like an ideal for me. He's been someone who rises above the ordinary. Well, I'm certainly convinced that he hasn't been ordinary. It's the rising above part I'm starting to question.

He spent part of his life chasing a crazy idea. Then, he got involved with a famous psychic. But that's not the half of it. He revealed that he has a history of using psychedelic drugs. Hearing that was almost like getting a body blow. Coming from anybody else, it wouldn't have been such a big deal. But I've put all my faith and trust in him. I just need to back up and consider the context. As I think about it, he wasn't trying to escape life. He wasn't looking for a party high. I totally believe he did it in the context of his path.

I started to let the unimportant become important. Perspective Linda, perspective. The astounding aspect of his past involved his descriptions of his teacher, which I wouldn't give to meet him! He must be an incredibly interesting person. I wonder if I could feel his power just by being around him. In retrospect, probably not. It's likely similar to what I've experienced with Bill. In other words, you don't notice so much until he turns it on. Then watch out, mama!

I'm still wanting context. What else can I learn about Bill as a person? How does he react to the frustrations we all experience? I would love to know more about what happened when he developed followers. The unpleasant truth is he has already set the stage. His plan is to eventually exit the stage left. He wants to keep my focus, quite appropriately, on Rick. Bill keeps telling me, in so many words, that he is nothing more than a shiny toy.

Rick's Journal

December 1

My path has been totally different from Bill's. I'm not making any judgment. In fact, I'm learning to genuinely appreciate the various ways that people make their way through their time on Earth. And there's even more to it. I'm developing the ability to move my ego aside in order to ease myself into vicariously experiencing how others deal with life's challenges. It especially helps that I've had several clients who have commented that I'm the first person who has really heard them. Additionally, when I enter into the persona of my trial opponents, I'm able to better anticipate where they might be going.

Bill has a checkered past. So what? Is that the worst he can offer? As a trial lawyer, I have heard things you wouldn't believe. I have no problem hearing about his frailties. It's a bit of relief since Linda sometimes seems to idolize him. If there was ever a situation that would lead me to be jealous, it would be in our sessions. I'm only saying that hypothetically since it's the last thing I feel. Bill is in it for us as a couple. I have mixed feelings about his plan to step aside. While I think it's right for Linda and me, I'm going to miss him.

It's fascinating to hear about Bill's teacher. Interestingly, his description serves to further deflect our attention away from him. He wants us to keep our views of him in context. It won't be long until we're on our own. All this talk about psychics and miracles has my head spinning. I still think of myself as being a regular, down-to-earth guy. But, do I really? Bill has cautioned us against getting overly caught up in roles and identities. Turns out, that's another useful lesson.

Tenth Meeting

"Since you're following a path I've already cleared in advance, I want to ask one more time about your commitment. You know, things I've never revealed about my imperfections. You've also seen glimpses of my perfection. You still have the option of looking for another way. Or, more realistically, you're free to make an attempt to return to a 'normal' life. There is no right or wrong decision. Just keep one thing in mind: normality is vastly underrated. Now, maybe you can see why I threw in that story about my wife wanting to have an average kid."

There was no wavering, no sign of hesitation. Linda spoke for the two of them by saying, "Stopping at this point would be equivalent to deciding not to breathe. You've done some things in your past that I'm pretty sure I wouldn't have done but showing us your dirty underwear isn't going to scare us off."

I chuckled, "I love the colorful way you put it, and I promise to make sure I keep my pants zipped from this point forward. Now that the preliminaries are out of the way, let's have some fun by exploring simple issues, such as the meaning of life."

Linda's expression was not as joyful as I might have hoped. "I'm really torn. I'm incredibly excited about our progress toward transformation. At the same time, I think we're about to lose you."

"Right on both counts," I assured her. "Our work isn't meant to last forever. But here's the good news. You will take my essence with you. You and I are not going to be joined in the way that you and Rick will be. At the same time, I will always be a part of you and vice versa. The two of you are meant to fly using your own wings. Just be careful not to look back too quickly. You might happen to catch a glimpse of me."

With a puzzled look, Rick acknowledged his confusion and consternation by asking, "Are you saying you're always going to be with us or not?"

"You got me, Rick. I apologize for that bit of tease. The fact is that the two of you will be on your own. Our incredible, beautiful, awesome relationship will end cleanly. I'm not saying that I will never see you again. Who knows? But it won't be the same. I respect you enough to watch your blossoming from afar."

With an anxious look on her face, Linda demanded, "But what if we need you?"

"As before, it will be up to you to sink or swim. I have complete faith in your ability to make the right choices."

Her expression changed to one of chagrin. "I guess there's no point in fighting the inevitable. But I do want to pick your brain for as long as you'll let me."

I smiled wholeheartedly. "Whatever I know or, at least, think I know, is yours for the asking."

This time, her brow wrinkled. "Oh, my gosh. There's so much that I want to ask about and so little time. Let me start with a big one. You told me about defining and changing constructs as one way of conceptualizing psychotherapy. I would love to hear about another."

"Excellent question. I only wish that I could provide a worthy answer. But I'll give it a shot. Just keep in mind that you asked about psychotherapy rather than transformation. In that vein, I told you that counselors frequently get bogged down on a personal level in dealing with the emotional baggage of their clients. In a way, that's positive. It means that they're invested.

"Unfortunately, it's incredibly easy for them to become enmeshed in the conundrum that their clients are experiencing. In other words, they can get caught in the same cognitive mouse trap. As you will remember, you can't find your way out if you've forgotten what the outside looks like. A therapist, on the other hand, is able to consider their problem from another level. It's the associated perspective that allows real alternatives to appear. But there's more. A therapist also must have the gumption to coax the client, with their express permission, out of their bubble."

"Seeing one client after another all day long and dealing with all their emotional issues must be incredibly wearing," Linda sympathized.

"And that's why many professionals end up taking the easy route. If they do the hard work to make inroads with their clients, what do you think happens?"

Rick was anxious to show what he had learned. "They immediately encounter resistance in the form of their clients' egos."

"Better watch it, Linda. He may surprise us by becoming a therapist as well. But kidding aside, you couldn't be more right. Clients keep writing checks at the end of sessions as long as they feel that they've been heard and supported. If their counselor appears to be adversarial or challenging, it can be a different story. On a similar line, are you aware that people only want to read editorials that support their own opinions? It's pretty much the same with counseling sessions. People gravitate toward comfort and seek people who support and maintain their view of the world."

Linda remarked, "You make it sound like it's almost impossible to do psychotherapy."

"You're not totally wrong. As a psychologist, part of my job is to recognize what people really want. Sometimes, they're looking for a sympathetic ear. And sometimes I provide it. Though, in truth, I find that sort of work incredibly boring."

"What's the alternative?"

"I look for any morsel of genuine interest when a client tells me they want to make a change. I probe to find out their degree of commitment and willingness to risk an alteration of their life path. To the extent I find it, I dive in with both feet. That's the type of work that I genuinely enjoy."

Linda grinned. "I remember that you mentioned your ADHD diagnosis. I take it you don't like to be bored."

"Very astute. I don't like to sit around listening to people as they recount the injustices they believe that they've experienced while justifying their own actions. To an extent, it's part of the job. I accept it as such. However, when I find people willing to move forward, I come alive.

"One of the ways I differentiate psychotherapy from counseling is simple. Counseling involves staying the course. It helps the client maintain stability and constancy as they encounter the inevitable stressors of life. In that way, it can be of considerable value."

"So, for the grand prize, what are you going to reveal?" As was becoming increasingly evident, Linda's struggles with impatience really did parallel my own.

"Sorry to say, I have no magical and all-knowing answer for you. All I can tell you is that the experience of providing actual psychotherapy is incredibly rewarding. It takes considerable energy because it requires an involvement with a client that challenges them to their core. The consequences of each intervention are unpredictable and can occasionally involve a degree of conflict. Doing psychotherapy is for big boys/girls only."

"I like that you've described the spirit of what you do. Of course, I would still like more specifics."

I chuckled as I said, "You're asking the 20,000-dollar question. If I had the answer, I would have to charge you more than 20,000 dollars. Let's think back to the work we did. My first task involved developing rapport. As it turned out, that went almost too well. Then, I had to assess your willingness to address the vague sense of discontent that was troubling you. In the process of doing so, I began introducing indirect and direct challenges in order to assess your openness to change."

"I truly love that you're making your point by talking about what I experienced. I'm still hoping that you can generalize it as well so I can use it with my clients."

"I totally get where you're coming from and will do my best. Here's where the skill comes into play. You must recognize the extent to which your client genuinely wants to make changes. Of course, most will say they do, but their natural desire will be to want the world to change in line with their expectations. If that's where they choose to be stuck, your job entails encouraging reality and acceptance.

"It's necessary to help them find that place within themselves, if it even exists, where they're willing to accept their responsibility for their predicament. Then, you must test the waters to see if they're ready to utilize their capacity to make actual changes in how they think and act. Only if all systems are going can you dive into therapy."

"How do you feel when you encounter a client who is genuinely willing to participate?"

"Linda, you'll find that it's one of the most rewarding feelings in the world. As I was saying, psychotherapy requires a huge amount of energy. At the same time, the expenditure is returned a thousand-fold. As you will discover, therapy stirs thoughts and feelings that then simmer in the broth of life between each session. Parenthetically, I read that last sentence somewhere and thought it sounded neat.

"In any case, your job then is to manage the excitement that you and your clients experience through the unpredictable and often bumpy road that appears in front of you. We all experience rare times in our lives that are especially poignant. As a therapist, you are provided the awesome gift of sharing such moments on a regular basis."

"Okay, I'm ready," Linda said half-seriously. "I just need to find a warm body so I can get started."

"Good luck with that," I cautioned. "There are lots of warm bodies out there. You'll find that few of them are willing to do more than pay lip service to making an actual change."

"Surely it can't be that hard. Don't most people want to improve their lives?"

"Of course, they do. But you're missing an important word. Can you guess what it is?"

Again, Rick was proud to show his attentiveness. "At the risk of showing up my partner, the word is 'comfort.' They genuinely want to change as long as it isn't inconvenient."

"Linda, you're going to have to start reserving a seat alongside you in class. I genuinely believe that we're in the presence of another budding psychotherapist."

Rick quickly demurred. "You've already got me a lot more involved in this whole feeling thing than I would have ever imagined. Please don't even joke about trying to make it my profession."

"Congratulations, Rick. You're a true man. You profess to live in a world in which feelings are reserved for the weak among us, namely women."

As expected, he wasted no time in backtracking. "Maybe I misstated. Are you sure you're not a lawyer? You're better at getting me to put my foot in my mouth than any of the opposing attorneys I've faced."

"Not my intent," I assured him. "Maybe I'm sidestepping the more difficult question that Linda posed. I guess I don't have a good, clear-cut answer as to what constitutes genuine psychotherapy. There are numerous ways of going about it, but ultimately, I would say that it involves purposefully taking on the ego, as we've discussed.

"I don't know of any other therapists who would phrase it in that way, but I think that most would acknowledge that there is a battle involved. Whether or not they have ever considered the process as an attempt to engage their clients' higher Selves, they certainly would have had to find a way to appeal to their clients' better angels if true progress were to occur."

Linda's Journal

December 8

I'm now in the middle of my first psychotherapy class. I've concluded that Bill and my professor are living on different planets. At the very least, they're speaking different languages. I guess all the theories that I'm learning in class will be of some benefit. I've got to say, though, it seems even more abstract than Bill at his worst.

Here's the thing. Bill has got me so excited about seeing clients that I'm about ready to pee my pants. It's something I've hardly dared to dream about. Now it's about to happen! As Bill talked about sharing poignant moments with clients, I felt an indescribable thrill running through my entire body. I've just got to remember to keep me out of my sessions.

When I'm sitting there with my first actual client, I can just imagine all the things that are going to be running through my head. I'm going to take my lead from something Bill said earlier. All the theories and techniques need to go out the window. Job one is going to be focusing on my client. I will hear their story and trust my brain to know how to respond. In a sense, the most critical aspect of therapy is the establishment of rapport. If my client doesn't believe I'm with them, nothing else I do will matter.

As I expected, Bill made it clear that he was heading for the door. I respect him enough to be clear about his exit. Of course, that's my head doing the talking. We will see how I handle it when the time arrives. I don't even want to think about it, so I think I'll just put that matter aside. Instead, I want to focus on the unimaginable opportunity to bond with Rick at a transcendental level. It's just around the corner.

Rick's Journal

December 8

I know that Bill is teasing me when he talks about my becoming a therapist. I can't believe I'm writing this, but he's got me thinking. My new way of relating to the clients I see in my practice is tremendously rewarding. Client meetings are no longer just a nuisance to get through. Now, I see them as an eye-opening opportunity to get to know another human being on a deeper level.

In a sense, there is a downside. My phone won't stop ringing. As it turns out, my clients are interested in more than just a check from the insurance company. Many of them feel like they've been jostled around by the system. My personal injury clients get bumped from one busy doctor to another, with no one really listening to them. It's not uncommon during our meetings to have them start crying out of a sense of relief.

And that brings me to another strange occurrence. What is this "feeling" thing anyway? I've spent years trying to keep my rational side in control. It's far from comfortable for me to allow emotions to enter the picture. And I'm talking about my own as well as my clients. I kind of wish we could do this transformation by taking on one change at a time. Of course, that's not how it works. It's the very antithesis of comfort and control.

Eleventh Meeting

"I continue to receive positive progress reports from Elizabeth concerning your work in marital therapy. Thanks for giving me authorization to speak openly with her. She is quite genuinely invested in what we're doing."

Rick couldn't resist asking, "And just what is it that we're doing?"

"Dad gummit, Rick," I said mockingly. "Now I'm going to have to reconsider all those 'A's' I was handing out."

"Just kidding. I certainly don't want to get a failing grade at this point. But you've got to admit, you've been taking us to your own version of Planet Nutso."

"And you're welcome. At least, I'm giving you one final chance to express your misgivings and ask any lingering questions. For clarification, our previous sessions involved cleaning up issues that each of you were dealing with. In a similar fashion, it's now important to address any marital concerns prior to the next step. Otherwise, lingering issues could become magnified as you would be dealing with each other at a greater level of intensity."

Linda's face was a contorted mask of conflicting emotions. "It would take at least a lifetime for me to come up with all the things I'm wondering about. But since you're throwing it out there, I would love to know more about your experiences with your teacher."

"Sure. As I believe I told you, his way of formulating the process of transformation was quite different. He liked to use scientific terms in his conceptualization. In the end, it really doesn't matter. The outcome is the same."

"But how did he learn to do transformation?"

"That's a great question. And you're going to absolutely hate my answer. I never asked."

For possibly the first time, she raised her voice. "What's wrong with you? Weren't you curious?"

"A better explanation would be to say that I was in awe. I had been searching through my life for someone who genuinely knows. Unexpectedly, I found him. I was caught up in his presence and, at the time, felt no need to go rooting through his past. I just knew that it was a blessing to work with him. I certainly agree, in retrospect, that it would have been a good idea to be a little more curious about his background. But it is what it was."

"Well, now that you've told me all about what you don't know about him, how about telling me what you do know?"

"Now we're getting somewhere. I unequivocally believe that he had a benefactor, though he didn't volunteer that information. And I do know an important way in which he honed his skill and promoted his power."

"While your answer isn't totally satisfactory," said a disgruntled Linda, "At least it's something. You may continue."

After providing her with a perfunctory bow, I continued. "There were so many incredible experiences I enjoyed while in his presence. I don't want to spend weeks reviewing them. I guess I'll limit myself to one that you might also be able to share."

Linda sighed. "As it happens, I have the time. There is nothing on my schedule other than 20 hours a day of grad school work. But, as you well know, your revelations take priority."

Rick agreed. "I don't want to downplay the capital murder case that I'm now defending, but I have my personal priorities. Don't rush on my account."

"As much as I appreciate your indulgence, I think I'll just talk about one experience for now. I had mentioned Carlos Castaneda and his experience with a medicine man. One of the things he wrote about was 'stopping the world.' I remember being enthralled by his writings and never, in my wildest dreams, ever imagined that I might experience the magical things he described. But I did. In fact, pretty much all of them."

Once again, Linda sighed. "I love it. But now I've also got to steal the time it will take to read Castaneda's books. You said things plural, so I take it that you had more than one unusual experience."

"The fact is, I could go through my experiences associated with Castaneda's writings almost one by one. The only thing that was missing was the psychedelic drugs. My teacher didn't find them necessary to guide me into transcendental experiences."

Rick was more than curious. "If he didn't use drugs, how did he go about it?"

"Since you haven't met him, you'll have to take my word for the power he possessed. He didn't use tricks, but one thing he did involve teaching me to access the intuitive part of my brain."

Linda interjected, "Bill, I'm so crazy about you, or maybe I should say with you, at this point, that I'm even prepared to endure sexist remarks. Are you going to say that he taught you to think more like a woman?"

In spite of the gravity of the moment, I couldn't resist a smirk. "You're giving women too much credit. Both sexes have been well socialized into dismissing their natural ability to tune in to what nature provides. I'm sure you've heard of omens. They're nothing more than superstition, right?"

Rick immediately agreed. "I think that the idea of relying on random signs is about as crazy as it gets."

"But here's the thing. When you decide to listen to nature and hear what it has to offer, you become attuned to a world you never imagined. Rather than thinking logically and dismissing something like the unexpected appearance of an owl, you begin to see nature unfolding in a totally different way. You find yourself communicating with the natural world in a manner that you would have never thought possible.

"Indigenous tribes in our own country shared a tradition of knowledge that allowed them to evolve in a way well beyond anything you might imagine. Their progress involved spiritual rather than material growth, so we tend to discount it. Can you even conceive of a society that values the success of the group more highly than the success of the individual? They were attuned to essence, whereas, in Western societies, we encourage ego."

Rick said, "I agree that we can't quantify spiritual growth. But through my life, I've been taught the value of getting ahead… beating the next guy."

"You've hit on it. The competitive world is great for material success. The capitalistic model allows the best ideas and the most efficient organizations to come out on top. But it also leads to an us versus them mentality. We totally ignore the worth of cultures that value mutual support and the success of the group over competition. The one thing that we have absolutely managed to accomplish in the United States is the alienation of people from just about every other country.

"But I digress. I wanted to describe a particular experience that I was later honored to share with several others. There is an actual place not far outside of Phoenix that allows for the experience of 'stopping the world' in Casteneda's terms. While it's a metaphor for jumping off the freeway of life, it was also a concrete experience for me."

"Okay, I've got things to do. You want to just cut to the chase?" Linda seemed almost embarrassed by her lame attempt at humor.

I continued unruffled. "As you approach this very special place on the road around sundown, you begin to notice an unusual luminosity. The darkening sky suddenly takes on an eerie glow, somehow seeming even more lustrous than midday. There is an other-worldly aspect as you begin to realize that you have entered an awesome, magical space. Have you ever heard people talking about having chill bumps? Well, that wasn't the half of it. Maybe someday I'll take you there."

Linda was beside herself. "Damn it! I wish I could believe you. First, you wouldn't take me to that healing waters place. Now, you're turning around and giving us a vague promise to show us something even better. I don't want to sound like a spoiled brat, but I would appreciate a specific date and time."

"You make a good and reasonable point. There are so many things that I want to share with both of you. As it happens, I continue to struggle with my mixed roles. As a therapist, I would never consider such a plan. Of course, wearing that hat, I wouldn't have disclosed so many deeply intimate facts about my life. For now, how about we just get back to talking about my teacher."

Linda sighed, but she couldn't hide the twinkle in her eye. "I'll let you off for now. Just don't even think about disappearing before you've made good on all the things we've discussed."

"Okay, I can appreciate your frustration. But allow me to get back on message. My teacher spent considerable time in an activity, or perhaps I should say an inactivity, that most people assiduously avoid."

"Okay, oh great man of mystery. Quit beating around the bush."

"Have you ever heard of sensory isolation tanks? They are designed to totally block out all sensory stimulation. You float in a pool of isotonic, body-temperature water absolutely devoid of light and sound. Until a few decades ago, neurologists believed that a person would die if deprived of all stimulation. Fortuitously, that turned out not to be the case."

Rick seemed puzzled. "Why would this obviously smart guy waste his time that way?"

"He found that the brain, deprived of outside noise, is able to wander inside itself and, ultimately, beyond the physical boundaries of the tank. Freed of all limitations, the brain can explore limitlessly. My teacher derived his theoretical model from John Lilly, a neurologist and inner-world explorer. Dr. Lilly's initial fame resulted from his work with dolphins. He later became fascinated with sensory isolation tanks, and he used ketamine, a strong sedative/hypnotic, to boost his inner journeys. The most notable quote in his book *The Center of the Cyclone (1972, p.18)* was:

'In the province of the mind, what one believes to be true is true or becomes true within certain limits. Those limits are to be found experimentally or experientially. When so found, these limits turn out to be further limits to be transcended. In the province of the mind, there are no limits.'"

"Sounds like quite a guy. Did he ever come out of the tank?" Linda asked innocently.

"Apparently, not often enough. He traveled too far on his inner journeys, and his ego ended up hitching a ride. He developed incredible models of awareness, but he lost touch with himself along the way. He ended up becoming obsessed with supposed communications with solid-state entities and became convinced that they were about to take over the world."

They were both flabbergasted. Rick was the first to speak. "You learned from a guy who learned from a guy who was psychotic? Remind me again. Where do you keep the door to this office?"

"I don't blame you at all, my man. At the very least, my story should further convince you that we're not playing around here."

Linda asked more constructively, "Are sensory isolation tanks dangerous? I think I've heard of them but know almost nothing about them."

"Like many things, they can be a useful tool. They lack popularity because, by definition, they aren't stimulating. On top of that, many people are fearful when asked to get into a tank that closely resembles a coffin. In fact, my teacher installed one in my office suite. My students were able to use it at no charge. Guess how many takers I had?"

Linda got a laugh out of that. "The way you just sold it, I think I can make a pretty good guess."

Linda's Journal

December 15

I'm relieved that Elizabeth has given our marriage a clean bill of health. I wouldn't have expected anything different. She's been fabulous to work with, and the few times Rick and I have gotten crosswise have been quickly resolved. I kind of wish that Bill would have become more involved in the growth of our relationship, but I'm sort of glad that he trusted Elizabeth to handle it. After all, he has unique skills. I think we're making the best use of his time and talents.

I can easily add another thing to my list of aggravations with him. How could he have not done anything to learn more about his teacher? What in the world? He spent his life hoping for a mythical person, one who actually knows. He meets him and then fails to ask any questions. I guess that I just have to somehow accept what Bill said. The guy was so awesome that it seemed superfluous to try to understand him.

What I wouldn't give to meet his teacher. Do I sound disloyal to Bill in writing that? I really don't think so. Bill has made it more than clear that I'm not his follower. He has downplayed his own importance from the start. I'm pretty sure I know what he's getting at. He wants me to be responsible for myself rather than simply relying on him. It is, after all, my life. I'm the one who has to deal with what I make of it.

It's interesting that his teacher had a different way of explaining the things that we've been going through. It's good, in a way. It underscores the idea that understanding is pretty much superfluous. It provides a frame of reference for talking to others, but who in the world else is going to be willing to listen? Maybe you could try telling them that you came up with your ideas while lying in a coffin. I somehow see an issue with that plan. It's also a good reminder that we get so caught up in our models that we lose sight of reality.

Rick's Journal

December 15

I don't like to admit it, even to myself, but I've been somewhat intimidated by Bill. In our last session, I decided that I was tired of letting Linda have all the fun. I got in a little dig of my own. Of course, Bill let it wash right off his back. It's hard to make male friends when you get older. It's too bad that our relationship is limited because I would really enjoy spending time with him.

I vaguely remember someone talking about Castaneda while I was in school, but I never gave the subject much thought. My interests centered on football, beer, and girls, though not necessarily in that order. I'm not surprised that hearing about the experiences of an anthropologist and some Mexican guru barely penetrated my awareness. I don't really have a problem with all the things I failed to learn in class. More significantly, the most important knowledge that was available just passed me right by.

I'm glad that it's not too late. Even if I had read about Castaneda's misadventures, they probably would have left me cold. Now, I know someone who can guide me through them. I have a whole new respect for mystical phenomena. Of course, how could I not since I've been exposed to just how salient and even tangible they can be?

If I had the time, I would drive the roads leading out of Phoenix to try to find that special place that Bill mentioned. As I think about it, the geographical location is not the critical aspect. Other people have probably driven that road many times. You must be in the right frame of mind to see and experience it. What I can do more constructively is to spend time becoming open to my intuitive nature. I will throw logic and common sense out the window during segments of time just to see what I can learn. As I release the censorship of my rational mind, I will open myself to what nature has to tell m

Bill has obviously gotten me rethinking many things I've taken for granted. I'm still struggling with a couple of my favorite preconceptions, namely competition and capitalism. I'm far from being ready to give up on either. However, I'm certainly reflecting on the value of a life and even a culture that approaches things differently.

Maybe there will be a point at which the human race can rise above, but we've got quite a way to go. In the meantime, I'm going to play by the rules laid out in front of me. That doesn't mean that essence and love for others will be far from my mind as I go about my daily life.

Twelfth Session

Since we're in clean-up mode, I would like for you to tell us more about quantum physics. You had teased that earlier."

"You're right, I did," I said, almost regretfully. I am a physicist, if only in my own mind. As it happens, my great intellect is limited to my forays into other realms. If only my math education had progressed," I mused forlornly. "Sadly, my mathematical prowess maxes out at adding double digit numbers if, and only if, I'm using a calculator. Otherwise, there is no doubt what my profession would have been."

Linda sighed. "Well, I guess that we're lucky that you're math stupid. At least you continue to find ways to make it easy for me not to idolize you."

"I don't want to sound like I'm bragging, but being hard to admire is one of my stronger traits. In any case, I did offer to expound on a subject I know little about, and you didn't let me forget about it. Thanks a bunch. Just realize that anything I have to say on the subject is readily subject to ridicule. I've got to admit, I'm glad that no one outside these four walls will ever hear my outlandish conjectures."

Rick joined in. "I can always use a good laugh. Give it your best shot."

"In truth, I love talking about quantum physics. I'm very lucky in that I have a friend who is a physics professor, and he occasionally indulges me. As it turns out, there can be a price to pay for having a great intellect. Without his wife to remind him, he would be likely to walk to class in his underwear.

"If you really want to dive into quantum physics and its relationship to consciousness, you might consider reading *The Emperor's New Mind* (1989) by Roger Penrose, Ph.D. I should mention that it's a bit outdated, but his manner of conceptualizing cognitive processes remains worth a read. With his incredible intellect, he describes the role of quantum phenomena in explaining how our brains work. The lessons you learn in high school about axons and dendrites are interesting but horribly inadequate when it comes to understanding how we think."

"How so?" Linda asked. I've been taking a deep dive into my neurobiology course. Don't tell me it's just a waste."

"Not in the least. Our basic understanding of neural transmission is interesting and certainly of value in its own right. Dr. Penrose, however, lays out a clear picture of the limitations of that model. Looking at the world through the lens of quantum physics, reality takes on an alien meaning. Even time doesn't work in the linear way that serves to maintain our sense of constancy and predictability. There is evidence time can move in a backward direction, at least at a quantum level.

Dr. Penrose makes the argument that, being limited by algorithms, artificial intelligence will never allow a computer to attain awareness. Artificial intelligence is incredible and will greatly shape our world. There is no question that machines can take in more information than us and perform calculations more quickly and effectively. We sadly have to cogitate within the confines of our very limited working memory.

"However, he argues that there is no reason to believe that digital machines can produce or reproduce consciousness. To me, that conclusion is important, though it is growing more questionable by the day. While reality might turn out to be reducible to nothing more than ones and zeroes, there is something more to us. For want of a better term, we have a soul."

Linda was highly engaged. "Not that it's unusual, but what you're talking about is a whole bunch more interesting than what I'm learning in class. I have a feeling that we could spend hours on this topic. I don't want to bore my loving husband, but I hope you'll tell me more."

"As you know, quantum mechanics takes over at extremely minute levels where the straightforward math of Newtonian physics no longer works. At that point, common sense flies out the window. We end up living in a world of fantasy. Except, it's demonstrably real. Without the strange world of quantum probabilities and apparent illogic, we wouldn't have modern technology.

To bring it home to our discussion, let me tell you about Heisenberg's principle of Indeterminacy. To give it a broad brush, the idea is that we can never predict what is going to happen, at least at the subatomic level, because our attempt to find out influences the outcome. You might have heard of the thought experiment involving Schrodinger's cat.

Rick was starting to become disengaged but was fighting to maintain his interest. "Okay, now you're going from physics to animal husbandry. You've already taken us throughout the universe. I guess I can hang on a little longer."

"Thanks, Rick. I'll keep it short to minimize any pain you might experience. But not so for the poor cat. It is lying unobserved in a closed box. As long as it's left alone, it could be considered to be both alive and dead, obviously a paradoxical state. There is no way to know until you open the box. In the way the experiment was set up, the act of doing so might or might not trigger a subatomic event that would then determine the fate of the cat. Through your curiosity, you would be determining whether the innocent cat lives or dies.

"Here's how it pertains to our discussions. As your awareness grows, you develop the ability to perceive and consider possible outcomes simultaneously. If you carry the idea to the extreme, you could potentially watch the world unfold through infinite dimensions. Every event would create a cascade of consequences that would then continue to cause further outcomes. You would be able to watch an unimaginable number of parallel universes created by the permutations of each act.

"If you're still with me, I'd like to mention an area that particularly fascinates me, though apparently no one else. There is a lack of demarcation between digital and analog realities. We live subjectively in an analog world. But science increasingly tells us that human perception somehow manages to make sense out of a strange world involving submicroscopic particles that spin in a whimsical manner. Further complicating the picture are photons that suffer from a genuine identity crisis. Our brains somehow translate the unimaginable array of information into something for our viewing pleasure."

"Okay," Linda said. "Now you're starting to lose me as well."

"My apologies. My inner nerd is shining through. I'll try to cut to the chase. Our experience of the world involves gradations. Rather than seeing things in black and white, we see colors. We feel various textures. We hear beautiful music. Our brain reveals to us qualities rather than quantities. Without getting too far into the Twilight Zone, there is even a genuine debate concerning whether numbers have a genuine reality of their own or whether they are simply tools we use to make sense of our world.

"What's disturbing to me is that we're now learning that so much of reality can be broken down into ones and zeros. The switch is either on or off. Nowadays, the beautiful scene you see when watching a movie is encoded as well as transmitted digitally.

"On a personal level, I'm fascinated by the increasing evidence that the qualitative world is nothing more than a human creation. Science tells us that whether we're talking about particles with different directions of spin or quantum fields, they either exist or they don't, i.e., ones and zeroes. Qualitative distinctions are creations of our minds. As you can see, the question of the veil becomes salient. Where is the demarcation between out there and in here?"

"While I can sort of appreciate your interest in that rather obscure topic, I'm not sure what it has to do with anything," Linda complained.

"Understood and accepted. But here's where it gets interesting, at least for me. The more we learn about the nature of reality, the more we're forced to conclude that reality is not as real as we would like to think. At least in theory, it may eventually be possible to create the entire universe simply by using a powerful desktop computer."

Rick shifted in his chair. "I'm not sure I really like this topic. Who brought it up anyway?"

"I totally get how it's outside of your comfort zone. It's the same for me. Did you know that reputable scientists once attempted, though unsuccessfully, to prove that everything we know to be real is nothing more than a hologram? Beyond this strange side trip I took you on, I do have a point. Thanks for indulging me. What I'm getting at is very basic. Here it is. Don't take things that are happening in your everyday lives too seriously. What we think of as being reality really isn't."

"While I'm teaching about something I know little about, I might as well continue in that vein. I'm sure you've heard of RAM or random-access memory. Computers these days have lots of memory on the hard drive. However, in performing complex functions, RAM is a limiting factor. It's roughly equivalent to working memory in humans. Maybe I should add that I know less about computers than I do about physics. Sorry about that.

"As we age, our working memory becomes even more limited. That's the reason that older people do better with routines. If everything is predictable, they don't have to tax their brains in determining how to deal with the unfamiliar. We talked earlier about habits, and there is an associated important lesson for all of us. The more we can establish routines, the better we are able to utilize our limited RAM/working memory in dealing with situations that are unpredictable. In other words, the more cognitive resources are freed up, the more prepared we are to deal with the unexpected.

"To take it a step further, that information can be useful in establishing patterns in our lives. For example, we know that exercise is something that could benefit us all, but most of us engage in it haphazardly. Which one of you wants to volunteer to get an 'A' by answering a simple question?'"

Rick was big on classroom participation and had no problem with the answer. "I'm sure it has to do with the ego. Wait a minute. I'm thinking about my own struggles with exercising. He slapped his forehead as he said, "Now I've got it! It's my ego that's gotten in the way."

"Care to elaborate?"

"When I think about going to the gym, I come up with a multitude of reasons to avoid doing so. I'm either too tired or too busy, or, quite honestly, there is something else I would rather do instead."

"Rick, I think you've just described the human race. There are things we would just as soon not do. If we allow our egos the freedom to avoid them, that's exactly what we will do. Now, let's go back to our discussion of habits. How can you use them constructively?"

"I think I've got it. I can make a choice to establish a healthy habit and incorporate it into my routine. If it's a habit, I won't think about it. My ego won't have an opportunity to talk me out of it. My ego wants to be comfortable, but I don't have to follow its lead. If something happens to throw me off schedule, I will deal with it and quickly resume my habit when I'm able."

"You obviously now have it down cognitively. The test will be in seeing how you put it into practice. It's possible to make a habit out of maintaining healthy habits. I recommend doing so. You can even incorporate that idea into your self-identity.

"I'll provide an example to show how dangerous it can be if you allow your ego leeway in determining your actions. I'm sure you've run across people who are chronically late. Oftentimes, their tardiness is due to an inner vacillation. Can you imagine the torture involved if you're lying in bed debating whether to get up and face the day? I was able to make my life much simpler when I decided that waking up means getting up, even on weekends. Don't muddle your RAM with thoughts that do nothing more than keep you stuck.

"People generally take little time in thinking through their lives. Rather than living automatically and reflexively, you have the opportunity to step back and think about how you want your lives to go. What healthy habits do you want to establish? Figure it out and then put your lives on autopilot. Just as in dealing with blips when you're working to eliminate bad habits, treat missteps as nothing more than part of the process. Our lives don't follow a script. It's the manner in which we deal with the inevitable deviations that determine our success."

I continued in a different vein, "I ran across something recently from my notes. It should be of value to you as we prepare for the next level of transformation. I can't locate the source, but I'll at least provide my scribbled notes from who knows when."

"Please do," Linda requested. "Any time that you can provide a step in the right direction, it's much appreciated."

"Okay, I'll give you what I have. At the very least, it will provide confirmation that others have traveled these roads before you:

'After transformation, the new being is out of step with the old. You have to overcome habits and routines that you can easily revert to when off guard. The new knowledge must be incorporated into your personality. It's akin to making a substance adamant, which is the goal of alchemy. It's necessary to withstand challenges. The new order must be maintained over the previous status quo, particularly with friends who think of you as before.'"

Linda was quick to comment, "I love this. Please don't stop."

"Okay, I'll provide another quote that describes the aftermath of transformation:

'The order in the heavens upsets the balance of earth forces that interlock and stalemate. It's necessary to learn to operate through your individual self without losing the sense of transcendence.'"

Rick seemed awed as he concluded. "You really didn't make all this up on your own, did you?"

"Since we're on a roll, I'll throw in a verse that, I think, is from the Bhagavatam, an ancient Sanskrit book of verses:

'The Atman or divine self

It is separate from the body.

It is one

Without a second

Pure, self-luminous

Without attributes

Free, all-pervading

It is the eternal witness.

Blessed is he who knows this Atman

For though an embodied being

He shall be free from the changes and qualities

Pertaining to the Body

He alone is united with me.'

"I wanted to share this information for a couple of reasons. First, I want you to keep it in mind as you progress. Second, it's important that you keep my role in perspective. While I'm not going to abandon you any time soon as Linda feared, I'm ultimately of little to no importance. I'm simply a seeker who found."

With her new-found cockiness, Linda couldn't resist a show of humor. "Okay, Bozo. Now that you've shown us that this wisdom has been around since nearly the beginning of recorded time, why don't you get out of the way and let the real teacher show himself."

"If only you could be so lucky. Like it or not, you're stuck with me. Blame the universe. The way I see it, God really does have a sense of humor."

This time, without asking, Linda got up and gave me a big hug. Rick couldn't resist joining in. I was glad that we still had work to do. I was really going to miss these guys.

Linda's Journal

December 24

How fitting it is that today is Christmas Eve. I'm looking forward to the best gift ever, as the next stage in transformation is right around the corner. Rick and I have come so far. I'm incredibly excited to start the new year on a new trajectory. Even as I write that, I must acknowledge that my excitement is bordering on anxiety. As Bill likes to remind me, I'm far from a finished product.

I guess I asked for a physics lecture, and boy did I get it. I'm so overwhelmed by all my questions that I regrettably detoured Bill off on a rather obscure topic. While the things he discussed aren't in my top ten areas of interest, I'll have to admit that he said he shared some provocative information. He was able to make his point on the tenuous nature of reality scientifically, just as he has done experientially. Mind you, I'm not saying that I love going off in that direction. It just seems like a concept that I might as well accept if I'm going to venture off to parts unknown.

Quite interestingly, he was able to bring it all back to our previous discussion concerning habits. Who would have thought that there was a way to get there from quantum physics? The things he said about RAM and working memory really do hit home. I've formed routines for almost every aspect of my life since I have to deal with suffocating time constraints. His earlier explanations led me to stop and think about how I go about my day-to-day life. Somewhat surprisingly, I kept discovering irrelevant and silly activities that were nothing but a waste of time. I love the goal of being an aware person, but it does require taking the time to stop and think.

Rick's Journal

December 25

This is a Christmas like no other. Every minute of every day is an unbelievable gift. I love it! So what if I don't understand half of what Bill said in our last session? At least I got the idea that he can back up much of what he's saying using both science and logic. Not that he needs to do that. My daily experiences tell me the things he is saying are real. The fact that he's blown holes in my concept of reality makes the whole topic cosmically hilarious.

His example of getting up in the morning really hit me right between the eyes. I've always said I'm not a morning person. How's that for 'is of identity?' I've said it to myself and others a thousand times in my life. And what was the result? I became a person who struggled to get out of bed. That misdirected self-identity stops right now! As with any change in habits, it's going to take some effort. Fortunately, I now have the self-discipline to accomplish it. I'm being propelled by some form of energy that I don't understand and don't need to.

It's amazing the difference it makes now that I have a sense of purpose in my life. Previously, I was more or less wandering through my daily routines. Like many people, I was doing what was right in front of me while, in the back of my mind, being preoccupied with waiting for the weekend to come. Now I realize how much I was cheating myself. To the extent that I can become fully involved in my minute-to-minute life, there is no such thing as boredom. I'm truly waking up and learning to live in the now.

Thirteenth Session

"Well, I might as well go ahead and tell you the "Big Truth.""

Linda shuddered visibly. "I'm not sure I like the way you say that. Maybe we don't really need to know. Please tell me it's just about politics.""

"Linda, your reaction is understandable. It's worse than what you might think but ultimately better. Again, it's all about perspective.""

"Well, go ahead and shoot. Just watch where you're aiming," she relented.

"My intent is to aim squarely at your head. It's that important. Let me begin by summarizing something Joseph Chilton Pearce wrote in his follow-up book *Beyond the Crack in the Cosmic Egg* (1973). Dr. Pearce made the argument that we admire the innocence of children, and then we do all we can to take it away from them. We insist that children join us in forming a concave egg of beliefs with fixed boundaries that conform to societal expectations. In so doing, we insist they sacrifice the natural childhood autism that allows their imagination to roam free.""

Rick seemed relieved. "It fits with what we talked about earlier with 'as if' thinking. While it's an important thing to consider, it doesn't seem to be such a big truth.""

"Rick, I'm only setting the stage. To continue, children don't really 'get' death until around pre-adolescence. When they do, they begin to accept a somewhat fatalistic and even adversarial view of life and the world in general. They sense a general hostility in their surroundings from which they cannot escape. The safety and protection they had assumed no longer exists.""

Linda offered, "Thanks for being Debby Downer. I've heard all that. If you don't have anything positive to say, it's better not to say anything at all.""

"As it happens, I'm only getting started. What that realization ultimately leads to is a recognition that, no matter how much we achieve in life, it's not going to be enough. The end result is always the same."

This time, Linda chuckled at her own edgy attempt at humor as she said, "You must be a hit at parties."

Ignoring her discomfort, I drove home the point. "That unimaginable realization can only lead to one thing…despair."

"You've certainly explained it. Now I think it's time for Rick and me to drive home."

"Here's the positive. It's that very despair that leads people to seek spiritual awakening. When they finally face the futility of life on this planet, they discover that they must turn their energies in a different direction. By coming to terms with the idea that nothing in this life is going to provide ultimate fulfillment, they discover something totally unexpected. In that very hopelessness lies the opportunity to seek the ultimate truth."

Linda seemed dazed for a moment before responding. "Now I get where we've been going. It's about Rick and me. It's also about something so much greater. I finally get the entirety of where you've been taking us, you scoundrel."

Rather than reacting to her comment, I continued, "Do you notice that it seems like we've been together forever, yet it seems like we just met?"

They both nodded enthusiastically. Linda announced, "You've really screwed with my sense of time. But there is something I've been toying with saying, and I guess I might as well come out with it. In some mysterious way, I equate it with knowing. I believe I've known you forever."

Rick appeared to be puzzled for a moment and then said, "You know, she's right. I hadn't thought of it quite that way, but she's got a point. I feel like I know you more than anyone except for Linda, and yet I hardly know you at all."

I sat and held hands with them as we shared a moment of brilliance and illumination.

After anywhere from 5 seconds to 5 hours, Linda finally broke free. "Can I count on you to explain what just happened?"

"Linda, if you think back, you'll realize that we were all luxuriating in the same space. You know it as well as I do at this point. In reality, we just entered a world where time and words don't exist. But I do think the question of how long our souls have been intertwined is fascinating, if unanswerable, given our current state of spiritual evolution."

Rick agreed. "A year ago, I would have been laughing at you. Now, I realize that we have a bond that has been forged across the ages. You are more than a brother to me."

I wasn't totally comfortable with intimate emotions, especially with men. It was one of my many areas that still required work, so I changed the subject. Rather than dealing with the opportunity for introspection and personal growth that the moment provided, I asked, "How about further questions?"

"Well," Linda ventured, "I wasn't quite done with whatever it was we were discussing, but since you offered. You gave me a taste of your thoughts concerning psychopathology. I'm also interested in the opposite. How would you define mental health?"

"I like that question. Society does tend to become overly focused on the negative end of the spectrum. The simplest answer to your question is flexibility. It's the ability to deal with life's challenges without being bogged down by previous reactions that may or may not have worked in specific situations. People tend to get in ruts. They react in the same way over and over to the point that they identify with that pattern. What's more, others reinforce the maintenance of those patterns through their expectations. They expect the grumpy old man to be unpleasant and treat him in a way that perpetuates his fractious mood."

"How would they act differently if they were healthier?"

"Do you remember the definition of a general-purpose computer? It's one in which no programs or courses of action are off-limits. A truly healthy person can examine each situation and determine the best way to proceed. For them, unexpected events represent an opportunity to grow and flourish. Like the rest of us, they still experience sadness, anxiety, and anger. However, they use such negative feelings as cues for constructive behaviors.

"I'm sure that you're familiar with the classic experiment on learned helplessness. Just as with mice, when a person is put in a situation in which nothing they do works, they become anxious and quit trying. Their limiting thoughts and beliefs offer no solutions, and they become depressed and miserable. Mental health efforts are then directed toward helping them escape that trap.

"I advocate for shifting more of our efforts to working with healthy people to encourage them to develop a competent identity. When things go wrong, they will then have the ability to utilize coping mechanisms rather than giving up. Hopelessness breeds homelessness. Feel free to quote me on that.

"As a corollary, I also believe in promoting a 'doership' identity. In other words, they think of themselves as having agency rather than anxiously waiting for things to happen. You've probably heard the maxim: If you have something that really needs to get done, assign it to a person who is busy. They are the ones who do."

I loved that Linda shared my almost romantic view of psychology and signaled to her that I was open to further discussion.

She said rather proudly, "We've been studying defense mechanisms in class. Each of them fits seamlessly with your definition of ego, even though the ego classically is thought to be an intermediary between the lustful id and the relatively inaccessible subconscious. Our discussions have made the various ways of self-defense used by the ego quite real to me. I can see how I have previously used each one. They all have the function of denying, falsifying, and distorting reality.

"Everyone who has had a psychology course has learned of them. But I think it's important to remind Rick of them since they could become useful in his trial work. They are sublimation, rationalization, repression, projection, intellectualization, and reaction formation."

Rick grinned. "I tend to turn off when I think I'm being lectured to. In this case, my reaction was totally different. I can tell that you're both passionate about the topic. And I can see that thinking about defense mechanisms can give me insight into both my clients and the opposing attorneys. Thank you."

Linda was now on a roll. "You mentioned that you had done seminars on transformation. I would love to learn about the kind of activities you included."

"Sure, I'll be glad to give you an example of an introductory exercise. In fact, let's do a mini-seminar just for the two of you."

Rick said, "I'm on board."

"Let's begin by recognizing that everything is energy or, in other words, vibration. In order to get in touch with that vibration, allow your breathing to turn into a very faint hum. Experience it and play with it. Find a sound that seems intuitively right for you. Allow it to gradually become louder. Open your mouth and let it flow, filling your body with vibration/energy. If any feelings want to come out, just let them happen. Let go of your need to control and just be the sound. Gradually, let the sound fade away while keeping it going inside you.

"Now let the sound guide you back to when you were an infant. You have no words to label anything. Everything seems new and interesting. Open your eyes and look around at a world you've never seen before. Don't try to label it. Just look at it and observe the profusion of colors and shapes. Crawl around like an infant, exploring and feeling whatever you run across. Now, crawl like an older baby until you run into a person. It's just another object to be discovered. Communicate with that person with your hands and by using baby sounds. Make your sound and let your partner get to know you by expressing it. Now stand up slowly and look at the world as an adult."

Both Rick and Linda seemed stunned. Rick commented, "Wow! That was such a simple exercise. But doing it with you and Linda was truly transformative. I experienced myself as a neonate and then as a toddler. It brought home the message of transcending words."

Linda added, "You really do have a way of making things magical."

I explained, "The trick is to encourage and allow people to suspend their logic filters. While we don't think about it or realize we're doing it, we expend considerable energy in maintaining the illusions that hold us in place. Interestingly, those constructs are necessary to a degree for everyday interactions. But, if given permission to release them in a social context, the results are often astonishing. In a group setting, that simple exercise can have profound effects."

Not surprisingly, Rick asked, "Where do we sign up for a class?"

"Well, I've got good news on that front. While you would likely enjoy participating in a seminar, you are well past that point. You and Linda are about to move into the big time. Do you think you're ready?"

Linda snarled, "Just try to hold us back!"

Linda's Journal

January 1

I'm beginning to wonder if Bill ever does anything by accident. It doesn't matter. How fitting it is that today is the first day of the new year. Rick and I are truly starting over in a brand-new life. Later today, we are meeting with Bill for an event that promises to be beyond belief. The descriptions of rebirth that I've heard about in various religions now make total sense. I wouldn't trade a thousand fairy-tale weddings for what Bill has promised. I'm chuckling to myself as I write this. How could I even think about making a comparison?

I'm glad that I was able to get in at least one more psychology question. It's so neat that Bill shares my passion! It's the first time I've heard anyone relate mental health to flexibility. As I think about it, his description makes a world of sense. If you can deal with whatever comes in life through a fresh perspective and a willingness to try a new approach, you're well equipped to handle anything life throws at you. If, on the other hand, your ego insists on sticking to the same unproductive ways of acting, you're going to experience frustration and a sense of futility.

As ready as I am to embrace my new career as a psychotherapist, I'm also going to dedicate a part of my professional life to providing personal growth seminars for the walking well. Why should people have to wait until they need intervention when we can teach and encourage positive coping skills right now?

As with many things in society, well-intentioned ideas become ingrained and then self-perpetuate. That's how we end up with unending poverty and an educational system that serves only itself. It just came to me. Bill's idea of flexibility as a definition of mental health also applies to government and society in general. We need leaders who can rise above and keep us from getting stuck.

I'm glad that he threw in a new idea for me to think about. It is serving as a diversion and allowing me to keep my excitement at a manageable level. Just barely.

Rick's Journal

January 1

It's hard to believe. We're here. The time is now. It's funny that I would express it as hard to believe. That's certainly a familiar thought for me lately. I no longer feel stuck in the roles of ex-jock, stuffy lawyer, and traditionally married husband. I am now FREE! I can play and live those roles happily, consciously, and interchangeably. I also know that I have a choice every minute of every day in how I want to play them. One thing is for sure. Those roles will never again play me.

I've never said it to Linda in quite this way, but I've worshipped her for a long time. Now that's about to stop. It's really kind of funny to think about it in that way, but it's totally accurate. I'm no longer going to be seeing Linda through a me-her lens. Our separation will come to an end as we join at a level beyond imagination and certainly beyond any words.

I sort of feel like I've unintentionally cheated during this process. It's not that there's anything I've done. Instead, it's more what I haven't had to do. I've certainly had my ups and downs, but I haven't experienced the despair that Bill alluded to. Maybe it was because of the gentle way he guided us. It's even conceivable that it's because of something my soul experienced at another time. I also benefitted vicariously from what Linda has gone through. In any case, I am now very familiar with the inside of the eggshell of reality. I've made a definite crack in the rigid shell and plan to break it wide open with Linda alongside. What we might find on the other side defies imagination.

Transformation

I began by making an obvious comment, "We've come a long way to get to this point. Care to make any final reflections?"

"Linda was first to respond. "I could talk all day about the things I've been through…the spaces I've experienced and my travels through the universe of awareness. Many times, I've wondered if there really is a there, there. And now we're here. You talked often about watching what you wish for, and you were right. I was way too attached to my hope of getting to this point. Now that it's arrived, I'm experiencing the equanimity that I first discovered what seems like a lifetime ago. I mean, part of me is tremendously excited, but I can watch that emotion and enjoy it for what it is. I want this time to be pure, and I'm not going to divert onto the myriad emotional roads that tempt me."

Rick looked at her with pure love in his eyes. "My whole life was leading to this moment. Like you, I didn't even know that it was even out there as a possibility. I'm so blessed to be with you." Somewhat begrudgingly, he acknowledged, "I'm even happy to share this incredibly intimate time with that character over there."

Previously, Rick and Linda had traveled extensively in order to select the place and even the time for the ceremony. Their research was worthwhile as they located an area with breathtaking beauty. More importantly, it was a place that was a conduit for awareness. It had a natural energy that practically vibrated under our feet. Not coincidentally, it was considered holy by the Native Americans, who were much more closely attuned to nature and Mother Earth.

We began with Rick and Linda standing next to each other, with me close enough to touch without intruding on their togetherness.

I volunteered my own feelings. "I feel awed by the unbelievable privilege of being here with two beautiful human beings/souls. I hope that you know that the things we have experienced have shaped my life in many ways, just as well as yours. I'm now a much more complete being, and the richness you have brought to my life is truly beyond anything I could ever express. I would expect that, for many ministers, marriage ceremonies become routine. What we are about to share is going to be anything but.

"Rather than asking if anyone present has a reason to object before proceeding, I want to ask that question to each of you for the final time. Please don't hesitate to mention any reservations or doubts. If there are lingering questions or any sense of uncertainty, now is the time to say your peace. We are, after all, talking about eternity. It's one thing to get married with good intentions, knowing there's a sky-high divorce rate. What we're about to do doesn't allow a legal recourse. Once you're in it, you're all in. And we're not talking about till death do we part. I want you both to be fully cognizant that we're talking about committing to a bond that will last until you finally merge as one with God."

Linda looked at me with loving and trusting eyes. "You know you're not about to scare me off. I'm committed to Rick, but not in the way most people think of the word. I have discovered him and loved him on levels most people don't even know exist. I know, with certainty, that he is my fellow traveler on the road to eternity. Once again, thank you for showing me and us the way."

Rick was done with all the pretenses. He was open to an extent that I had never witnessed, being simultaneously completely vulnerable and invulnerable. "You've given me the chance to truly meet and share with this awesome Being in a way beyond imagination. How could I conceivably hesitate? I'm ready to become One with her."

The sun was making its appearance, and the birds were singing. Then, everything came to a conspicuous stop. The world stood still in anticipation.

"There are obviously no words to describe the next step. We can talk about it afterward, but please remember that wrapping it with words would only diminish it. Any future discussion needs to be limited to solidifying and incorporating the experience at the heart of your mutual Beings. As much as I cherish the word, ineffable, it's an absolute dud in its ability to express what's about to happen."

I asked them to face each other while holding hands and began intensifying the energy. The pure and growing energy emanating from the three of us caused the sky to become ablaze in a bright, multi-colored celebration. The trumpets of heaven sounded, beginning as a low rumble. The complex vibrations gradually combined organically to a crescendo that included and transcended all earthly instruments.

"The ethereal glow that grew and grew was beyond description as Linda and Rick united in absolute bliss. The bond that had served to link them together disappeared as they melded in a brilliant flash of light and love. There was no longer a distinction between Rick and Linda. They were truly One.

While it might sound melodramatic or maudlin, the truth is what it is. Linda and Rick now truly Are. I wept.

Postscript

Hidden between the folds of his flowing, white robe, Rick had carefully tucked two airplane tickets. For Linda, it was going to be the surprise of a lifetime. He just hoped it wouldn't end up being a prematurely shortened one. Want to take a guess as to where they were headed?

My work with them was not done after all.

Bibliography

1. Bach, R. (1970). *Jonathan Livingston Seagull.* Macmillan Publishing.
2. Bach, R. (1977). *Illusions: Adventures of a Reluctant Messiah.* Delacorte Press.
3. Dass, R. (1970). *Be Here Now.* Lama Foundation.
4. Lilly, J. (1972). *Center of the Cyclone: An Autobiography of Inner Space.* Julian Press.
5. Pearce J. (1973). *Beyond the Crack in the Cosmic Egg.* First Pocket Books.
6. Pearce, J. (1971). *Crack in the Cosmic Egg.* Inner Traditions/ Bear & Company.
7. Penrose, R. (1989). *Emperor's New Mind: Concerning Computers, Minds, and the Laws of Physics.* The Oxford University Press.
8. Ritter, N. (2022). *Truth Beyond Words: A Teaching Novel.* Self-Published.
9. https://www.amazon.com/Truth-Beyond-Words-Teaching-Novel-ebook/dp/B0BK2YY5ZC
10. Yogananda, P. *(1946). Autobiography of a Yogi.* Philosophical Press.
11. Special thanks to Julio Gea-Banacloche, Ph.D. for his consultation concerning quantum physics.